The
Golden
Highway

by

Anthony Ashpitel

ANTHONY ASHPITEL

ISBN 978-0-9569003-2-6

Publisher: Anthony Ashpitel
Email: tonyashpitel@btinternet.com

Updated in 2011 from an original novel by Anthony Ashpitel

This book is dedicated to my wife, Anne, who is a boundless source of help and encouragement.

AA

ANTHONY ASHPITEL

Prologue

(20th December: 0530 - 0730)

The motorway was almost deserted in the pre-dawn of that winter's day and the security man could see only one other car when he took the slip road to join the eastbound carriageway. As he moved into the slow lane, he adjusted his speed to a sedate sixty and found this kept him some five hundred yards behind the other vehicle. He was in no great haste to arrive at his destination so he settled down to a leisurely twenty-mile drive.

Occasionally, a patch of mist would loom in his headlights, momentarily blocking his view of the red tail-lights ahead, but otherwise there was nothing in that black world to distract him barring the twinkling of the lane markings. Gradually, he fell from listening to the inanities of the early morning radio programme and found his mind wandering back to those thoughts, which had dominated his attention for so long.

Ironically, he felt a marvellous sense of peace. It was a new experience for him and one to be savoured. For forty of his fifty-eight years Edward Simmonds had lived mostly on the fringes of the criminal world or sometimes, as of late, well and truly in the middle. Now he had decided to call a halt. More than that, he was going to the police with a tale that could only alienate him from his previous associates.

He knew, full well, what the outcome of this action must surely be; he had no illusions. However, if it was necessary that he should spend a long time in prison rather than stand by and see many innocent lives placed in jeopardy, then so be it. In an hour, it would be over, or perhaps that was too naive; he could visualise very well a long and difficult future with, in the beginning, the trauma of massive media coverage. It was this last which provoked his one regret: that his family might suffer for his actions.

When the twinge of pain he felt at this had subsided he tried to relax again but soon found his mind straying back to the events behind his decision. He tried hard to subdue such memories but met with very little success. Eventually, he gave in to them and his mind returned to the night almost a year earlier, to the time when he had been foreman of one of Hargreaves' motorway construction gangs.

As he fell into reverie his awareness of his surroundings diminished to the point where only his subconscious was involved. Because of this, he failed to notice the two spots of light in his rear-view mirror, which heralded the approach of the truck. However, it was unlikely, even had he been aware of its presence at such an early stage, that he could have avoided the incident which was shortly to occur and which would end in the loss of life.

Like a silent film the actions of the past played across his mind in vivid sequences. He pictured the five heavy trucks and their massive escort of police as they sped through the darkness towards the ambush. He saw clearly the gang's deployment at the crossroads where the convoy was forced to slow. They hadn't stood a chance. The slam of the gas-charges as they hit and penetrated the thin layers of metal had soon been followed by the disintegration of the orderly, almost military string of vehicles into a disorderly circus, as drivers succumbed to the gas and cars and trucks ran haywire.

Not one man had died in the fracas, though this was not something the gang had delayed their flight to check. They left it to the newspapers to later assess the score.

The security man's mind then raced to another scene, pausing only for the briefest moment to remember the cross-country dash and camouflage operation that had followed the hijack. He saw the clearing that, under the lightening sky, became the roughly gouged furrow of an embryo motorway. There, too, was the vast and newly excavated hole into which they drove the five trucks. Then there was the 'fixing' operation to establish the exact location of the cache, so necessary because soon the spot would appear no different to any other for some miles to east or west.

It had been his job to operate the GPS and theodolite: the former to mark the exact position of the cache, the latter to measure its exact depth. In the gloom, their previously agreed landmarks had been difficult to discern but he could still remember his relief at picking out the important reference point of a signpost some distance to the north, the datum they were using. In the magnified picture through the viewfinder he had even been able to make out the legend printed on one of the pointers: 'Peterboro' 9m'.

He had to hand it to the Top Man, the only name by which the gang knew their leader. It had been his plan and it had worked perfectly. It was only when he thought of what was about to happen that he felt weak again and began framing his opening statement to the police. "The recovery operation of a lost box will commence on the twenty-seventh of December," he would say, and watch their reactions closely. He felt it would be interesting to see as he had included in the line the code word used by the police for the dragnet, which had unsuccessfully hunted the gang: 'Operation Lostbox'.

His return to full consciousness was gradual as he first took in the noise from the radio, with its latest news headlines on the Middle East and the Petrodollar crisis. He reflected that it seemed just one tragedy after another: already, barely ten years into the new millennium, the situation around the world was proving no better than the last in terms of tragedies. Certainly, it didn't justify the wild celebrations of hope attending the fireworks at that juncture. He shook his head. 'How depressing', he reflected, aloud, and turned his attention back to his driving.

His reaction as he looked ahead was of mild surprise for now he was barely fifty yards behind the front car. Checking his speed, he found he was down to fifty and decided he would overtake. In his rear-view mirror, he saw the powerful lights of a truck and, though it was only a short distance behind, he decided he had plenty of room to pull out.

It was as the manoeuvre was still in its infancy that he became aware of a sense of unease. A glance in the mirror confirmed the basis for such feelings. The truck had increased speed rapidly and was now very close to his offside rear bumper. He could make out the truck's outline quite clearly, in spite of the glare from its headlights. The backwash of light also illuminated the cab's yellow and blue paintwork. It was then that a flash of recognition suddenly brightened his eyes, prompting a deeper feeling of unease.

He was still reasonably calm, however, and felt that his reserve of acceleration and a degree of safety-mindedness on the truck-driver's part would be enough to avoid complications. However, things began to move too quickly, even though his mind was racing and stretching each second.

His first inkling that the situation was dangerous came as he heard the deepening growl of the truck's engine simultaneously with his own bid for acceleration. Then he felt rather than saw the truck move alongside, cutting off his avenue of escape. Terrified, he applied full acceleration in a desperate attempt to squeeze through but heard the truck's engine now grow even louder, followed swiftly by a crash as it nudged his car towards the other.

In the subsequent fight for control, he momentarily glimpsed the occupants of the other car. There were two of them: a rather frightened-looking, elderly couple.

In desperation, Simmonds slammed on the brakes. As if reading his mind the truck-driver dropped back a few feet and was there to nudge him forward as he decelerated. In order to regain some semblance of control he had to release the brake smartly and re-apply the accelerator.

With sweat glistening on his face now, he tried once more to accelerate past the front car. Again, he was thwarted as the truck nudged into his off side. A moment's thought ruled out any idea of overtaking along the hard shoulder, too, for the obviously terrified driver of the front car was slewing in a wide zigzag, which effectively blocked such a route.

It was then that Simmonds knew all hope was gone. He knew the truck-driver had his car's capabilities measured to the inch and could only be waiting for the right moment to suit his purpose.

Immediately he reached for the mobile phone on the dash mounting, but it wasn't there. In the collision, it had dislodged and tumbled into the foot-well on the passenger side. It could have been miles away, for all the chance he had of reaching it. It was then that he reached a shaking hand into his pocket and withdrew the ever-present notebook. With one hand on the steering wheel, the other traced, in an all but unintelligible scrawl, the opening line of his statement intended for the police. It had required a tremendous effort of will to control his hand but the task was soon completed. Then, all he could do was await the inevitable.

He didn't have to wait long.

Three hundred yards behind the three vehicles, the driver of a small van watched in amazement as the final scene of the incident played out. The patches of mist were thicker and more frequent now and he had some difficulty at first interpreting what he saw. However, even the mist couldn't disguise the truth for long and, as he saw the truck begin to push the two cars across the hard shoulder to the depression beyond, he felt his anger rise.

For a moment, knowing how powerless he was to stop what was happening, he contemplated sounding his horn in a futile gesture of defiance. His next thought was to stop and help the injured, assuming there would be any survivors.

His third thought was more selfish but he couldn't resist it. It was the instinctive urge to flee. Before his accelerating vehicle had even passed the truck, now only a shadow in the mist, he heard the crash of metal on metal but he did not pause to wonder at the devastation he was ignoring.

It was his intention at first to get completely away and forget anything had happened. A glance at the sleeping woman in the passenger seat did nothing but reinforce the idea, but when he had progressed some distance from the scene and his nerves had almost ceased to jangle, he was plagued by feelings of guilt.

He passed several motorway emergency telephones without stopping. He reflected it wouldn't be wise to use those. Instead, he took the next exit. Several miles on, he entered the village of Grafton and pulled up alongside the public call box. Then he quickly doused the lights and quietly climbed out of the van.

It was at that point in the night shift when time seemed to stand still. With only an hour to go to changeover, the clocks seemed to stop.

The hands were pointing to three minutes past seven when the ringing telephone nudged the 999 operator into the semblance of wakefulness.

'Emergency services,' murmured the operator.

'There's been an accident,' said the van driver. 'Two cars are off the road. I'd passed them before I could stop and...'

The man had been talking very quickly but the duty man was used to it. 'Where are you calling from, sir?' he interrupted.

'It wasn't here,' responded the caller, too quickly.

'Yes, but we can work out the position from where you're calling from,' persisted the policeman, gently.

'I'll *tell* you where it was. It was about six miles from the Langton Junction, along the eastbound carriageway towards Ipswich.'

In the operations unit, the typed message was already being transmitted to the nearest police and ambulance services and, because he suspected it would be difficult to get information out of this particular caller, he had ticked the Fire Brigade box as well.

Suspecting that it was the shock of what he had seen which prevented the caller being more co-operative, he decided to try the soft approach.

'Now please listen carefully,' he began, gently. 'If we're to get help of the right sort to the injured we must know everything you saw and, if we're to get this help to the right place, we must have your position as a reference...' Suddenly he stopped speaking, an action responding to the sharp click he heard as the distant receiver was replaced.

The emergency operator shook his head and wondered at the technology, which could pinpoint a mobile phone to a very small area when they no longer had the same for public call-boxes. Perhaps, he reasoned, with too many services chasing too little money in these depressed times, the decision had been made to let the system which they had used to provide instant number reporting of public call-boxes to go. Perhaps, the saturation in wireless communications, whereby, seemingly, every six-year old and older now had their own personal communications device, meant the limited use of public-callboxes no longer warranted the necessary expenditure. Perhaps, he thought. Then he stopped reasoning, as he took another call and responded, 'Emergency services....'

Back in the van the man turned to gaze at the still form of the woman and was gratified to see she was still asleep. After a few seconds, he took to staring ahead through eyes that saw nothing, and felt the sickening guilt return. Then he quickly drove the van onto the road. In a few minutes, they had re-joined the motorway and the anonymity of a denser wall of mist.

Chapter One

(22nd December: 0900 - 1130)

Three days later, at ten in the morning, the motorway carried a steady stream of traffic on both carriageways. Beneath a clear blue sky only the sun's low angle gave the traveller a clue as to the season, until he or she rashly opened a window to the near freezing air outside, when there could be no doubt.

From the heated comfort of his car, Bailey took in the scenery. The Cambridgeshire countryside was not the most inspiring, but it wasn't the low, flat fields that caught his attention. Instead it was the motorway itself, meandering in spite of the seemingly clear country ahead and fashioned like a causeway in that its wearing surface was some twenty feet above the plateau that supported it. He thought of the enormous cost of such a highway - more a measure of Britain's commitment to trade in the Euro-zone than to alleviate the overloaded and inefficient traffic routes in the south. This much he had learned from the banner headlines of a jubilant press at its opening - or partial opening - some nine months earlier.

As he stretched his neck, the better to see a section of motorway that was partially blocked from view by a lorry, he felt the searing pain again.

Gingerly, he fingered the lump on his head and allowed a curse to escape his lips. Then he frowned at the pain this brought and remembered the cause of the bruised and broken skin.

It had happened only that morning as he had prepared to leave his flat for his new job at the service area. He had still been clambering into the pale blue one-piece overalls, which the company issued to all its security men, when he had answered the doorbell. Now, with the gift of hindsight, it wasn't difficult to see where his mistake had lain in this action. Had he not been in such a hurry to leave, he might have been more alert and not succumbed so easily to the attack by two masked men, which had rendered him unconscious.

The motive for the attack was difficult for him to establish. Although at first he had discovered his wallet was missing, his subsequent visit to the kitchen in search of something soothing had revealed not only the wallet, fully populated and next to his mobile phone, but a note as well; all three in clear view atop one of the working surfaces.

The scribbled message was to the effect that there had been a mistake as, upon checking his identity, they realised they had assaulted the wrong person. As a measure of his gratitude for their concern, he had called the police and handed them the note as evidence.

With his hyper-suspicious mind, it was possible to conclude various motives for the incident. The two most obvious were that, indeed, it had been a case of mistaken identity, or that the note was merely camouflage for the theft of something he hadn't yet missed. Various other ideas came to mind including one that assumed old adversaries had tried to get even. He wasn't too convinced of the feasibility of this because a quick mental check failed to produce the names of anyone who was in a position to resume hostilities. Besides, the hefty blow on the head had been the only real injury he had suffered in the attack and this just didn't indicate the working-over he would expect.

Considering himself fallible, he spent a few more seconds checking his conclusion. The result was the same. It was still the second possibility, the one of theft, which interested him most and he spent the remainder of the drive in deep thought on the subject.

The 'Trucker's Place', serving Benwick Motorway Service Area's westbound commercial drivers, was situated on the ground floor of the two-storey service complex and was entered via a discreet door on the Lorry Park side. As transport cafes went, it was quite spacious; the fifteen-or-so customers then present going very little way towards filling the place.

Behind the substantial counter with its festoon of steam pipes, Banjo Crane surveyed the plethora of unused tables and looked forward to the promised stampede when the stretch of motorway to the coast was finally complete. He knew the road building was behind schedule, as was the reconstruction of the eastbound side of the service area. He could see more layoffs coming in spite of their already much reduced staffing quota and it almost made him wish for the windswept roadside tea-van he had sold for this, a warmer job.

Despite the seasonal drawbacks of his roadside hut, he had enjoyed his time selling tea and sandwiches - where he had attracted the nickname Banjo for his own particular method of sandwich making - and he had enjoyed chatting with the regular truckers and 'reps'. He still managed to keep in touch with the drivers who regularly used the 'Trucker's Place' too, but the size of the place seemed to take something away. He sighed then, lost in thought during the quiet period. He was becoming discouraged. He could feel it. Perhaps it was the boredom. If so, it could only get worse because, with the Christmas holiday coming up, the place would shortly resemble a graveyard except for the tiny trickle of drivers, and of course the strays and hitchhikers.

With this latter thought, his gaze shifted to the figure of a man sat hunched and alone some way from the only other signs of life, a group of drivers chatting after their meal. As far as he knew, Shughie had never picked up a hitchhiker in his life but it was certain that if anyone were on the road this Christmas, it would be the quiet scot.

As if sensing he was under scrutiny, the man turned slightly in his seat. Quickly, Banjo averted his gaze and began, nervously, to tidy an already perfectly stacked mound of crockery. He didn't know why, but Shughie made him nervous. Perhaps it was just that he couldn't understand a man who was so insular. He knew he wasn't physically frightened of the man, but Banjo didn't look up again until he heard a hail of hellos from the group in the corner and saw, closing the door, a tallish man with fair hair he recognised as a driver who was popular with the truckers.

'Been away awhiles, Don,' observed Banjo, in an acceptable form of greeting. 'What's wrong? Don't like the food here?'

Don returned the smile. 'So that's it. That's why I've been coming here these past months. You sell food!' he replied, in mock surprise. 'S'funny, I'd never really seen the connection...'

'Okay, unless you want your next meal in Peterborough General, gimme yer order in a civil tongue,' demanded Banjo.

While he waited for his order, Don went over to the group of drivers. At the end of the semicircle, and nearest the door, sat a young man with red hair who, with a uniform of pale-blue and a lapel badge proclaiming him to be an assistant security-man, stood out from the other, less formally-dressed men. Being some distance from the centre of the group, he added little to the conversation but his presence didn't appear to be resented by the others.

ANTHONY ASHPITEL

'Where yer bin this past fortnight?' asked a large man in the centre of the semicircle, as the newcomer approached.

'The wife. Complications with the baby,' he answered. 'Her's alright though now. It's due anytime.'

'Yer heard about Eddie, then?'

'Yeah. Shame,' said Don. 'Some bloody loony, no doubt.' He jerked his thumb at the distant figure of Shughie. 'Is he still playing his silly games?'

'Still the cowboy,' affirmed the large man, who went into a crouch and lowered his voice at the same time. 'Seven days a week. God knows what he's haulin'.'

'What day's he on?'

'No idea.'

'I do,' said the assistant security man, from the end of the line. 'He started again the day before the accident. That's four days ago.'

'Why d'ya ask?' questioned the large man.

'It pays to keep well clear of men like him. Four days without even a normal night's kip. Who knows what might happen with him on the road,' answered Don.

As if hearing enough, although it was doubtful that the import of what had been said could have carried that far, Shughie rose from his chair and turned for the door. He was of medium height but rather thick set, though none of his bulk was fat. Under the thatch of unruly black hair, his face suggested an age in the middle twenties but a closer

20

look at the eyes put a few more years onto that assessment.

Quietly, he left. As he made his way to his truck all eyes followed him, none more intently than those of the newcomer, Don.

At twelve minutes past ten Bailey's battered-looking sports car slid into the staff car park to the rear of the Trucker's Place. When he had emerged from the car's warmth he paused for a few seconds, after locking the door, to look around him at the 'village' which would be his stamping ground for the next few days.

The nearest building was the services complex, which housed the cafeterias and shops normally found together on such sites. It was connected - by a glass and concrete concourse spanning the motorway - to another, similar, construction that was so far incomplete. It was a large building, two-storeys high and by far the most imposing of any on the site.

By turning his head to the right he could see beyond the lorry and car parks to the high screen of dense shrubbery where, beside a gap, stood a sign reporting the way to the motel. Further round to the right and only a short distance from the slip road, which re-joined the motorway, was a single-storey building that was well advertised as the Police Post by the garishly coloured patrol cars parked outside.

Bailey turned back to face the complex and, as he did so, he was mentally drawing a plan of the site and added to it the detail from his memory, of the fuel station and the fenced compound of the maintenance depot which he had passed on his arrival.

He was feeling the cold now, dressed only in his overalls but, before he moved off, he scanned the facing wall of the complex. On the ground floor was a door almost exactly in the middle, marked Trucker's Place, and to the right of this a large window. To the left was another door bearing the legend 'Staff Only' and further left another large window. On the first floor were several small windows, one of which framed the upper half of a young woman.

Satisfied that he had the perspective of the place right, from the model and drawings he had seen earlier, Bailey walked over to the staff entrance. Ahead of him stretched a narrow corridor with nothing other than one door in the walls on each side to break the monotony of this tunnel, which ended in a steep flight of stairs.

At the top of the stairs, he found himself on a very small landing faced with a choice of two unmarked doors. He took the one on the left, which brought him the choice of two corridors, at right-angles to each other, but this time he was saved the mental strain of making a decision. Along the corridor straight ahead he could see the girl again.

'Mister Bailey, isn't it?' she called. 'I'm the receptionist, switchboard operator and general dogsbody around here. I saw you arrive and recognised the ghastly uniform.'

She led him into a small room, which owned one window and an inner door. A telephone switchboard on its own table, desk and a filing cabinet made up the sum total of furniture but an attempt had been made, with festoons of tinselled decorations, to bring a touch of Christmas to the otherwise stark decor.

'Mister Hickson wants to see you right away,' she explained, and opened the inner door for him.

The spaciousness and contents of the manager's office surprised the security man for it resembled more the office of a draughtsman or architect.

Upon taking the proffered seat, indicated by a silent wave from the figure, which didn't even look up from the study of some papers, Bailey looked around the room. On the wall behind the substantial desk was a large plan drawing of the motorway service station. On the one opposite the windows was an artist's impression of the project that was recognisable as such from the little he had taken in on his approach only minutes ago. But the large model of the site which lay on its own table seemed to have only the central strip of motorway to identify it with the present project, for the proliferation of model buildings gave it the look of a small town.

He would have scrutinised the model further but he heard the ruffle of papers and felt obliged to return his attention to the man behind the desk. A single glance supplied Bailey with the salient features of the man and he saw that his new employer was around fifty years old and, though not handsome by any means, was lent a certain distinction by the cut of his neat greying hair and smart clothes.

The manager waved his arms wide. 'Impressive, isn't it?' he said. 'It's not something you'd expect for a tin-pot service station, hmm?'

'From what I've seen so far, it isn't exactly the smallest in operation, even now,' responded Bailey.

'Quite so,' commented Hickson, and Bailey realised the manager was nervous. 'The observation is merely relative, you understand, relative to what it is going to be. The reconstruction of this old service area is no small undertaking.'

Bailey nodded.

'But I rush ahead. First, we'll talk about you.' The manager retrieved the file he had been reading earlier and placed it in a central position on his desk before opening it.

'Your record is impressive,' he said, nodding. 'You've done a lot of security work and I should estimate your qualifications to be in excess - far in excess - of those demanded by the job here. I find this strange.'

'Strange?' queried Bailey.

'Don't worry, your job is safe - you passed the agency interview with flying colours, I assure you,' responded Hickson, quickly, misreading the security man's tone. 'But I have a question. Call it simple curiosity. I'd just like to know why you accepted such a low-key position?'

'This is confidential?'

'Absolutely,' confirmed the manager.

'It's simply a matter of security - in the other sense of the word. In the past my work has necessitated a tremendous amount of travel and a generally unsettled way of life,' he explained. 'I see this position as a chance for long-term employment - with the satisfaction that can bring - together with the opportunity it affords me to settle down.'

'Settle down?' exclaimed the manager, sitting bolt upright. 'What are you, er...thirty five, forty?' He made to pick up the folder.

'Thirty-eight.'

'Thirty-eight and you make it seem like retirement age,' laughed Hickson, suddenly, to Bailey's eye, more relaxed.

Perhaps he'd bought the story, thought Bailey.

'Well, be that as it may, we're glad to have you, Bailey, I must confess.' Hickson paused, then looked straight at Bailey. 'There's not a drink problem is there?' is asked, sternly, eyebrows wrinkled intensely. 'I won't tolerate drinking on duty.'

Perhaps he *hadn't* bought the story, after all, reflected Bailey, unfazed. 'No. No drink problem,' he replied, assuredly.

Hickson nodded curtly, and sat back in his seat. 'When we were forced to hunt for a new security man – and at such short notice - I was certain we would need to do with someone temporary or have to call in one of the larger security firms. I feel your enrolment will be to our mutual advantage, I'm relieved to say.'

'Thank you,' responded Bailey, who at the same time sighed inwardly. But he, too, had a question. 'My predecessor...' he prompted.

'Yes?'

'Do we know yet what happened?'

'An accident,' shrugged Hickson, bending forward to reach for a pair of spectacles. 'A collision between two cars. Beyond that, nothing. Fire destroyed the lot.'

'Fire?'

'Yes, it was so bad, apparently, that they're still sifting for a clue to the cause - beyond the obvious one of collision. There wasn't enough left to bury of Eddie...er, Simmonds' body...'

'I'm sorry. Of course, you must have known him well,' cut in the security man, noting again the nervousness in the manager, which could not be confused with grief or embarrassment. 'Excuse me for being so inquisitive,' he added, smiling. 'Put it down to my job.'

'Yes, yes,' agreed the manager, holding the spectacles to his face with both hands. For a moment he held them quite still. Then, as if emerging from deep thought, he looked up at Bailey. 'Let's take a look at the service area on the model,' he said.

Both men rose and walked over to the model on the table. In a few seconds Bailey began to see something more recognisable as Hickson removed various blocks of polystyrene from the model.

'We're still in stage one of redevelopment although there are seven stages before completion at the end of the decade,' explained Hickson. 'Unfortunately, we are already some weeks behind schedule. Even stage one of the reconstruction on the other side of the motorway is far from complete even allowing that it is policy to finish one side of the service area before starting the other. '

'Why is that?'

'So that you keep your front money to a minimum by paying for the construction of only half of the motorway service area - MSA we call it - which, when completed, should attract some of the money to finance the building of the other half,' he responded. 'It also means that if traffic loads don't live up to expectations, you can always plead for a change of plan with the Department of Transport, reduce the size of the other half of the complex and therefore the cost.'

'Good thinking.'

'Good business,' corrected Hickson.

'But why the delay?'

Hickson paused before replying to Bailey's question. 'This is also confidential,' he said, at last. 'It's a foundation problem, which is being investigated at the moment. Nothing major, you understand, but sufficiently worrisome to bear further investigation.'

For some minutes the manager and Bailey discussed the present layout of the MSA. Gradually, Bailey became aware of a mounting enthusiasm in the other man as they talked. It was obvious now that Hickson was almost fanatically keen on the development under his charge and Bailey was no longer surprised at the appearance of his office.

Presently, Hickson began to talk of future developments. 'Take a look at this page,' he directed, tapping a printed page, which was stuck to the wall above the model. 'Traffic loads - vehicles per mile - projected for the next twenty years. No doubt you have heard through the press of the potential for this motorway?'

'To the point where some people have named it the Golden Highway, you mean?' responded Bailey. 'Yes, I've heard something of it, although I've been abroad in recent months and don't have the full picture. It sounds exciting.'

'Exciting? It's terrific!' amended the manager, with feeling. 'In your time here you will see this place swell to the point where its daily population is measured in many tens of thousands. This won't just be a place to stop for petrol or a bite to eat. In years to come people will visit us to do their monthly shopping or for a night out.'

Hickson saw the doubt in Bailey's face. 'Not convinced? Well, perhaps you would like to put your own construction on the following facts,' he said, and drew the non-believer's attention to a large map that had escaped Bailey's attention earlier because of its location on the wall behind the chair he had used.

'This motorway is shaped like the letter Y.' Hickson traced his finger along a broad, coloured, line that had been applied to an Ordnance Survey map. 'It connects the industrial midlands - and via the M1 and M6 motorways, all points north and south - with these two ports.' He tapped the map. 'A brand new ferryport just south of Great Yarmouth, or rather, it will when the final section of motorway is completed, and, via the other arm of the Y, Harwich.

'Together, those two ports will draw seventy per cent of cross-channel traffic within fifteen years. Why? Because at the moment the Straits of Dover, by far the most popular crossing point on the Channel - due to its narrowness - is like Oxford Street is at this time of year, but all year. Which means that ferry services at that point are reaching capacity. That's the first point.'

Bailey watched keenly as the manager, flushed with enthusiasm, resorted to ticking off on his fingers as punctuation for his observations. 'Secondly,' he continued, 'all traffic using Dover and travelling to or from points north of London must use the ancient and overloaded roads of that region...'

'M2 and M25 are ancient?' challenged the security man.

'No, just inadequate at present - and for the foreseeable future,' responded Hickson. 'Add to that the excessively long detour often undertaken by hauliers who, in order to get their goods from the Midlands to Northern Europe, send them first south to Dover, across the Channel, and then hundreds of miles north. The advantages of a direct route, albeit with a longer sea crossing, must be obvious.'

'But surely the Channel Tunnel...'

Hickson sighed deeply. 'Putting a tunnel under the channel doesn't mean your traffic problems evaporate. Even when, if ever, they sort out the high-speed link this side of the channel, we still need to get the rail links through the spine of England if we're to see the Tunnel begin to fulfil its promise. As it is, more roads will have to be built, which will devastate Kent, and further escalate the bottlenecks in the London area.'

Bailey was nodding in agreement by this time but it didn't stop the other man driving his point home. 'It makes economic sense not only to the road-haulage firms but to the local authorities who see their A and B roads - and sometimes unclassified roads - take an expensive beating from the so-called juggernauts.'

'Yes, I see that,' said Bailey, feeling he was expected to actually say he was convinced. 'But how does the shopping arcade fit into all this?'

'Consider, first, what will happen when that final section of carriageway is completed and the road-haulage companies are fully geared to working this route.' Hickson, pencil in hand, indicated with a sweeping motion on the map the two-way traffic along the motorway. 'Millions of tons of cargo will pass between Northern Europe and all points in the UK along this route.'

He smiled as he turned to face Bailey, with a hint of conspiracy in his eye. 'There are only four MSA's on this route and this is the nearest one to the coast. It is also situated right in the middle of East Anglia which, having a population that is not concentrated in major cities, has not attracted shops of the discount variety in any great number. Again, the cost of transport has been largely responsible for this and the inhabitants have sometimes suffered by having to pay high prices for poor selection.'

'So you set up a couple of large shopping arcades - one to each carriageway, use the economy provided by transport which is passing your door anyway and you're in business,' supplied Bailey.

'Big business,' corrected the manager. 'Hyper-markets, too. We have the space already allocated behind each half of the MSA. We'll be within reach of every car-owner in East Anglia who's prepared to make a two hour *return* journey once a month to obtain his goods in bulk.'

'Fascinating,' proclaimed the security man, and meant it. He had heard it said that East Anglia was the only region of Central-Southern England that had escaped concentrated development. He now realised that this was a statistic with a very short future.

'And the other amenities,' continued Hickson, replacing the lumps of polystyrene onto the model. 'Conference halls, banqueting and general hotel facilities; hotels and motels, entertainment: a city without the impedimenta of private dwellings.' He pointed to the two largest blocks, one on each half of the MSA. 'Multi-storey amenity centres with everything I've just mentioned and more.'

Bailey was tempted to scoff when he heard ballroom-dancing and banqueting on a motorway service station but changed his mind when he realised these were merely spin-off ideas of an enterprise which strived to win a large slice of the region's food and entertainment market. He was impressed but he had one query. 'Surely, drink must be a problem.'

'It is, and we still haven't satisfactorily cracked that one. We're praying for prohibition,' he said, and laughed, fully at ease discussing what was obviously a subject dear to his heart. 'But seriously, we're wondering if coach trips could be afforded a privilege of some sort. It's a bit vague at the moment, although we're all agreed that drivers should not be tempted to drink alcohol on the MSA.'

'You've got a motel on here,' said Bailey. 'That's new, isn't it?'

'Experimental, at the moment. It's a small affair with only fifteen rooms and, until the other complex is completed, on this side only,' responded Hickson, deflated slightly now that they had returned to talking of the present. 'Incidentally,' he added, 'you've got Simmonds' old room. Which also reminds me: his next of kin will be along this afternoon to pick up his belongings. They're still in his room, I'm afraid.'

Mention of the old security man seemed to have cooled the manager's enthusiasm even more and Bailey noticed the nervousness was back in evidence.

Hickson returned to his desk then. When he had resumed his seat he looked across to Bailey. 'The assistant security man will help you settle in and show you round,' he said. 'I'll get him over here to meet you.'

With that he bent to the intercom. 'Tell Davies to come and see me, straight away. You'll find him in the usual place, if I'm not mistaken,' he instructed, a business-like tone back in his voice again. He turned from the intercom when the girl had acknowledged the order and said, almost to himself, 'He'll be in Banjo's. Wants to be a truck driver.'

'What's the staffing level here?' asked Bailey.

The manager thought for a moment before answering. 'I can only say it's the same for security as it is in every other department at Christmas time,' he responded, eventually. 'That is, too low. There will be just the two of you on duty until the twenty-seventh, when Williams and Wyatt relieve you for the New Year holiday period. On the sixth of January you will revert to full staffing. That is, all four of you.'

'Two?' exclaimed Bailey. 'Just running the CCTV suite will…'

Hickson smiled. 'You're used to a more sophisticated security organisation, Bailey. This is the Trufood Company, with, at present, only a medium-sized service area to operate. The staffing levels are low, even by my expectations, but the numbers are worked out by head office, not me. As for CCTV, that would be nice but not essential at this stage of development.'

'But how did this Simmonds run a security schedule on just four men? You need at least two per patrol - the two man rule - and then at least three shifts...'

The manager held up his hands. 'All right, I see your point. But I think you may be overreacting,' he interrupted. Then, quietly, he said, 'This is a fairly peaceful location still. The motorway police are always at hand, too. They've got a Police Post here, permanently manned. It is only over this fortnight that we are down to two men per seven-day duty period.' He paused and shrugged. 'Besides, Simmonds coped.'

Before Bailey could respond to the barbed comment, they heard a knock on the door and the manager shouted, 'Enter!'

'Ah, Davies,' he said, as the red-haired assistant security man walked into the room, 'I want you to meet your new boss.'

ANTHONY ASHPITEL

Chapter Two

(22nd December: 1130 - 1330)

Bailey decided against going straight to the motel and had Davies take him on a tour of the MSA instead. The more they talked the more Bailey grew to like the cheerful young assistant and a rapport developed rapidly between them.

Their first call was at Bailey's car. The thin material of his overalls was no protection against the low temperatures outside and he gladly retrieved his bulky parka from the boot.

'Some heap you have there,' remarked Davies, looking at Bailey's car. 'Could do with a wash'.

'You're volunteering?' asked Bailey, who, looking back at the vehicle, had to admit that the rakish wedge appeared forlorn and uncared for, clothed in mud and grime.

Davies shook his head. 'It's more an excavation job. You're sure it's a car under there?' he asked, smiling.

'I think so,' responded the other man, not quite truthfully. Even had he not known beforehand, the car's breath-taking performance would have told him that something out of the ordinary was housed beneath the sloping bonnet. As it was, he had been given a full briefing on the machine and knew that major chassis and brake tuning had accompanied

36

the insertion of the three-point-five litre engine with its attendant turbo-charger.

'Where to first?' asked Bailey, shrugging into the parka as they moved away.

'I think a circuit would be best,' replied Davies, taking a quick look around him. 'Which makes the Police Post our first call.'

There followed a two-hour hike during which Bailey was introduced to some thirty people. As Davies had promised, they first took in the Police Post and met the morning-shift Sergeant. He was pleasant enough but gave Bailey the impression that he thought civilian security men were mere amateurs. True or false, the feeling didn't inspire conversation beyond the barest formalities. Or was it just that the policeman was more interested in the portable TV discreetly placed in a back room which distracted him periodically, with its programme on current affairs.

'Bloody OPEC,' he said, to no-one in particular, 'Wanting proof that America can back up the dollar with gold reserves. Bloody cheek. Should drop a bomb on 'em.'

Davies smiled and shook his head. 'Nuking them is his usual reaction to anything he doesn't agree with,' he explained, quietly.

Bailey made to leave and the pair were soon walking along the boundary road, past the motel's screen of foliage, towards their next call, the maintenance depot.

There was no sign to indicate its use but inside the large compound - on the front of the one, large building - was the name 'Hargreaves', a name Bailey had seen at several points along the motorway.

'Surely the Highways Agency or Department of Transport look after maintenance?' thought Bailey, aloud.

'They do,' supplied his assistant, 'but only after the motorway has been completed for a full year. Until then it's the contractor's responsibility to see that all is in order.' He nodded towards a scene of high activity by the side of two enormous hoppers. 'They're getting ready now. The DoT's Senior Engineer for this motorway will arrive for his turnover inspection at the beginning of January.'

'But the motorway isn't even finished.'

'It doesn't have to be,' responded Davies. 'Motorways are built in *sections*. This section will be one year old in January.'

Bailey smiled, impressed by the depth of his assistant's knowledge. 'You learn an awful lot being a security man around here', he said.

'With an ex-foreman for a boss I could hardly fail to,' responded Davies, referring to Simmonds.

By this time they had arrived at the double-doors of the large corrugated building. Inside, they passed by several gritting vehicles and small vans before they turned into an office marked 'Clerk of Works.'

'You're the Clerk of Works?' asked Bailey, of the small man to whom he had been introduced, indicating the sign on the door.

'No,' smiled the small man. 'No posh titles for me. He'll be a Department man appointed for when they take over in the new year. I'm just the contractor's foreman.'

Bailey nodded. 'What's security like around here? Anything ever go missing?' he asked, feeling he ought to be seen to be taking his job seriously.

'No, lad,' responded the foreman. 'Beyond the gritters and maintenance vans which we park in here for safety, there's nothing out there 'cept the two forty-ton hoppers and fifteen hundred tons of grit and rock-salt.'

'What about tools, lanterns...and your motorway signs?'

The small man pointed through the office window into the inner area of the building. 'They're all locked-up in them chacons.'

They talked for a few more minutes but apart from the foreman making a call to the met. office for a weather-check, Bailey found nothing of interest in their conversation. Inevitably, the topic of the ex-security man's death came up and Bailey decided it was time to leave.

On the way out he passed another room in which some twenty or thirty people were gathered. He asked Davies for an explanation.

'Mostly standby crew,' he answered. 'Between November and March the foreman 'phones up for the weather forecast twice a day. In readiness for bad weather they have an extra work-shift to back-up those out on the motorway. They also do extra patrols to check on fog patches or other dangers.'

Although the main reason for the guided tour of the MSA was to familiarise Bailey with its layout and operation, another major reason was for identification purposes. It wasn't sufficient to merely inform the various supervisors and foreman that a new security man had arrived on the scene for, when a prowler is sighted at three in the morning - in company uniform or not - he is necessarily viewed with some suspicion if unrecognised. It was in order to prevent such false alarms that they briefly called upon the supervisor of the fuel station on their way back to the complex.

Their visit was shorter than either had expected because no sooner had Bailey been introduced than the man had to leave in response to the gesticulated movements of a filling hose which a short but large old lady was holding in one hand - a toy poodle in the other. As the noise and movement of cars on the fuel area was quite intense they decided against waiting for his return and left.

As they zigzagged their way across the car-park to the complex, Bailey looked ahead at their destination. The main entrance to the complex was in the wall facing the motorway slip-road he had arrived along that morning. It took up some fifteen feet of the wall close to the left-hand edge of the building. The area to the left of the building - the goods delivery area and boiler-house - was screened from view by a short high wall.

They paused, at Bailey's insistence, before they arrived at the separating wall. His attention had been caught by a group of workmen gathered around what looked like a portable pump. 'What's all that about?' he asked, raising his voice above the noise the machine made.

'Foundation trouble,' answered the assistant security man, simply.

'Hickson mentioned something about that. Didn't seem to want to discuss it.'

'Shouldn't wonder,' called Davies. 'Reckon there's been a balls-up of some sort.'

In the warmth of the main building, and to the accompaniment of piped music in the form of 'The first Noel' rendered by Bing Crosby, they first visited the shop and then the restaurant before making the last call of the morning at their office. Throughout the tour so far, Bailey had noticed two things above all else - that Davies was well liked by everyone on the service area and, as indicated by the countless inquiries and references about the old security man, so had Simmonds.

The office was a narrow but long room at the end of the manager's corridor. Being on the first floor and at the end of the building, it had a good view of the parking areas and, in the distance, he could make out, beyond the screen, an L-shaped two-storey building that was the motel. Inside the office was a small desk with a filing drawer upon it alongside the ubiquitous PC. At the far end of the

41

room a camp-bed had been made up and, beside it, wrapped in brown paper, stood a pair of bottles.

'What's that?' asked Bailey, pointing, and there was an edge to his voice.

'My camp-bed,' said Davies, hurriedly. 'Unlike you, I don't get a room on site. I've got a flat in Peterborough but I sleep here between rounds at night.'

Bailey was unimpressed by his answer and it showed in the glance he directed toward his assistant.

'The bottles?' asked Davies. 'Christmas cheer for the troops.' The hint of humour in his speech did little to hide his nervousness.

'Then save it for next Christmas,' said Bailey, evenly. 'No drinking over the duty period. With only the two of us, we can't afford the luxury.'

'You're the boss,' confirmed Davies, glumly.

'Now let's get the rounds schedule organised. Then we'll go to lunch.'

The cafeteria was conveniently located for the security office, it being only a short walk past the manager's quarters, then down the corridor which branched off to the right just before the tiny landing, and out through the other door onto the concourse. An alternate route was through the other door on the landing that led to the kitchens serving the cafeteria. But, as the use of this latter route was frowned upon, the two security men went the long way round, picking up a situation report from 'We Three Kings of Orient are...' *en route.*

It seemed to Bailey that bright red was the dominant colour in the decor of most MSA cafeterias, Benwick being one of them. He had never had the reason for this explained to him but, as he looked around the cafeteria, he found the glare from its overuse to be almost intimidating. He wondered if, perhaps, this wasn't the very psychology behind its use, to ensure that visitors to a cafeteria so treated would spend as little time as possible within its confines, thereby freeing space for more paying customers.

If this was indeed the theory, there was no requirement for such treatment in Benwick's cafeteria. The large room before him seemed almost deserted even though his eye estimated that some three hundred people were present. This was Benwick Motorway Service Area in pre-flood days, before persuasive measures to increase customer turnover were needed. An indication of its present level of usage was the deployment of small portable barriers that corralled patrons into a small section of the total floor area.

Nevertheless, Davies, who led the way, ignored the cordoned area in favour of a table in the corner where the cafeteria jutted out over the motorway by some fifteen feet and where it was separated from the restaurant by a ceiling-high concertina of dividers.

'Some sentimental reason behind your choice of this table?' queried Bailey, sitting down. 'Or are you just allergic to carols,' he added, referring to the piped music.

'No, just the view,' replied his assistant, nonplussed. 'I always eat here. When I'm not in Banjo's, that is.'

Bailey looked behind him. A large plate-glass window revealed the neat lines of the motorway stretching away into the distance towards the east coast. 'Of course, you're interested in becoming a truck driver,' he said, turning back to face Davies.

'Buying myself a share in a big rig from the money I make from this job,' supplied Davies, proudly.

'This can't be the quickest way of accumulating the money.'

'As an assistant security-man, you mean? No, it isn't', he replied, nervously rubbing an enormous jade-coloured ring. 'But I hear a lot of *experience* talked in Banjo's. It's all part of the plan, you see...'

Some plan, thought Bailey as he spent the next ten minutes hearing how Davies and his girlfriend would first get their HGV licences - she was almost through her training - and run their own haulage business. Bailey had to admit the plan was unusual and challenging which, naturally, he found quite interesting but he was grateful for a halt in the young man's enthusiastic tirade caused by a man's arrival at their table.

'Hello, Larry,' said Davies, only slight disappointment showing at the interruption.

'This seat taken?'

'No,' replied Davies. 'It's yours.'

The man Bailey saw was about his own age but a little taller than his five foot ten inches and perhaps a little heavier.

'You'll be the new security man - old Eddie's relief,' said the newcomer.

Bailey nodded. 'Ian Bailey,' he said and stretched out a hand.

'Lawrence Braidwood,' returned the man. 'My friends - and those who dislike me interrupting their life story,' he shot a glance at Davies, 'call me Larry.'

Davies smiled in acknowledgement.

Larry hadn't finished his introductions, adding, 'I'm the foreman with the construction gang down the line.'

'Though he spends most of his time over here, it seems,' said Davies, mischief in his eyes.

'This is where the girls are, isn't it?' he protested, in mock astonishment.

'You'd think so. Most of the construction gang seem to live here,' continued the young man. Then he frowned and said, 'That's a point; I don't seem to have seen many today.'

'Christmas holiday,' supplied the foreman. 'It'll be quiet now until the New Year. At least, I hope so - I'm the relief plant manager for the period.'

'What are you here for, today,' asked Davies, grinning, 'or is it personal?'

'We had a vehicle breakdown this morning,' replied Larry, himself trying to suppress a smile as he faced Bailey. 'Would you believe it? My first day as Plant Manager and I get a breakdown.'

'What was it?' cut in Davies.

'The Contractor. Broke down on the motorway.' Larry was obviously far from upset and treating it more as a joke.

'Bloody hell,' cried Davies, 'that's the biggest tractor there is. Where is it now?'

'Oh, we got it off the motorway, all right. Just. It's here in the lorry park. I've already had the police have a word about it,' he answered. Then he shook his head. 'The worst of it is that it was on its way for a scheduled service.' He must have found something funny in this for he grinned.

As their conversation progressed, Bailey discovered that the foreman considered a sense of humour - however inane - essential in his line of work. The security man had time later to reflect upon this outlook. For now, he could understand the need for humour during great civil engineering projects, where vast amounts of manpower and machinery and materials are needed to construct new highways against the clock. That was difficult enough, add failures in supply or machinery and - worst of all - the weather, and difficult could turn into the well nigh impossible. Finding your motorway line several feet under water for as far as the eye could see, or faced with mud-stranded vehicles whose recovery required men sorely needed for other tasks - and all against the clock of time and money - was not funny at all. However, as you cannot easily insure against 'acts of God' such things must be suffered and, when the hard-slog of rectifying them has been accomplished, then it is better to laugh at them than to cry. However, there was one subject which Larry did treat with reverence: Edward Simmonds.

'Good man, that,' said Larry. 'Did you know I took over from him as foreman? Yes, I did. He'd been looking around for a nice quiet job for some time and, because he'd been with Hargreaves for some years, he got the job of security man when this place was built. I could always count on his advice.' Then he smiled. 'I wish I had it now with that bloody brute out there.'

'What do you use it for?' asked Bailey, hoping to get them off the subject of his predecessor.

'It's a shifter, really. We use it for hauling machinery out of the mud.'

'It's a Scammell Contractor, capable of hauling up to two-hundred tons on the drawbar,' put in Davies.

'That's when it's used properly,' corrected the foreman. 'But we just use it as a shifter.'

Bailey showed great interest in the construction of motorways and asked the foreman many questions on the subject. Soon, pieces of cigarette packet bearing explanatory diagrams littered the table.

After some time Braidwood glanced at his watch. 'Look, I'll be on site tomorrow morning if you want a look around. It's only thirteen miles away and with it being quiet just now there shouldn't be any problem. Fancy it?'

'That's kind of you,' said Bailey. 'About ten?'

'You're on,' confirmed the foreman, 'But I must go now. I hope to find out today what the matter is with the brute - although I won't be able to move it till tomorrow, in any case.'

'Why's that?'

'Flat battery. Bloke who was driving it drained the box,' he answered. 'See you later.'

'Quite a character,' announced Bailey, when Braidwood had gone.

Davies nodded.

'Shame about Simmonds,' said Bailey, after a few seconds of silence spent contemplating the congealing dregs of coffee in his cup.

'Eddie? Yes,' agreed Davies. 'A good man.'

'Too good.'

Davies frowned. 'How do you mean?'

'I just get the impression that he was just too good to be true. No-one, it seems, has a word to say against him.'

'Oh, he was no angel!' said Davies, smiling mischievously, now that he realised what Bailey was inferring. 'His past was murky, to say the least, and quite a police record to go with it, too. But since old man Hargreaves rescued him he's been - was - on the straight and narrow.'

'Sure?'

'Course I'm sure,' said Davies, a little brusquely, his complexion rapidly assuming the colour of his hair, 'and boss or no boss, you're talking about a special friend of mine, Mister Bailey. What's more, the man is dead. Surely you have the decency to allow the dead to take their pasts with them?'

'Sorry. Stupid of me,' placated Bailey. 'With my background you tend to become a little cynical.'

He didn't allow Davies the chance to ask just what Bailey's background had been because he was already getting to his feet to leave. Calmed, Davies followed him and they left the cafeteria to the accompaniment of 'The First Noel'.

Chapter Three
(22nd December: 1330 - 2030)

The duty-roster Bailey had worked out for Davies and himself was simple: one or the other would be on duty at any one time. This meant that the duty person would be out and about around the MSA during the period of his duty while the other relaxed or slept. Beyond this, the only other generality in the scheme was that the day shift would be the longer of the two periods, although Bailey inserted safeguards to ensure his personal appearance on duty at irregular intervals. This policy had noticeably irritated his assistant but drawn no direct comment. Davies' outburst in the cafeteria, in response to what he saw as another example of mistrust had been, in reality, a reply to perceived slights on both of Simmonds' and Davies' competence.

Bailey reflected upon this as he looked around the previous security man's room at the motel and felt it would be interesting to see his assistant's reaction to his plummeting respect for Simmonds as a security man.

The room was like any other modern hotel room with fitted wardrobes, bathroom *en suite* and beds - except that this one had only a single bed when commonly new hotels went for the more versatile combination of a double and one single to each room. A glance through the window over to the other wing of the building told him why this was so; there was no doubt to his calculating eye that the neat rows of doors and outside stairways were spaced at much wider intervals than on the end of this wing.

This alone was not a point to draw the temper of the red-haired youth. Bailey's thoughts moved to another aspect of the accommodation, which caused him misgivings as to the efficiency of his predecessor. Why was it, he wondered, that a man who is in charge of security would choose such a room as this. It is on the first floor, has to be entered via an internal staircase - past the watchful eye of the office porter - and, through provision of only one window, had a field of view little greater in azimuth than to reveal the front of the motel and some waste land beyond. What was more; there was no fire escape from the tiny landing outside his door.

The prospect of having to use such a room made Bailey feel distinctly uncomfortable. He felt trapped by the thought that each time he entered or exited the room he must do so via only one, readily monitored route - through the office. It meant he must be seen and, discarding whatever feelings the staff may have regarding the morality of it, the one thing a security man must ensure is that he may come and go completely unannounced and, hopefully, unobserved.

In Bailey's covert line of work such freedom of movement could mean the difference between life and death - *his*. Therefore, he must do something about it. What he intended to do was a distraction, but a necessary distraction, all the same.

Bailey turned from the window and, as he did so, he was struck by his own solitude, an emotion he felt at the outset of any operation. As usual, he would work alone, his first objective being to carry out a survey of the area and personnel. This was no mean feat in itself. Then what? Simple, he reflected with derision: narrow the field down until you're certain of your suspects and have 'cracked the case', and then raise the alarm for his boss, Rider, to take the glory when all the messy work was out of the way.

Bailey knew he wasn't being very fair to Rider. The type of job Bailey was usually picked for, and the current one was very much a case in point, could only be carried out by a man working alone. It was to Rider's credit that he always seemed to choose the right man or men for the task in hand.

The truth was that Bailey preferred to work alone as it meant he only had himself to worry about. Besides, planning was simplified when there was only one. Like when, for instance, he was concerned for his own safety. The situation of this room was a suitable case for treatment. It just would not do, he reflected, and began surveying the other wing again.

The motel was a two-storey affair, fashioned in an L-shape, with the proportions about the same as for the letter. The shorter wing housed the offices, nearest the end wall on the ground floor. Above this was located a storeroom and the room in which Bailey now stood. Completing the wing were four more rooms - two up and two down - each with its own individual access, with those on the first floor served by recessed stairways. Each of the four rooms and all ten in the other wing had windows to both front and rear, with those on the first floor equipped with fire ladders.

His survey complete, Bailey decided he preferred the ground floor room at the end of the other wing. It would provide him with inconspicuous access and exit. The problem he faced was how to accomplish a change of room in as innocent a fashion as possible.

After some brief thought, he rested the matter unresolved to look more closely at his immediate surroundings again. The manager had been right about Simmonds' things for they were everywhere and it was here that Bailey got another glimpse of his predecessor. Wherever he looked, he found everything neat and in its place. Nothing marred this neatness but there were lapses in the arrangement of certain items. Again, Bailey felt something was wrong.

He didn't see it at first, but when he did, it was clear to him that there was discord between his conception of a neat-and-tidy 'everything in its place' man as outwardly revealed throughout his belongings, and the lack of logic so obvious in the *positioning* of various objects. Surely, such a man would not leave his suitcase by the door when there was a perfectly functional stowage above the wardrobe. Could the same man leave his shoe-cleaning kit on a chair under a towel, or not find time to use the cabinet above the basin for the arrangement of at least some toiletries, rather than struggle with a bulging soap bag?

But Bailey had no time to reflect more on these oddities as he was interrupted by the telephone, the ringing of which did nothing good for his aching head.

'Mister Simmonds' next-of-kin,' said the manager's voice, when Bailey answered, 'is on her way over to you now to collect his belongings.'

'She?'

'Yes, *she.*'

The phone clicked into silence.

Bailey was again warned of the woman's imminent arrival by the sound of the duty motel porter's voice that prompted in him further speculation as to the fitness of a predecessor whose quarters were inadequately soundproofed. Perhaps that was being too critical, he reflected. Such a parameter belonged more to his, Bailey's brand of professionalism, not that of Simmonds' world. However, this reinforced in him the need for a change of room.

The porter's voice became quiet suddenly at a point Bailey judged to be at the foot of the stairs. Then he heard the sharp but muted clack of heels, on the steps of someone moving up. He moved towards the door.

Through his investigations of Simmonds, he saw in his mind's eye a picture of a daughter who was clean, neat, every-day and homely. It took only the time required for both eyebrows to arch to their limit for him to know that his preconceptions were very wrong.

Her eyes were blue, accentuated in their allure by the complement of suntanned skin in a fine-boned face framed by near-black hair, which would have tumbled to shoulder-length but for the restraining influence of a white woollen hat. A *retroussé* nose and even, white teeth added character to complete a beautiful portrait. Added to this her use of artistic clothes draped casually about her lithe frame produced a woman whose presence brought Bailey the nearest he had come to sweating palms for almost as long as he could remember.

Even so, he frowned. He frowned in sympathy with the frown she was wearing and he realised with relief that whatever troubled her would also blind her to his discomfort.

His introduction met with a handshake and the response, 'Anne Simmonds,' delivered in a flat voice.

'Coffee?' he asked, noting that not only was she upset but she was shivering - her clothes not having apparently been chosen for any insulation value.

'Thank you,' she answered. 'I've come to collect my father's things.'

He watched her as she looked around the room. 'I'm afraid they need packing yet,' he said. 'But sit down, please. You're not in any hurry, are you?'

'No, no hurry,' she replied, and again Bailey was conscious - perhaps overwhelmed would be a better word - at the sadness in the woman's eyes.

Again, she looked around the room, as if trying to see something that wasn't there. 'Mister Hickson told me you are my father's replacement.'

'Yes, I took over today,' said Bailey, bending over the collection of tea and coffee things, which nowadays passes for a dumbwaiter. Then he turned and said, gently, 'Look, are you feeling all right?'

'Thank you, yes,' she said, quietly.

Bailey wasn't satisfied. 'I can go away for an hour or so if you want to be alone...to...collect up your father's things.'

'No, please don't go, Mister Bailey,' she said with urgency, looking directly at him for the first time. 'I don't think I could take it... the room...all at once. Not yet, anyway.'

Bailey touched her arm reassuringly. 'Worry ye not, milady. Bailey will stay here as long as you want,' he said, with a smile.

For the briefest of moments, she smiled also and Bailey came over just a little light-headed, which the professional in him put down to the cranial injuries he had sustained in the attack at his flat. Perhaps that also explained away the weakness in his knees as he went to the corner where the electric kettle was issuing an ever-expanding cloud of condensation.

As he returned with the coffee, the woman looked up at him. She must have seen something in his expression for she said, 'Is something the matter?'

Bailey pulled a face of indecision and paused before answering. Then he sighed. 'It's just that, although I never knew your father, I've seen photographs and heard opinions of high esteem from everyone around here - but I still can't match the image of you as his daughter. I see the likeness but you seem from different worlds.'

Anne nodded and looked down at her coffee for a few moments. She made a number of attempts to find the words before eventually she sighed and said, 'Perhaps what you have just said sums it all up. You see, I never knew my father - apart from the early years, and perhaps not even then. It's a long story about the selfishness of youth and too many things found out too late.'

'Harsh words for someone,' remarked Bailey. 'Yourself, perhaps?'

'The very same.'

'Would you like to tell me about it, Miss Simmonds?'

'It's Anne, and it's a sad story.'

'I'm Ian, and I like stories.'

It was a mixed-up story she told him, and Bailey had difficulty in separating fact from innuendo between the sobs. He gathered sufficient information to form a broad outline however, and promised himself another try at the detail later.

Anne Simmonds, it seemed, was the younger of two daughters. Up until the age of ten, her glimpses of her father had been rare, as he had worked mostly away from home. Bailey applied to this what he knew of Simmonds' past and surmised that such work had probably included several stays in HM Prisons. But he didn't break her narrative to seek confirmation of this, preferring to remain silent and allow some thread of connection in her confession - for that was what it was.

Ten was a bad age for Anne as it marked the point in her life when her mother died of cancer and she was entrusted to the care of a boarding school. Throughout her six years there her father had kept a low profile, appearing only infrequently at holidays. It was as well that he did so, as in the young mind of his daughter - confused by the trauma of such upheaval in her surroundings - he was to blame for her mother's death, however baseless this accusation was in truth.

When she was almost seventeen, she left school to live with an aunt who had totally replaced her father in her affections. Her looks and figure were now such that she was able to supplement the money from the part-time job - taken while she waited to go to university - with what she earned from several modelling assignments. As it was, she later left her college prematurely for the more lucrative prospects of a model and was now to be seen modelling the creations of a London-based fashion house.

In the nine-year period since she had left boarding-school she had had little communication with her father, although her earlier conceptions of him had mellowed to the point where she was ashamed now of her harshness. But it had been *so* long and she couldn't quite bring herself to make the first conciliatory move. And, of course, she never had.

The story was almost the same with her sister who, at eighteen years of age when their mother died, had gone out into the wide world and within two years was married. Again, letters and visits had been infrequent but Anne had attended the wedding and this had helped forge a rather fragile bond of kinship between the three - Anne, her sister and her brother-in law.

It was a sad story and Bailey could understand some of what the girl was going through as she sought now - too late - to discover this person whom she had never really known.

When her last sobs had subsided, Bailey took back his reassuring arm and stood up. Then he went over by the window and looked out across the motel courtyard.

'I'm..I'm very sorry to have bothered you like this,' she said, behind him. 'I'm not normally emotional, it's something I've learned to live without. Please excuse me.'

'Not at all,' he answered, his tone dismissive. 'But do you think it is wise to pursue your plan, knowing how much it upsets you?'

His reference to something she had said at one point in her story, about finding out more of her father and his life, brought a slow, determined nod of her pretty head.

Then if that's the case,' he said, 'I suggest you get a good night's rest first. You're far too upset to pursue the matter further today. Are you staying in the area?'

The girl looked up, dazed. 'No, I only drove up this morning.'

'Then why not take a room for the night here at the motel. I'm sure the management will defray expenses in your case.'

The girl looked indecisively around the room.

'I'll pack everything and deliver it to your room,' he said, reading her mind, then added, 'when I, er, pick you up for dinner at seven.'

She smiled then, which momentarily illuminated the patched make-up. 'You seem to be taking good care of me, Ian. I'm truly grateful. You're right about staying - I don't think I could face the drive back just now. But just one thing...'

'Yes?'

'I pay my way.'

'As you wish', said Bailey, making for the telephone. 'I'd better check there's a suitable room.'

Once he knew it was the young lady who wanted a room, the porter was most amenable. It was then easy work for Bailey to have *his* preference met and was assured the ground-floor end-room of the north wing would be reserved for her.

'Is that a good room?' she asked, puzzled that he should take the trouble to obtain a specific room.
'The best I can do,' he replied, and that also have echoed his private thoughts. He had taken the first step towards changing rooms by booking the girl into it. With luck he should be able to investigate its suitability when he called there during her stay. But at the very least he had saved the room from other tenants until the morning when she would leave. Of course it was only a step, and he needed to give the matter much more thought, but he knew that his impromptu action was the best he could do for the moment.

It was almost 1630 hours and time to do rounds when Bailey finished packing his predecessors' belongings. It wasn't merely through their awkwardness that he found it necessary to leave out a pair of gumboots. On his tour with Davies he had picked up a lot of mud on his shoes and, as he had stupidly forgotten to bring any protective footwear with him, it was a chance he couldn't pass up. Having noticed that Simmonds had the same shoe size as himself, he decided his need was greater than Anne's and, with his next rounds due very shortly, he felt there was no time like the present to try them out.

Outside the sky was already as black as it would get that night and, indeed, had been only marginally less so when he had escorted Anne to her room an hour earlier. A light breeze had also sprung up which though not of significance on its own, added to the general discomfort caused by the close to zero temperature.

His rounds alone began with a tour of the boundary fence. This had no security merit as such but merely indicated the shape and extent of the MSA territory. Bailey's interest in it was merely to help him learn the lie of the land on his beat. He cast his torch-beam over a broad strip of ground for over a mile of boundary fence on the unfinished westbound complex, before returning to the eastbound side.

Security patrols bored Bailey, which made him no different from the thousands of other people who carried them out each day. He found himself easily distracted from the process of checking doors and windows so, when he heard the steady beat of the boiler-house pump, he was drawn to it like a moth to a flame. Perhaps surprise was also a factor in his interest. Davies had already mentioned earlier that work in the boiler house was ordered to cease at 1600 each day as the pump's hoses were considered a safety hazard to pedestrians, strewn as they were across a section of the dimly lit car park.

As it was he found the four men in the boiler house were in the process of wrapping up for the day when he entered. Even as he crossed the threshold he heard the faltering rhythm of the noisy pump as it died.

'Working late,' observed Bailey, his tone purely conversational.

The nearest man, thickset and busy disconnecting hoses, dropped the heavy brass connector at his words. ''Strewth, you frightened the hell out of me!' he exclaimed, but not Bailey noted, before he had spent a whole two seconds scrutinising the newcomer.

'Sorry, just doing rounds,' placated Bailey. 'I'm Eddie's relief.'

'Oh, I see,' replied the man, bending to resume his task. 'We're just a bit late tonight.'

'Snags?'

'Yeh, that's it. Snags. We don't normally run over 'cos the bobbies don't like it.' He straightened again, his task completed, and looked at Bailey. 'That's why you gave me a fright. I thought it were them,' he said, and added a mischievous grin.

Behind the man - and two others whose hair glinted wetly under the single arc lamp - was a gaping hole in the floor. From his position by the door, Bailey could just see far enough into the hole to see that it was filled with water to within three

63

feet of the concrete floor. Only inches from the edge stood the large boilers and control consoles, all covered in a thick coating of dust.

'How high will the water rise before it stops,' asked Bailey of a fourth man, having noticed that the water level in the hole wasn't steady but inching upwards.

'About six or seven inches from the top,' replied the man. 'You can just see...'

But his words were lost to Bailey as the sharp, tinny voice of his radio interrupted them.

'Yes, Graham,' answered Bailey, to Davies' call.

'Break-in reported at the main store. You know where that is?'

'On my way. See you there,' he responded, not sure where the main store was exactly but aware it was somewhere in the main complex. As he ran from the boiler house he reckoned on having time to remember its location on the way. Too late, he remembered it was next door to the boiler house and found himself almost immediately among a group of dark shapes who seemed over-quick in diverting their energies from the main store to himself - but heavily.

In the ensuing struggle three thoughts broke through to his consciousness as he went into automatic action. The first was to note Davies's arrival into the fray, which was fairly soon after his own. The second was that although it was obvious that two men could not hope to overpower what seemed to be a gang of leather-jacketed youths, it seemed their attackers were pulling their punches - painful as they still were. Finally, Bailey became aware of another arrival, of a figure vaguely familiar and who proved the turning point in the scuffle for, suddenly, seconds after his arrival, the gang broke off and fled into the night.

'After them,' gasped Bailey, but it was doubtful that he, Davies, or the third man - who he now made out to be Braidwood - could have given chase, as all were in various postures on the ground.

Slowly they got to their feet, aided by the four workmen from the boiler house who had noticed the incident only when they saw the gang running past the doorway.

'Welcome to your new job,' wheezed Braidwood, rubbing his chest through the heavy jacket he wore.

'Thanks,' said Bailey, his breathing returning to normal. 'But really, thanks for your help, I appreciate it.'

'It was just luck I happened along,' he replied. 'I was on my way to wind up the work in the boiler house when I saw you.'

'Lucky for us,' put in the assistant security man.

Bailey turned to Davies. 'How are you, Graham?'

'Think..I'm all right. My head has been proved to be softer than concrete,' he said, rubbing it, 'but I feel I've been luckier than I have a right to expect.'

Bailey was examining the lock of the main store by this time and noticed it was still secure. 'Well, at least they didn't get in here,' he said.

'Shouldn't we inform the police post and start a search?' inquired Davies.

'No, I don't think so,' replied Bailey, as they moved off in the direction of the main entrance to the complex. 'Besides, they're probably somewhere between here and the M1 by now. Did you catch a glimpse of a face, either of you?'

The reply was a unanimous *no.*

They parted company with Braidwood at the entrance to the corridor that led to their office, at which point he announced he would visit the cafeteria in search of aid and sympathy.

'Close shave,' observed Davies, as he closed the door of the security office.

Bailey shook his head, instantly regretting it. 'We were too lucky,' he said, a wince the only sign of his discomfort. 'It was just a roughing up. A lesson - for me, perhaps.'

'A roughing up? A lesson? What do you mean?'

'You saw me examine the lock on the door and heard me say it was still secure. It was and there were no signs of tampering or even marks on the wooden door,' he said. 'Which means they were waiting. Who reported the incident? Anonymous was it?'

Davies nodded. 'Telephone call. Man said there was a break-in in progress at the main store. I just reported it to you exactly as it came in.'

'As I say, it was some sort of lesson.'

'But why?'

'I don't know yet, Graham. I'll just have to wait and see. Perhaps they want to scare me off,' said Bailey, confiding to his assistant his true thoughts, but as an exercise in collaboration he was wasting his time. His thinking was wrong.

The restaurant on Benwick service station was a rectangular affair walled on three sides in smoked-glass. The whole sat squarely on the concourse over the motorway together with the two cafeterias - only one of which was yet in use - adjacent to it. Although only a single, removable, glass wall separated users of the cafeteria and restaurant, they were further distanced from each other by a difference of some fifty per cent in prices. However, the facilities could not be considered comparable. The choice was simple: multi-coloured plastics, for anything from furniture to cutlery - and some would include the food - was the province of the cafeteria, and; soft-lights, carpeted comfort, prompt waitress service and well-prepared food from a rather long - if alcohol-free - menu, was that of 'The Britannia Room.' Of course, the bill from the latter could still be a shock to those who ignored the warning menu on the door, but at least the smoked-glass prevented outsiders from seeing your tears.

And then there was the view.

'I've often eaten at motorway restaurants,' said Anne, looking delectable in a creation which Bailey would have sworn there wasn't room for in the case he had brought from her car. 'But this is the first time on a cross-motorway affair - and at night.'

Bailey followed her glance to the road below where the lightly loaded carriageways twinkled with red, white and amber lights. 'Wait until this motorway really gets going as an international route,' he replied, 'and you'll be able to witness the spectacle of an all-night traffic jam.'

Bailey felt good as he sat across from the girl, with three-quarters of a fine meal inside him. But although she was the main reason for this, a warm bath and a change out of the ridiculous uniform had played its part in dismissing, temporarily, the worries of his job - whether overt *or* covert.

It was while he was turning back from his view of the motorway that his glance took in the approach of a uniformed figure and his contentment suffered its first blow. He reflected that the last thing he needed when in the exclusive company of a beautiful woman was an intrusion from the law. That there was no doubt an intrusion would occur was made plain by the sergeant's determined step in their direction.

When the introductions were over, Sergeant Brennan got quickly to the point of his visit. 'It's about the incident earlier,' he announced, the strong voice matching his military bearing. 'You were involved in a dust-up with some rough-necks, weren't you?'

Across the table from Bailey, Anne suddenly sat even straighter than the correct posture she normally adopted and her eyes widened in concern. 'You never mentioned it to me?' she said to Bailey, surprise in her voice.

Bailey shrugged a shrug which he hoped would convince her that such occurrences were merely an aggravating fact of life and, therefore, below comment. 'Just a reported break-in,' he explained, addressing himself to the sergeant. 'Several unidentified youths who turned their attentions from the main store to me, and later, my assistant and Mister Braidwood.'

'Braidwood? The General Foreman from the construction site?'

Bailey nodded, saying, 'He helped us out. Lucky for us it was, too.'

The sergeant gave an odd look as if he was surprised at this, but his only comment was, 'Well, you live and learn,' said mainly to himself.

There followed a short question and answer session in which the last shred of factual information concerning the incident was aired. Finally, Brennan put away his notebook having written nothing in it whatsoever. Throughout he had been politeness itself, asking his questions in an unemotional way. Now he had finished, his tone became conversational.

'The manager tells me there are only two of you here over the Christmas period. That's going to prove inadequate if another incident like this one occurs,' he said, tapping the breast pocket which contained the empty notebook,' so we'd better put a little more into liaison between our two departments. Otherwise, I may not be able to bail you out in an emergency, simply because I don't have all the facts.'

Bailey nodded but grinned at the same time. 'Okay, message received. I consider my wrist well and truly slapped,' he added. 'And I'm grateful for the offer of co-operation. Most sensible.' It was as close as he could bring himself to appearing to co-operate, which was stupid of him, as he was later to require a high degree of co-operation from those at the Police Post.

'Did you know my father?' asked Anne, of the policeman.

Brennan smiled. 'Yes, I knew Eddie quite well,' he replied. 'He used to come over to the shop for a chat on his rounds.'

As Brennan recounted his friendship with Simmonds an atmosphere developed among the three which could best be described as *chummy*. Anne and Bailey prevailed upon Brennan to stay for some coffee with them. Although he protested that he had the 'eight 'til two at the Police Post' and that he had only called by to check the facts of the incident before taking over his shift, he showed no sign of moving.

Inevitably, they got around to talking about the policeman and his work on the motorway. Both Bailey and the girl were interested in what the sergeant had to say; Bailey for background on his 'patch', and the girl because she wanted to soak-in any information on any subject which bore relation to her father's memory.

'It must be frightening,' said Anne, 'being in the middle of a motorway accident with car speeding by within inches.'

Brennan smiled. 'Like anything else, there's a procedure we follow that keeps us safe. Things aren't as haphazard as they may appear.'

'What procedure is that,' said Bailey, genuinely interested.

'Ace card. It's been around a bit but it works.'

It was as Bailey probed deeper about the *Ace card* system of dealing with motorway incidents, which the police employed, that they all became aware of Braidwood's presence in the restaurant, making the same beeline towards them as the sergeant had, almost half an hour earlier.

'Pull up a chair, let's have a party,' suggested Bailey, with only feigned heartiness. Entertaining though the sergeant had been, and as Braidwood also could be - in his anecdotage - Bailey naturally preferred to be alone with the girl and was vaguely irritated that such a situation was unlikely to occur for some time.

'Thanks. I might do that,' said Braidwood. 'But first I must spoil everyone's fun by talking a bit of shop with Sergeant Brennan, here.'

'It's fixed?' queried Brennan, his tone noticeably cooler now.

'Not yet, sergeant. But at least we now know what the problem is and we'll have the necessary parts here by tomorrow afternoon,' explained the foreman.

'Well, I suppose it's the best we can expect. But I want that thing out of here - and back on the construction site where it belongs - as soon as possible.'

He turned back then, to the couple. 'And now I must be getting back,' he smiled. 'But first, that Ace card thing.'

'Yes?' said Bailey.

'You could always accompany a patrol on an emergency call-out.'

'An accident?' prompted Bailey. 'You can fix it?'

Brennan chuckled. 'Not the accident. I can fix it so that you can go with them - follow in your car. But only if a call-out occurs on my shift.' He looked then towards the motorway below. 'And if there is one thing I can guarantee in weather like we're expecting,' he continued, gravely, 'is that an accident will occur - sooner or later.'

'Just tip me the wink and I'll be with you,' said Bailey.

'All right, that's settled. Use your own car to follow the patrol vehicle and keep well back. Then join the policemen at the scene,' he advised.

He turned to the girl. 'Nice meeting you,' he said. 'It's been a privilege. If there is anything I can do, just let me know.' After adding an apology for disturbing their dinner, he quickly left the restaurant.

'Still working,' observed Bailey, directing his attention towards Braidwood.

'About an hour's work, then I'll call it a day,' replied the foreman. 'Unlike some. What is this, a holiday camp?' he added, indicating Bailey's non-uniform clothes.

Bailey grinned. 'Privileges of being the exalted head of security. Anyway, though Davies is on at present, I'll have a wander around in an hour or so.'

'Keen as that, eh?' said Braidwood in mock seriousness. 'I thought we had police to watch over us. But if you insist...'

'Talking of the police, you seem to have upset them,' said Bailey, then seriously, 'Why is he so impatient for you to get the Scammell back to the site?'

It was Braidwood's turn to smile, although he considered there to be an open-season on smiles anyway. 'A little problem of tax and insurance,' he replied. 'Like there isn't any. It didn't need it when we used it purely on-site. How was I to know it would break down on the brief trip to the servicing centre?'

They laughed at his misfortune - as he had intended they should - and then Bailey belatedly introduced him to Anne. Once she discovered that Braidwood, also, had known her father it unleashed another barrage of questions and an answering volley of anecdotes from the foreman. Not only was Bailey having to share the girl's company, now he had almost become excluded from the conversation as Braidwood regaled her with his stories. Bailey found himself noticing other things in the restaurant. For instance, he could see the waitress who had attended their table was becoming just a little impatient at their long stay. Shortly, she was joined by another waitress who had been busy at the far end of the room until then. The response from the latter, to what Bailey saw as agitated mime, was ill-suppressed mirth.

Still wearing a broad smile, the little woman moved towards their table. Bailey watched as she approached and saw that she had a slight limp. She was a small woman, just under five feet tall, and – though he couldn't know it yet - would only admit to being be fifty-five years of age, a figure that just didn't add up, given her history.

'I think we're about to be thrown out,' said Bailey.

'Wha...,' said Braidwood, interrupted in mid-sentence. He followed Bailey's glance and saw the woman. 'Oh, it's Lela,' he revealed. Then, within her hearing; 'Lela, my bonny Polish love.'

'Hello *darlink*,' she responded, which Bailey later found was her favourite impersonation of the Gabors, whoever they were. 'You are making Joyce very unhappy,' she added, with finger-wagging emphasis.

'Never mind Joyce, my love,' he implored, while Bailey and Anne sat back and enjoyed the exchange. 'Let me introduce you to these nice people. Lela, treasure of Benwick service station, this is Anne, and this is your new security man, Ian Bailey.'

'Please to meet you,' said Lela, trying to affect a curtsy but not being very successful, 'and a happy Christmas to you both.'

Then she straightened and hit Braidwood a blow across the head with the back of the hand. 'Treasure of Benwick, phut. Cheekee monkee!'

Braidwood laughed. 'I think I'd better get back to the Scammell, it's too dangerous around here,' he said, pretending to fend off more blows.

'And I think we may have stayed too long, as well,' said Bailey, and saw the glint in Lela's eye before she turned and beckoned to the other woman to come over.

In a second or two Joyce was with them and, apart from another bout of fun - with Braidwood the predictable catalyst - the trio were soon on their way out of the door to more calls from Lela of 'Happy Christmas'.

As he closed the door behind them, Bailey chanced to look over to where the two women had been joined by Hickson, the manager, who had appeared from nowhere, and seemed to be berating them.

'Doesn't like them chatting with the customers,' explained Braidwood, watching the same scene.

'So it would seem,' confirmed Bailey, as they walked along the concourse. 'He seems very upbeat about this place but something about the place seems...'

'A bit run down?' prompted, Braidwood. 'I take it you've had the sales pitch?'

Bailey nodded.

'Unfortunately, Hickson is still of the notion that this place is going to compete with the Channel Tunnel. The lack of investment is no accident. The race has been lost. All those models in his office are just broken dreams. We'll be lucky if we finish the road.'

Bailey frowned. 'He seemed quite convinced...'

'Delusional, more like. While they were waiting for the high-speed rail-links to the north to be announced there was some hope, but the road hauliers have got into the habit of factoring the cost of going around London via the M25 – and the hell that can be – to the M2 to Folkestone and the tunnel. The game is lost. They'll get some trade this way, for sure, but it's no longer the Golden Highway that they've been touting for years.'

This was depressing, thought Anne, who decided to change the subject. 'Isn't Lela fun?'

'Ah, another character completely,' said Braidwood, smiling. Then, seriously, he added, 'She hides her disability well.'

'What do you mean?'

'Lela is a war-hero, or should that be heroine,' he explained. 'She came over in '38 as a young girl, before Poland fell to the Germans. She later trained as a spy or courier, or whatever. Lied about her age. Went back at the age of 17 in '44.'

'That's fantastic. Is that where she lost her leg?' queried Bailey.

'*Lost* her leg?' exclaimed Anne. 'I saw her limping, but...'

'You're very observant,' said Braidwood, and Bailey saw a strange look accompany the remark made to him. Bailey took notice of this and decided it would be better to limit his observation skills in future, to those that befitted his current role.

Braidwood was still talking. '...and she lost her leg when she parachuted into Poland. She lay in deep snow with a broken leg for nearly two days. Without proper treatment she contracted gangrene and, though they took the leg off well above the diseased part, she eventually had to have it cut off above the knee.'

'Incredible,' said Anne. 'What happened to her then?'

'It proved something of a blessing, apparently,' he continued. 'For the war effort, at least. Looked even younger than her age and could move around without suspicion. She did long tours of the military garrison towns collecting information. She came out of the war undetected, too.'

'And she seems *so* cheerful - and wishes everyone a happy Christmas.'

'Yes, it's called courage,' agreed Braidwood. 'There's a funny thing about Christmas, too. You see, it was on Christmas Eve that she was dropped into Poland...'

They had arrived at the main entrance to the complex by now and they stopped in order to finish their conversation before going out into the cold. Braidwood continued, without faltering. '...She hasn't said so in so many words, but I get the impression she feels that by carrying out a warlike act on that day she violated the spirit of Christmas.'

'You mean she thinks losing her leg was a punishment?' asked the girl.

'Hm. Something like that, and her preoccupation at Christmas time with the spread of 'goodwill to all men' is a sort of penance.' He suddenly shrugged himself out of the serious tone of voice. 'I could be wrong,' he said, 'after all, it's only my opinion. But whatever we say, she's a very warm and lovable old girl.'

'And not looking at all bad for someone who must be well over seventy or even eighty', observed Bailey.

'Well, if sixty is the new forty, and we all need to work for longer, nowadays, perhaps eighty isn't so old anymore?'

They parted then, Braidwood explaining that one of his men was taking a battery back to the Scammell so they could test the electrics. Bailey walked with Anne towards the motel.

Chapter Four
(22nd/23rd December: 2030 - 0430)

The tachometer of Bailey's car 'blipped' to three-thousand-five hundred revolutions as he changed up into fifth gear, then it settled to a quiet one thousand short of that. Even so, the speedometer read out a shade over the legal motorway limit, which was a problem because the flashing blue light of the police Range Rover ahead in the darkness was gradually disappearing into the distance. Bailey remembered that the sergeant had instructed him to keep well behind the police car, but surely not so far that he lost contact, he reflected, and so he applied gentle pressure to the accelerator.

He had been on his way to do an impromptu rounds, as announced to Braidwood in the restaurant, when Davies found him. 'I don't know what it's about,' said his assistant, short of breath from running, 'but the sergeant wants you to get on the westbound carriageway as fast as possible.'

'That's quick,' said Bailey, surprised. It was only an hour since Brennan had mentioned the trip and only half-an-hour since he had left Anne at her room in order to change back into uniform for rounds. 'Still, sooner can occur just as often as later,' he added, cryptically, and pausing only to thank Davies, ran towards the car park.

'Try keeping you mobile on,' shouted Davies, his tone sarcastic. Then to himself, he said, 'Might save me running around like a lunatic,' as he finally got his breath back.

But Bailey was long out of earshot.

Bailey was still wondering at the frequency of accidents when he noticed the patrol car moving over to the fast lane and slowing down. Bailey followed suit and was soon up with the other vehicle, which he saw was negotiating one of the gaps occurring in the crash barriers at two-mile intervals. Judging the oncoming traffic very nicely, Bailey followed the other car onto the westbound carriageway.

As they sped along the outside lane Bailey tried to remember the *Ace card* routine - an interest in which was the reason for his being on the road. *Ace card* was a mnemonic, a memory aid, with each letter indicating a word that formed a step in the procedure for dealing with emergencies. He recollected that it applied to the driver of the police vehicle, not the other member of the team.

A stood for *approach*, which for obvious reasons would never be attempted against the direction of traffic on that carriageway. The letter *C* meant *Caution signs* of which they carried a number. At a distance of nine hundred yards from the accident site they would place a road sign, and the same for six-hundred and three-hundred yards. At one-hundred yards they would deploy cones and - at night, as now - flashing lights, which would lead traffic clear of any obstructions.

Examine scene was the wording behind *E*, and the driver must assess the situation, check for injuries and report what he found to the operations room by radio. The second *C* of the mnemonic was for *casualties*. First aid was the priority, then removal from danger to the hard shoulder. Here the next letter, *A*, reminded the driver to check that *ambulance* or fire brigade assistance had been summoned.

At that point in his reflections his concentration was broken as he spotted a group of flashing amber lights in the distance and wondered if this might be their destination. Almost immediately, he got confirmation of this as the police car rapidly slowed to a stop and the policeman from the passenger seat got out and placed a sign: 'Police - Accident.'

Within seconds of setting off again he had stopped to erect another sign, 'Police - slow,' which was followed by another shortly after that. Then, when Bailey was close enough to see the outlines of several vehicles at the accident site, the policeman off-loaded a number of cones and lights before the driver drove the car nearer the scene.

For a moment the driver did not leave the vehicle. Bailey could see someone leaning towards the driver's window and, after a short conversation, the policeman picked up his microphone and began speaking into it. Then he got out of the Range Rover. Bailey followed.

Five vehicles were lined up on the hard shoulder but only two of them were damaged. The other three cars had stopped to help. The most seriously damaged car was a small saloon made even smaller by being concertinaed at both front and rear; an amendment of design that prevented Bailey identifying the model. The near side rear door was open wide but the other three were firmly secured, enmeshed in the car's framework.

There were two casualties, both from the small car. One was the driver who the policeman found to be dead, still trapped in the car. The other was a girl who had been taken from the rear seat by helpers and placed in the warmth of another car. As he walked with the policeman along the neat row of cars, Bailey remembered, amazingly in the circumstances, that at least there was no requirement to implement *R* of the Ace card procedure; to *remove obstructions* from the road. The wrecker's trucks would take away the damaged vehicles - when the fire brigade, yet to arrive, had freed the body from the saloon.

As they waited for the ambulance and fire engine, the policeman took a look at the girl. Her physical injuries were slight with only a wrenched arm and superficial cuts to her face where flying glass had caught her. It was here that Bailey felt the greatest sympathy for the job of motorway police - or any member of the emergency services, for that matter - for he must carry out a detailed investigation, on the spot, to establish the cause of the incident. That was the final letter in the mnemonic, *D, detailed investigation* and Bailey did not envy the policeman's task. He could understand the grief of those who survived accidents, when others hadn't. Such was obvious. But he couldn't understand how someone could face tragedy several times a day and knowing, perhaps, that one half of a family is dead, even bear to talk to the other half who survived. Oddly enough, it went some way to making him understand why the police were so keen to halt behaviour that could cause accidents.

When he had finished examining the girl, having done his best to reassure her throughout, the policeman left her in the care of a woman witness and turned away to join a group of men some way off.

'I've never seen driving like it,' protested one man.

'Stock-car racing it was,' said another.

A third man started to say something but was drowned out by the approach of both ambulance and fire engine. As they came to a halt, their sirens muted at the same time, the policeman left the group for a few seconds in order to brief the crews. When the girl had been taken, sobbing and still in shock, to the ambulance, which took off immediately, the firemen began their grisly task of cutting out the body of the car driver.

Gradually the policeman directed his questions to get the facts. He realised from experience that people take a little time, after a shock, to talk in anything other than superlatives and adjectives. His patience as usual was rewarded and one man began to describe just what had happened.

'I suppose we were well bunched up, mainly because of the antics of this truck-driver who kept changing lanes,' he said. 'Nobody could tell what he would do next so eventually we hung back, I suppose.'

'What did the truck look like? Shape and colouring?' queried the policeman.

'Black and white cab, I think,' said the man.

'No, it weren't,' said another, small man. 'More like yellow and black. Big thing it was.'

'Container or tarpaulin,' prompted the policeman.

'Oh, definitely tarpaulin,' replied the first man, but casting a questioning glance at the small man all the same.

The small man nodded in confirmation. 'It just pulled-up sudden-like and this car,' he gestured towards the badly damaged vehicle where firemen were wielding hydraulic cutting equipment, 'went in the back of it. The other car went into the back of the first car and then all hell broke loose. We had to push the wreck onto the shoulder.'

'Did the truck stop?'

'Not on your Nelly,' he exclaimed. 'Gone like a flash it were. Never knew they could go so fast.'

'Anyone chance to note the truck's number, or any name on the side?' asked the policeman, but not holding out much hope of an answer. He had resigned himself to overwhelming statistical evidence that number-plates became invisible when accidents occur.

'I did,' said a female voice, and the men turned around to see an old woman with a hand raised for attention. 'I wrote it down.'

'Thank you,' said the policeman, unable to hide fully the mild surprise he felt. He took the note from the lady. 'Is that a U or a V,' he queried.

'It's a V...VDR,' she said. 'Sorry about the writing...'

'No problem, madam,' said the policeman. Then he turned to his colleague, who had joined them after laying out the cones and lights, 'Send that through, would you, Jimmy?'

'Well, that seems to be it,' he announced, returning his attention to the group. 'Thank you for your help. If you will just return to your cars I'll take names and contact details before you go on your way.'

By the time another ambulance had arrived, to transport the freed body, a wrecker's truck was waiting to take the gutted car onboard. The other vehicle, a large saloon, was found to be virtually unscathed though the driver was predictably upset. Even so, he refused the offer of a police driver to take the car to the service station and, instead, drove onto the motorway himself, the last vehicle - apart from the Range Rover and Bailey's car - to leave the scene.

'That's it,' said the police driver. 'See what you wanted to see?'

Bailey nodded. 'And a little more,' he said. 'I don't know what they pay you - but it can't be enough for this sort of job.'

On his return to the MSA at 2220, Bailey locked the car and made straight for the motel. It was peaceful now though colder, which made him move all the quicker. Once through the gap in the hedgerow the wind dropped away and he felt more comfortable. It was this that halted his scuttling run, allowing a more leisurely pace. Now he could lift his head to see where he was going instead of relying almost exclusively on blind navigation.

It was then that he saw it: a perfectly innocuous figure that was negotiating an exterior staircase to one of the motel rooms. But to Bailey's hypersensitive alarm system it was more than that. He saw that the figure's destination was the room next to his own but, more than that, his memory recognised the shape and gait of the burly man, although he didn't know from where.

Without breaking his step, Bailey continued towards the motel office, where he let himself in as quietly as possible and padded over to the counter. Once there, he reached behind the desk to the tray of registration cards and checked the room adjacent to his. His perusal was to no avail for no memory bells tinkled at the name he saw. However, the room plan did reveal one useful piece of information in that it confirmed the sign displayed outside the office: No Vacancies.

''Ere, what's the game?' challenged the corpulent office porter, appearing from an inner room and grabbing the card.

'Just doing my job,' responded Bailey, sternly, 'like any good security man should.' He had wanted to avoid being caught reading the register but no great damage was done and his explanation was plausible.

Recognition flashed in the porter's eyes. ''Course. Yes. I forgot,' he said, and Bailey noticed he peered, suggesting a need for glasses.

With that Bailey turned and headed up the stairs to his room. Inside, he threw off his coat and shoes and lay on the bed. There was serious thinking to be done and it was as well to be comfortable as it might take some time, he reflected. Besides, his head felt ready to burst.

He lay there for an hour before he suddenly sat up, swung his legs off the bed and walked over to the window. He had a plan for changing rooms *and* discovering from what period in his past the man next door belonged. First, he needed to see if the girl was still awake and, as he looked across to her room, this appeared to be so because a light shone in the window.

Now for the next part, he thought. Knowing the light could go out at any minute, he had to work fast. His plan required that he leave his room twice if he was to succeed without inviting suspicion, and that also meant his trips must be legitimate. Quickly, he donned his parka and shoes.

The suitcase containing Simmonds' belongings was still on the floor by the door and Bailey scooped it up as he left the room. It had been his intention to delay handing it over to the girl until the morning as he hadn't wished to provoke further tears by taking it to her as promised before dinner. Now the task had become a necessary chore.

He paused again at the office counter on his way out. When the porter appeared, Bailey told him that he was taking Simmonds' belongings to his daughter's room and he would like her warned by phone of his imminent arrival. Sulkily, the porter grunted that it would be done.

Outside, Bailey walked a few steps towards the girl's room before he stopped and looked back towards the office. He was gratified to see that the porter had his back to him and was engaged in the task of using the telephone. Immediately he saw this he turned sharply to his right and headed out through the gap in the hedgerow towards the car park.

There were few vehicles about now and even fewer on the adjacent lorry park. Near to the dividing causeway of paving slabs was parked the largest vehicle present, which Bailey at first mistook for an overgrown wrecking truck. That is, if you ignored the slanted, bulldozer-like blade on the front. In the dim light it was difficult to discern detail but he could still make out the spaced letters emblazoned across its front: *Scammell*. So this was the 'brute' Braidwood had spoken of, reflected Bailey. It was a brute, too, being about thirty feet long and sporting tyres with a diameter over three feet. The high snout of an engine cover and a large cab indicated it was an old design but the impression given by this and the short platform atop the double-axle was *power*.

Bailey took all this in at a glance - slow that it was - but soon found himself at the rear of his car with other things on his mind. The sole reason for his choosing to deliver the suitcase at this time of night was as cover for this call to his car. Specifically, he had called to collect a small package from the boot.

It was no ordinary lock on the boot lid because what was contained inside was luggage that was very much out of the ordinary and one thing he just didn't need was a thief finding he had the means to start a minor war. Not that Bailey expected to be in a position where the full potential of the equipment was required, but he felt an awful lot better for its being available. It took only a minute to move the covering of clothes to one side - the majority of his clothing was still there - and retrieve the small package from its protective case. Then he slipped it into his parka pocket, re-locked the boot and headed back to the motel.

'A little formal, aren't we?' said the girl, with a smile as she opened the door. 'I promise I wouldn't have been offended if you'd just turned up on the doorstep without warning.'

'It gives the porter something to do,' replied Bailey. It was true: it had both distracted the porter from his change of direction and fixed in his memory that Bailey had left on a legitimate errand.

Given that she had had some five minutes in which to dress, the girl wore a silk night gown and her hair was turbaned under a hotel towel. 'Thank you for bringing the things round,' she said, and Bailey realised that the smile that had greeted him, and what she said now, bore an undertone of strain.

'I thought it would be better if I brought them now as you may leave tomorrow when I am off the service station,' he said.

'Oh, where are you going?'

'The construction site - a tour. I arranged it earlier with Braidwood.'

'Oh,' she said, again, her eyes darting glances around the room with a little wildness about them. 'Er, coffee?'

Bailey was mindful of his need for sleep as he was due on rounds at 0100, but the girl seemed genuinely to want him to stay. So he agreed.

She seemed to relax a little then. She talked about her life modelling and Bailey gave a completely rewritten history of himself.

Throughout this conversation Bailey managed to make a thorough survey of the room and even excused himself to use the bathroom so as to investigate its interior. None of this indicated a lessening of his interest in the girl. This was just the result of years of experience and it might be said that when he took in the number and location of windows, the positions of the three beds and even the curtain rail, which divided the room, it was a task carried out in automatic only. It was a matter for his subconscious alone.

He found he admired the girl very much, and not only for her obvious beauty. He believed her to be an outwardly confident woman - if her father's death was discounted - honest, and straight speaking. He was aware that perhaps he liked her too much and in some masochistic way was glad she was leaving in the morning as it would allow him to concentrate on his job, as well as keep her away from a potentially dangerous situation. For once he regretted his work and thought it would be so much better if he were to return to London with the girl and really get to know her. It was therefore with understandable unease - and an amount of Chauvin distaste - that he spent the latter half of his hour in her room seeing his assessment destroyed.

Anne would never win fame as a seductress, Bailey was sure. She had no flair for such behaviour. However it seemed nobody had bothered to acquaint her with this fact, which is why she crowded into that half hour a parody of the art which had no place outside theatre farce. Even the ploy whereby her gown was allowed to fall away from her languidly crossed legs - to be discovered and replaced with theatrical deliberation - was used repeatedly. Again, her eyes, still unable to entirely hide their wildness, would glance suggestively and in exaggeration.

Perhaps his reaction would have been hypocritical if it had not been for the fondness he felt for her. Also, it was so obviously a 'come on' that he spent more time wondering *why* she was putting on the show rather than being receptive to *what*. Even so, he was looking for a reason from entirely the wrong direction.

He left at 2345, using the excuse of rounds to free himself. When he had gone the girl turned from the closed door and her face transformed into one that was hardly beautiful, so tragic was its countenance. Slowly, she walked over to her bed and sat down. Her hand reached under the pillows and came out with a badly creased envelope from which she withdrew a letter.

It took no more than a minute to read it for the speed with which she turned the pages suggested she had read it many times already. And, like those other times, she now burst silently into tears. But her anguish was deeper now; it was twofold. To the contents of the letter must be added the embarrassment and hurt she felt at the failure of her awkward, girlish overture to Bailey, who could not realise that what he had witnessed was really a cry for help.

It was with an almost physical effort that Bailey wrenched his mind from the girl to concentrate on the next step of his plan. Lying on his bed with just the glow from the headboard light for illumination, he ran through the pitfalls. After a minute-or-so he gave up. He felt tired now and this was another demanding influence on his attention. As a precaution against unscheduled sleep he turned to the built-in clock radio, and set it to burst into life at 0050.

It was while he was adjusting the volume of the radio that he paused to listen to what the announcer was saying. A glance at the clock told him it was a minute past midnight and therefore he was hearing the latest new bulletin.

'...which is thought to be connected with the state of unrest in the Middle East. However, the American Secretary of State will stay in Britain for two days before he continues his tour of European allies.'

Bailey, sat on the edge of the bed now, nodded silently.

The announcer continued, 'Weather in mid-Atlantic is characterised by a deep low-pressure area which is concentrating the efforts of the government weather service. Already the westerly gales are causing problems on the western coasts of the United Kingdom and inland areas can expect gale force winds and snow over the next day or two as the gales move east. It is looking very much like a white Christmas...'

'And on that cheerful note...' murmured Bailey, switching off the radio, but he did not finish the sentence. Instead, he turned off the light and lay back again.

Within a minute he was asleep.

Bailey carried out the first half of his 0100 rounds - the partly completed complex on the far side of the concourse - with a meticulousness that was not characteristic of him. Such overcautious checking was not prompted from any late keenness on his part for the job but merely to provide the maximum opportunity to establish whether he was being observed. He had experienced the odd feeling that he was being watched almost from the start, but it wasn't until he had begun to return to the concourse that he saw him.

To have evaded detection for as long as he had was a measure of the man's professionalism. Unfortunately for him, he had not made allowances for the limitations on his mobility caused by size. Eventually it had dulled the keenness of his surveillance to haul his large frame around and he had thrown some caution to the wind in order to keep in contact. Only a single glance had been needed for the security man to know it was his next-door neighbour.

With his patience rewarded, Bailey did not delay in crossing the concourse for it was too cold to dally without very good reason and the cafeteria had the means to thaw his chilled frame. As he walked, he plunged a gloved hand into his parka pocket and withdrew the package he had retrieved from his car. Surreptitiously, having no means of knowing just how closely he was being watched, he transferred the package to his trouser pocket.

What had prompted such action was the change of plan Bailey had just decided upon. His original intention had been to start a fire in his own room, suitably engineered with the use of the package to appear the result of an electrical fault. But he knew that it was likely that suspicion would be attached to him even before forensics experts could confirm this cause. Now he had another idea. He'd start a fire in the room adjoining his, which would not only destroy his own room because of its proximity but also that of the burly man. It would also raise the question of why a client of the motel had not been in his room when it burst into flames at two in the morning.

'Silver Bells,' sung by Doris Day, was the duty Christmas ditty as Bailey approached the cafeteria. There were, perhaps, twenty travellers seated in the cordoned area of the cafeteria, each looking to be a member of the walking dead. Bailey bought a coffee and chose a table close to the counter before removing his hat, gloves and parka. After some five minutes the man who had been following him entered the cafeteria, no doubt driven into its warmth by the cold and the fact that Bailey looked to be settled. While the man was still at the counter, Bailey went up to the man operating the cash register, leaving his things at the table.

'D'you mind if I use the staff toilets?' he asked, within the burly man's earshot. 'It's a bit of a walk to the public ones.'

'Sure. You know where they are? Through the kitchen, on the left through two doors,' replied the youth.

Once out of sight, he increased his pace until he was almost running and he only slowed to a walk when he was approaching the motel. He ignored the office and instead took the stairs that led to the room next to his own. Then his left hand reached into his uniform jacket and into a pocket that wasn't usual on the standard garment.

The locks on most hotel rooms would never be a match for Bailey's skill, principally because the frequency that hotel keys are lost or stolen means either cheap, easily replaceable, or expensive programmable versions are employed. The one he tackled now was of the cheap variety – the Hickson touch, he reflected - and within the minute he was sliding silently into the room.

The first check he made, by the subdued light of his penlight, was of the window and he was gratified to find that the curtains had been drawn. In the second sweep of the beam he saw something glint on the far side of the room and by the wall which divided this from his own room. A closer investigation revealed it to be a piece of equipment of a type that Bailey had seen before.

It was comprised of two boxes joined together by a short length of cable. The larger box was a tape-recorder while the other, which was in position against the wall, was an extremely sensitive microphone of a type that Bailey recognised, to which was attached a pair of headphones. Simply explained, the device was modern technology's answer to the eavesdropper's upturned glass. Bailey pressed the rewind button on the recorder, first noting the counter reading so as to be able to reset it to as it was before. Then he pressed the playback and heard a rerun of the news he had listened to at midnight, the quality of sound being as good as that he had experienced in the next room.

It was an odd feeling he had when the recorder played back the words: 'and on that cheerful note', but it wasn't the recognition of his own voice which was responsible for this. It was the choking sensation caused by the placement of an iron bar around his neck.

At first, Bailey went through the usual controlled sequences to free himself from his assailant's grasp. Squirming and trying to place his elbow in the man's gut proved a dismal failure for the man just tightened his grip and this effectively halted any movement of Bailey's torso. An attempt to jab his heel into the man's shin was even less effective as the man felt it coming by the shift in his victim's weight and he just lifted the foot a couple of inches while he leant against the wall for stability. Instead of what he had intended, Bailey found that the back of his leg connected very painfully with the toe of the man's shoe.

Bailey was conscious of two things by this time: he was fast running out of tricks and slowly choking to death. He nevertheless continued struggling, a little more wildly now, as the survival instinct was growing stronger. But although he could hear the man's breathing becoming progressively more laboured from his struggles, Bailey knew he would be a long time dead before the man gave up from exhaustion.

A third thought penetrated his woolly consciousness. This was a death-trip. Bailey had seen the surveillance equipment and therefore knew he was being shadowed. To avoid the rumpus that his release could create, the man must get rid of him. It was most likely that the man's superiors considered Bailey to be merely a danger from the point of being meddlesome and therefore unaware of his true employers.

Slowly he reached down a hand to a tiny slit in his uniform trousers, hidden in the join of material, which ran down the outside of his thigh, and withdrew what appeared to be a knitting needle. Again, he was thankful for the alterations he had had made to the uniform prior to his arrival at the MSA.

In hand-to-hand combat it would not be a contest, Bailey knew. He couldn't hope to deal with the man whose arms were squeezing the life out of him. Nor could he execute the man, even with the needle, while in his present position. That is why he first jabbed the implement into the man's groin, which had the desired effect of releasing him. Then he turned and drove the needle under his assailant's chin and deep into his brain.

The man was dead before he hit the bed but only because Bailey had caught and deflected him before he could fall, twitching, to the floor. Then Bailey allowed himself a few moments to recover physically while his brain continued to race.

Feeling a little better for his rest, he now knew what he must do. The man's death would not be an embarrassment if he paid attention to detail. That is why he next stripped the body and arranged him in the bed as if he was sleeping. Then he removed the needle and replaced it in its sheath.

His next task was to short-circuit the tape-recorder supply lead, which would blow the fuse in the plug and leave a nice black mark on the wall-socket cover. He then unscrewed the socket cover and poured some powder into the recess from the package he had brought with him and replaced the cover and plug. Again, from the package, he drew a miniature circuit tester, of the type that generates an electric current, and attached it to the tape-recorder supply lead. One revolution of the handle sent electricity down the line to the wall-socket which started the powder smouldering. Within ten minutes there would be a moderate blaze in the room. It was time for Bailey to get out.

His first call was the cafeteria where he retrieved his things. He was surprised, on checking his watch, to find that he had been away for only twelve minutes. Then he was on his way back to the motel, this time by way of the office.

He had to bang on the counter to get a response from the porter this time. The portly figure arrived quickly, however, although his dishevelled appearance indicated that he had been asleep.

'I've just finished rounds,' said Bailey. Then he sniffed the air theatrically. 'Can you smell burning?'

The porter's first reaction to this was alarm, which blew away all vestiges of sleep from his face. 'Burning? Burning?' he challenged, before he began sniffing. In no more than five seconds he was satisfied. 'No, I can't smell anything.'

Bailey wasn't surprised. His own sense of smell was quite acute and *he* couldn't smell burning either. But he said, 'It must be me. Imagining it, I suppose. Oh well, goodnight.'

In his anxiety to return to slumber-land the porter didn't even reply but Bailey felt sure that whatever was on his mind wasn't complimentary anyway.

The porter's attempts to get back to sleep again were in vain. Even when the fire had finally been extinguished at 0315 his frayed nerves began to jangle from reaction, and continued to do so to the end of his shift.

Bailey hadn't been gone more than five minutes when he returned to disturb the porter's sleep again. His entry was a little noisier than before, but then his reason this time was to raise the alarm for a fire in his room. With all the noise he was making, mostly directed at the porter who he insisted should wake up, Bailey totally confused the poor man. This served Bailey's purpose by convincing the porter that he had fallen asleep again. So disorientated was the man that he later said nothing of the five minute delay between the security man's 'discovery' of the fire and raising the alarm. It was difficult to believe any of the porter's statement as he had been incited to such a pitch of terror that throughout he adopted the reasoned behaviour of a headless chicken.

The seat of the fire was situated on the wall, which divided the two rooms, and therefore Bailey felt confident there would be a period of some minutes before any other rooms - and therefore lives - were threatened. Even though he could reasonably expect help to have arrived before then, he personally evacuated the nearest rooms and raised the alarm on the rest.

Somehow, the porter managed to carry out the tasks assigned to him by the security man and the first fifteen minutes saw the arrival of the manager, Davies, two policemen and the fire brigade. At a safe distance, clad only in nightwear and blankets, stood the motel's clients - their number swollen by the presence of travellers who could not resist witnessing the spectacle.

For ten of the above minutes Bailey, Davies and the two policemen attacked the fire with portable extinguishers and, eventually, a rather ineffective fire hose. Amid the confusion nobody noticed that the operator of the hose, Bailey, was controlling the nozzle so that it remained of limited efficiency. When he felt sure that enough damage had been done to the burly man's body to blur the cause of death, the fire-fighting usefulness of the hose greatly improved. Finally, the firemen arrived and with typical efficiency had doused the blaze in less than ten minutes.

During the twenty-five-or-so minutes it had taken to extinguish the fire, the manager was to be found reassuring the motel's inhabitants. Although immensely relieved at the minimal damage caused outside of the two rooms on fire, he still had the chore of re-housing three people from the water-damaged room below the one so recently inhabited by the burly man, and he exercised all his charm in accomplishing a change round in the accommodation.

The initial investigation into the fire took place in the manager's quarters, attended by all those who had had a direct part in dealing with it. In his written report, Bailey listed the occurrences from the time of his 'noticing' the smell of burning, less of course the four-and-a-half minutes he had spent encouraging the fire.

'And now I'll try and get some sleep,' he said, handing the report to Hickson. 'There's nothing else, is there?'

'Nothing that can't wait until the morning, Bailey,' replied the manager. 'But where will you sleep now that your room is gutted?'

'Oh, I'll find somewhere,' he answered, and left the room.

Chapter Five
(23rd December: 0430 - 1330)

The dawn was just breaking as Bailey left the girl's room. It was 0730 now and he was on his way to the security office. The clear sky of the previous day had given way to a grey overcast but the temperature had risen slightly.

It had been a shamefaced Anne who had answered the door at four-thirty in the morning. In response to Bailey's request for a bed, she had readily agreed and then disappeared to her own bed again, having drawn the central curtain across to form a dividing wall.

Too tired to investigate her change of mood, he had flopped down onto his bed and slept. When he awoke, he dressed quietly and left the room without disturbing her.

Davies was waiting for him when he arrived at the office. From his vantage, he had been able to watch Bailey's approach across the car park.

'Coffee?' he asked, as the security man shut the door behind him.

Bailey nodded and moved over to the rounds book where he glanced down the entries on the last page. 'No problems, I see. You may as well get your head down. Remember, you're on again at ten until I get back from the site.'

'Don't I just know it,' replied Davies, and Bailey could see the puffy ridge of skin under each eye, caused through lack of sleep. 'What I wouldn't do for a decent bed,' he added, looking down at the camp-bed, 'and one of those things you share a room with.' A laugh escaped him as Bailey aimed a playful punch at his arm, in response to the reference to Anne.

''Course it beats me why you changed rooms, at all,' continued the assistant security man, as Bailey stared at the motel. 'You've much more space in the girl's room.'

Bailey knew from experience that it is a symptom of tiredness and strain to talk a lot, especially when the pressure is off and the prospect of sleep very near. He could even allow that Davies would talk a certain amount of irrelevant nonsense as he began to relax, but surely not the rubbish he was talking now.

'You're not making sense,' he said bluntly.

Davies repeated what he had said, almost word for word, but still Bailey looked at him with a concern that showed. 'Look, I moved into the girl's room, from my own, when the fire destroyed it,' he said slowly, and it was obvious from his tone that his estimation of the assistant was suffering a decline.

'Oh, I didn't realise that...'

'Well, now you know,' interrupted Bailey, roughly. Then he turned back to his perusal of the motel. He could quite plainly see the two blackened holes that had once been the windows of the two first floor rooms. He assumed they would be boarded up today, after the experts had had the opportunity to inspect them.

'It's just that I thought you'd taken over Eddie's room,' Davies persisted, 'the one the girl's in.'

Bailey had been all set to round on his seemingly stupid assistant, his patience and interest in the subject being now at an end. Instead, something clicked in his brain and diffused his temper, allowing curiosity to take over. 'What was that again?'

It was Davies' turn to sigh and wonder at the mental keenness of his superior. 'The girl's room used to be the one her father used. I was surprised you would change rooms for a smaller one, that's all.'

Bailey was quiet for a moment. 'Let me get this straight,' he said. 'The security man was billeted in the room now occupied by the girl - *not* the one that I moved into.'

'That's what I said,' confirmed Davies, patiently. 'Which is why I took longer than I expected to find you with the motorway message,' he added. 'When I couldn't get you on your mobile, I phoned your room but a girl answered. I couldn't understand this so I was on my way over to investigate when I intercepted you on rounds.'

Bailey nodded slowly, but didn't say anything.

'I'm surprised the manager didn't tell you,' added Davies.

'So am I,' agreed Bailey, but he was wondering why Hickson had gone to such lengths to hide what - as Davies had just proved - was a too-easily discovered deception. And why plant the security man's belongings around the room? Was this just camouflage to further fabricate the ruse? It would be interesting to hear what the manager had to say.

But for the moment he didn't want to involve Davies in this and so he changed the subject of their conversation. 'I've had a word with one of the police sergeants,' he began, 'and he shares a fear that the beating we took yesterday might be more than it seems. Like me, he has no concrete views but he asked that a higher degree of surveillance is undertaken on rounds, and that we should liaise closely with the police.'

Davies nodded. 'What are we looking for? Anything in particular?'

'That's just it, we don't know,' responded Bailey. 'All we can do is keep our eyes open a little wider and put into the rounds book all our suspicions. As the trouble started at the main store, we could begin by checking that more frequently.'

'Okay, boss.'

'And now I'm going back to the motel for a shave,' said Bailey, and this time a warning look dissuaded Davies from making any disparaging remarks.

ANTHONY ASHPITEL

Bailey paused on his way back to the motel to pick
up some breakfast from the cafeteria. As he watched
the woman carefully pack the sandwiches and
coffee he reflected on his sensitivity concerning
Anne. He had almost added to his parting shot in
the office that he was going to the motel to say
goodbye to the girl, but had decided against telling
his assistant lest it attract further ribald comment.
Why should he worry what Davies might say about
him and the girl? He was being silly, he knew. But it
was *why* he was being silly – not an emotion he was
prone to - which disturbed him.

Anne was dressed and all was tidy in the room
when he arrived, but he noticed that she had made
no attempt to pack.

'I brought you some breakfast,' he said, smiling.
'A sort of thank you for letting me stay last night.'

'Oh, thank *you*,' she responded. 'But you
shouldn't have bothered, it was the least I could do
for someone in your predicament.'

Bailey started to arrange the food on the small
table. 'What time are you leaving?' he asked.

'I'm not.'

'You're not?' exclaimed Bailey, at once elated and
confused at her words.

Anne shook her head. 'I'm staying here for a
couple more days.'

'But why?'

'You know why: my father.'

'You mean you want to stay and upset yourself some more,' said Bailey, and it was a statement rather than a question.

'If I must,' she responded, slowly. 'But I don't think it's likely. I feel stronger now.'

Bailey could see his plan falling apart. If the girl stayed she would keep the room and he would have to make do with something unsatisfactory. Besides, he was confused by her insistence that she stay when he could see no logical reason for her doing so. Perhaps that was it: *she* was illogical and was guided in her decision by purely emotional reasons. It was possible, but Bailey couldn't quite see it as the whole reason. Therefore, he became suspicious. What was more, he wouldn't give up the room without a battle.

'I'm afraid the room is already booked out to someone for today,' he said gently. As her head came up to question him with a glance, he added, 'Me.'

'You're joking.'

'I'm not,' he said. 'I booked it last night.'

The girl's shoulders slumped. 'It doesn't matter. I'm sure there will be another room available.'

'That's just it, there isn't another room,' he persisted, not liking himself very much now. 'They book up early at this time of the year. It's a welcome break in the journey. This was the only room available, *then*.'

It should have been enough to complete her dispatch, but she wasn't finished. 'You're determined to force me out. *Why?*'

'I'm not trying to force you out, at all,' returned Bailey, an edge creeping into his voice. 'Although I admit there can be little benefit in you staying.'

'Shouldn't I be the judge of that?'

Bailey shrugged his shoulders.

Sensing she had the initiative, she sat up straight but the tone of her voice became smooth. 'Couldn't I stay here - in your room - for a day or two?' she reasoned.

'Do you think the management would tolerate such an arrangement?' parried the security man. 'A few hours for a displaced person is one thing, but setting-up house...'

'We're both *marginally* over eighteen. What can they do?'

Bailey said nothing.

'Look, I'm sorry about my behaviour last night,' she continued, a note of pleading in her voice, 'I'm embarrassed and not very pleased with myself. If I could, I would explain. But I promise if I can stay...'

'Okay, I'm convinced,' said Bailey quickly, in the hope of interrupting what he knew she would say. 'When you want something you can be quite determined, can't you.'

The girl slumped back again. 'Thank you,' she said.

'For the breakfast,' he added.

Bailey had two places to visit before he left for the motorway construction site. His first call was to the security office where he woke his assistant. Then he left and entered the manager's outer office.

'He's on the phone to head office at the moment,' whispered the girl, even though the inner door was shut.

Something must have shown in his face for the girl moved between him and the door. 'He left word that he isn't to be disturbed until he's completed the call,' she added, hurriedly.

Though irritated at this, Bailey didn't want to force his way in and, anyway, he was due at the construction site within the half hour. He could always catch him later.

'May I use your phone? Internal,' he asked.

The girl indicated the telephone on her desk. 'Please do.'

'How's the motel filling up?' he asked the motel manager, after identifying himself. He was aware that he had earned some respect since helping to put out the fire and this was proved when the man answered his enquiries without hesitation.

'We've ten booked for tonight of the thirteen rooms remaining,' he answered, 'though we expect a full house by lunchtime.'

'Put me down for the one at the end of the wing, will you? The one on the ground floor.'

'Of course,' answered the voice. Then there was the sound of a laugh. 'Don't go starting any fires though, will you.'

Bailey allowed the man his little joke and brought the call to an end. He was quite pleased at the way things were turning out after the upset to his plan caused by the girl's staying. He now had his room and could also keep a close eye on Anne who had aroused his suspicion by her insistence on staying. At least, that was all he would admit she had aroused.

As he left the manager's outer office Davies joined him, on his way to do rounds. They then walked together as far as the main entrance of the complex, where Bailey reminded his assistant to put all suspicions in the rounds book. Bailey then left the building and crossed the car park to his car.

Davies didn't immediately leave the spot where he and Bailey had parted. Instead, he watched his boss get into his car and drive out of the car park. While he watched he became aware of a tall, powerfully built man who was following the car's progress very closely. Whether the man was merely admiring the sports car's lines or something of greater significance was impossible for Davies to know. But the fact that the man then quickly left his position at the main entrance and moved inside the building while speaking into his mobile phone, seemed suspicious.

Davies made a mental note to include the man's antics in his rounds report. Unfortunately, the assistant security man never returned to the office.

Much of the success or failure of Rider's operations rested upon the briefing he gave to his agents. Only very occasionally was his preparation defective and this invariably occurred when an operative had to be sent in immediately, and therefore cold. Given the luxury of one or two days' notice, his team could provide an intensive course that saturated the operative in background information. But it took a very special brain to absorb and retain such a forced flood of facts, and when added to the other qualifications required by their role, such men were selected from a very short list indeed.

Bailey was such a man. He remembered the vast majority of the information presented to him at his briefing. This is why he had known something of the layout of the MSA and the *Ace card* system. He knew quite a lot about motorways, too. He could quote from memory the chain of command employed by the main contractors, for instance, from Hargreaves and his Board of Directors - though their executives - and all the way to the labour-force.

In his mind's eye, the security man selected the areas of responsibility for just one of these executives, the Chief Engineer. It was this man who had most to do with the actual road-building, having his own Head Office and Site Office, together with their own organisations.

It was the site organisation that Bailey would see on his tour and, as he drove along the lightly loaded motorway, he concentrated on refreshing his memory of this. He knew that the Chief Engineer would rarely visit the site, leaving overall charge there to his Site Agent. In a similar way, the Department of Transport's man, the Engineer in charge of the project, was normally too involved with planning and other work to be in attendance on site. So the Engineer in charge would leave the tasks of monitoring and checking the contractor's work to his assistant, the Resident Engineer.

Below the Site Agent, the site organisation split into three groups, each supervised by a manager. There was the Site Office, where the wages-clerks and timekeepers worked; the canteen, where the kitchen staff prepared meals; and the Sub-agent's Office, where the Sub-agents - assisted by section - and junior-engineers, would detail the work of the labour force. Their instructions would be issued to foremen and gangers - the senior foreman being known as the General Foreman, or Braidwood, as it was on this site. They would supervise the work of plant operators, drivers, tradesmen and labourers.

He even knew how to get to the construction site, which was not immediately obvious to the uninitiated as it meant some manoeuvring was required at the last junction and around the barriers at the end of the open section.

But such knowledge was only background information, which he must supplement with actual experience. Rounds of the MSA had revealed the actual layout of the service area, and accompanying the police car on its emergency call showed him something of how they worked. His visit to the construction site would fulfil the same purpose in respect of the motorway.

Beyond the barriers, the motorway continued for some three miles before the mini-village of accommodation and site offices came into view. The collection of caravans - of varying ages from ancient to merely old - were clustered about two new portable offices of the type which are jacked to a level position above uneven ground. In the background, man-made mountains of aggregate and other materials provided protection from the wind on three sides while the raised causeway of the motorway protected the fourth. Dotted along the skyline were items of mechanical plant, various machines that had the look of prehistoric monsters. And, like the rest of the scene today, they were still and silent.

He had eased the car most of the way down the uneven track to the office before he saw any sign of life. Then, as he was negotiating the last in a series of potholes, he glimpsed a figure coming out of the cabin.

'Hello, I'm Jim Kingston, one of the foremen around her,' said the spryly built man, when Bailey lowered his window. 'Larry told me you were coming. Just park-up and come inside.'

The interior of the rectangular building was cleaner than Bailey had expected, considering that the wind had blown the lighter materials from the storage mounds and coated everything outside with a patina of light dust. But that, he presumed, could be because they had had opportunity to tidy things up now that the majority of people were away for Christmas. There was one element of untidiness, however, in the shape of a dishevelled man who slouched against the wall behind Kingston.

'Where's Larry,' asked Bailey, conversationally. 'Busy?'

'That's the size of it,' confirmed the foreman. 'He had to go over to the Plant Depot at short notice. He asked me to look after you.'

'That's fine with me,' smiled Bailey.

'Good. What I've got in mind is for Joe here,' Kingston's thumb jerked back over his shoulder, 'to take you on a tour in the three-wheeler. Ask him anything you like.'

He slid from his perch on the desk then and added, 'When you get back I'll tell you a bit about how we operate.'

'Thanks. I just hope I'm not putting you out,' responded Bailey, and although he seemed far from elated at the prospect of being Bailey's chauffeur, the untidy man didn't say so.

It became obvious after a walk of a few hundred yards that Joe was no conversationalist. It was also obvious that unless the vehicle they were to use was somewhere over the horizon, there was only one other they could be heading for. Kingston's mention of a three-wheeler had conjured up the picture of a tiny runabout in the security man's imagination. What stood before the two men was as different from this picture as a double-decker bus is from a go-kart. The machine was enormous.

Each one of the three bloated tyres stood higher than a man, the tread of each as deep and corrugated as those on a tractor. Connecting the front wheel to the four at the rear was a long but slim 'boom', that was suspended at least five feet from the ground, and stretched for maybe fifteen- or twenty feet before it met the rear wheels. Towards the rear wheels the 'boom' had a fixing point, as indicated by the four bolt holes and scarred paint where something had once been bolted on. Well away to the side of the vehicle a wide, to Bailey's eyes, bulldozer blade was located, bearing the same colour paint in places as that of the three-wheeler, which he imagined was the missing appendage. Above and behind the rear wheels of the monster stood a high-sided glass cubicle, which was the cab.

Bailey and his guide climbed the ladder and clambered into the confined interior. The security man noticed that there were two seats. One that facing out over the single wheel had before it a small console containing the usual driving instruments. The other faced in exactly the opposite direction, and the attendant console was there for the control of a hydraulically-operated contraption at the rear of the vehicle.

'That's your seat, there,' said Joe, proving not only that he had a voice, but also something more sinister. For as he spoke the Bailey was exposed to his evil-smelling breath.

Eventually, when the alarm bells in Bailey's head had stopped jangling, the answer flashed across his brain. The same warning bells had sounded on the previous night when he had encountered the burly man. As then, he felt he knew the man from somewhere. The difference now was that he knew where he had met them before - and smelt the man's breath - when they had attacked him at his flat.

It required several seconds of sustained willpower for Bailey to quell the urge to bounce the man there and then. He knew that it was not the right time. That would come later, he was certain. In the meantime, he would watch the man very closely to ensure that no sequel to the attack could take place. Turned sideways on, as he sat on the rearwards facing seat, he monitored everything the man did as they lurched away from the site.

Underway, the throb of the engine was so loud that it prevented real conversation, which suited Bailey fine. Although this also meant that a spoken travelogue was out of the question, Bailey could occasionally pick-up a word or two as his guide pointed out some detail. This, too, suited the security man for the scenery told its own tale as they trundled alongside the motorway.

The tour lasted for an hour in which time Bailey saw the various stages of motorway construction, albeit in reverse order. As they moved east towards the coast, the vast curve of highway was worn away, layer by layer, until only the raised causeway was left.

As they progressed, the occasional mobile phone mast punctuated the course of the road but otherwise the scene was a moonscape, dissected by the scar that was the course of the embryo highway.

Traveling beside the highway, the lane markings and cat's eyes were the first to go as they passed the point where such work could no long be carried out. Then a layer of the wearing surface, carefully rolled bitumen, ended in a jagged edge, followed by the bottom layer a half-mile later. Long shifts of the concrete base were bare then until they, too finished abruptly in a neatly angled line.

For security against the lurching of the three-wheeler, Bailey used one hand to hold on to a fixed bit of the cabin at all times. The other hand was plunged into his pocket. This was no accidental arrangement, for the GPS receiver application on his mobile phone recorded their track faithfully and, when Bailey's interest in a particular piece of landscape was piqued, he clicked a button to record the position.

Keen not to reveal a heightened interest in the view, Bailey's eyes narrowed to inspect the course of the motorway from this point onwards with increased vigilance. The satellite surveys, both radar and Magnetic Anomaly Disturbance (MAD) had quite clearly revealed the infrastructure of the motorway right up to where the reinforced concrete petered out and that around the 'furniture' of bridges and reinforced conduit further on. Unfortunately, this same reinforced lattice acted like a faradic cage and prevented these tools revealing what lay beneath. Bailey's covert study was directed towards disturbances of any kind and he was rewarded on a grand scale as almost the entire landscape was disturbed in a sea of ruts, gouges, and large pools to exercise the three-wheeler's excellent low-density ground traversing qualities. Also, unfortunately, none of the disturbances that he could yet see stood out as being out of the ordinary – for a motorway in the making.

The separation of concrete from the sub-base aggregate coincided with the place where a half-formed road bridge spanned the motorway route. Amid the scaffolding and reinforcing bars could be seen the plywood shuttering into which concrete would be poured, strengthened by a framework of reinforcing steel mesh. The vehicle tracks that criss-crossed the area around the bridge foundations seemed particularly numerous and, it seemed to Bailey, a logical place for him to inspect later, unobserved, and so he pressed the button on his phone again.

It was some time before the aggregate layer fizzled out but when it did the edging stones, cemented into place so that the concrete spreaders could run along them in railway style, also ended. After that, only the heaped earth sub-grade of the causeway remained to cross the landscape of East Anglia.

There was little point in going any further so Joe deftly reversed the three-wheeler and they started back, splashing along the same route. Now that he was no longer concentrating on the motorway, in addition to his driver, he could see the things he had missed on the way out. Items of machinery dotted the landscape and Joe would occasionally point to one and add an accompanying explanation of 'drott', 'grader', 'scraper' and other terms.

As they progressed, Bailey's eyes continued to watch the ground for signs of disturbance, but eventually gave up as almost the whole of the strip of land alongside the motorway was churned up by earthmoving machines. He reconciled himself to having taken a largely wasted trip. Yes, it had been interesting but, beyond identifying Joe as one of the ungodly, he felt his trip had moved him along in his investigation very little: only the view of the area around the embryo bridge had grabbed his interest unequivocally. What he had to admit though, was that this trip gave him a very good, if not indispensible introduction, to the lie of land, which would hold him in very good stead later.

Instead of returning directly to the spot where the vehicle had been parked, Joe turned towards the multi-humped storage area, and, with an explanation that Bailey heard as 'have a look at the dump,' the three-wheeler growled its way up the first incline.

The 'dump' was criss-crossed by roughly hewn tracks with, off to one side, a large but shabby complex that Joe called the Mixing Plant. He spent some time touring the area and seemed to be enjoying himself as he tried for steeper and more dangerous angles on the higher tracks. The machine reacted very well to these antics but occasionally Bailey felt uncomfortable as a particularly critical angle was reached, when he felt sure the vehicle would topple over. And, of course, Joe knew this.

After a while Bailey decided that if he was going to risk his neck at the hands of this driver he would do so in pursuit of some useful purpose. So far, Joe had avoided the high passes on the edge of the storage area furthest from the site. Bailey realised that the vantage afforded by one of these high points would enable him to view the surrounding area, which just might turn out to be profitable. The plan, unfortunately, was not converted into action. Whether Joe considered it to be a challenge he didn't care for, or whether it really was 'unsafe' as he claimed, he didn't try but instead turned the vehicle towards the cluster of caravans.

Outside the office, Bailey's shout of thanks was lost in the roar of the three-wheeler's engine as Joe gunned the engine and moved up the incline without a backward glance.

Kingston was much more voluble that Joe, and he answered the security man's questions knowledgeably and fully. It was obvious the man enjoyed his work and Bailey was taken with his enthusiasm for civil engineering. However, he felt that things were becoming a little too technical for his needs when the foreman launched into a lecture on the California Bearing Ratio - a formula worked out to assess the bearing capacity of different materials. It appeared to be a vital consideration in the construction of any road or structure, to know the CBR of the ground upon which something was being built. Bailey had no doubt that this was so, but the technicalities were beyond his requirements and so he returned the conversation to layman level by stating that they appeared to have foundation problems at the MSA.

'Hmm, so Larry was saying,' responded Kingston, catching breath at the same time. 'I never go over there myself, but I hear it's water problems.' Then he smiled, and added, 'Which only goes to prove the necessity of carrying out a thorough survey before starting work on foundations.'

Having made his point rather neatly, the foreman paused just a little longer than it took to draw in a breath and Bailey seized upon the change to make his exit. He had been grateful for the tour, and thanked Kingston for his information, but as he drove back onto the motorway he promised himself another visit to the site - unannounced, unaccompanied and a little more selective in the areas to see.

Returning to the MSA Bailey felt a little happier than he had before visiting the construction site. Until then he had found little that was of significance to the job in hand - outside the dead man's room. Now he knew who had been responsible for his attack and, although there were still many questions he couldn't answer, he felt certain he was in the right area.

He concentrated on the one overriding question: *why* had they visited him at the flat? There could be only two possible answers: to take something, or, equally possible, plant something. But *what*? He didn't pretend to know the answer and, for the moment, he didn't worry overmuch about it. Their very proximity to his chosen area of operations tied in with his suspicions and that was the real reason for his satisfaction.

When he pulled onto the MSA he noticed that the sky was darker now, which was a little premature for only an hour after noon. As if sensing a change in the weather, the swollen throngs of travellers - on the way to their Christmas venues - moved quickly to and from the complex.

Although he was hungry by now, he entered the complex by the staff entrance and climbed the stairs to the manager's office.

'I'm afraid he's still busy,' said the girl.

'So am I,' replied the security man, and went into the manager's office.

Whatever it was that had been keeping the manager busy it ended then, for as Bailey walked in he was replacing the telephone.

'Ah, Bailey,' he said, smiling. 'Have a nice trip?'

Bailey nodded, surprised. 'You seem to know everything that goes on around here', he observed.

'It's surely my job,' replied Hickson. 'But there's no secret to it. Davies told me an hour ago. Which reminds me...'

The manager glanced around the well-stacked desk and extracted a blue covered folder that he gave to Bailey. 'You may not have had the opportunity to read the company regulations, but let me tell you it states quite clearly that security staff are not to drink alcohol whilst on duty,' he said, his tone officious.

'Davies? Drinking?' said Bailey, with a frown. 'Surely not.'

'I'm afraid so. I didn't mention it to him myself because he didn't appear to be drunk. But I could smell it on his breath.'

It was Bailey's turn to become officious. 'Leave it to me. I shall be having words with young Davies, I assure you. And although it would be unwise to further reduce our skeleton staff over Christmas by taking any higher action, he certainly won't do it again.'

'I'd appreciate that, Bailey,' responded Hickson, and he visibly relaxed. 'Now, what have you come to see me about?'

Bailey was back on an even keel now which was proved by his cool tone as he addressed the manager. 'I came here to ask why you changed the security man's quarters before I arrived.'

Hickson cleared his throat and sat upright in his chair at Bailey's words. 'Change of rooms?' he asked, innocently.

'Don't play games,' chided the security man, realising that he was in the strong position of being virtually unsackable for the next few days. 'You swapped the Simmonds' room from a large to a small room. You also tried to camouflage your actions by pretending that the smaller had always been the security man's quarters - even to the extent of re-distributing his things around the new room. The simple question, therefore, is *why*?'

Hickson sighed then, which wasn't the reaction Bailey had expected. Alarm or shame he could understand. Such emotions would have fitted in with what he suspected. But a sigh? Bailey began to feel some unease.

'So you found out,' began Hickon, unnecessarily. 'I told Head Office this would happen. Once they set a precedent with Simmonds it would be difficult to change...'

'Do you mind talking some sense?' demanded the security man.

'The room. The one Simmonds had. It was a three-bed room.'

'And?'

'And, this is a business,' said the manager, raising his voice. 'Here was an employee - single - who was using a room designed to accommodate three. If it hadn't been for his friends at Head Office I would have moved him to the single room long ago. It was simple economics.'

'So when he died you made sure the next security man would be put right at the outset,' supplied Bailey. There was only one more thing to ask and he had the feeling that he already knew the answer. 'Why then, did you go to all the trouble of not only transferring his belongings to the new room but re-distributing them as well?'

Hickson gave a feeble smile. 'A little ruse on my part. A deception to convince the new security man,' he said, nervously. 'But you see the sense behind the change, don't you?'

Bailey had been right in his assessment of the manager's probable answer to his question. 'Yes, it makes sense,' he said, turning for the door. 'It's good business.'

But for all the logic the manager had just demonstrated, Bailey could not believe that he would spend his time re-distributing a dead man's belongings around another room just as a 'little ruse'. Added to what he had seen in the now gutted rooms, this disbelief seemed to confirm that the manager's story had no place in truth.

He hadn't made it through the door before he stopped at the sound of the manager's voice. 'Oh, Bailey. One more thing,' he called. 'Where are you sleeping?'

Bailey turned to face him, and smiled, saying, 'In my room, of course. The old one.'

Bailey's preliminary search of the complex was without success and so, hoping to combine lunch with looking out for his assistant, he made for the cafeteria. Amid a crowded section of the room the security man ate his meal in some haste. Perhaps it was the intimidating décor, which made him want to be elsewhere, the bustle, or the repetitive drone of carols, louder now to overcome increased noise from the diners. However, it was really a worry for the safety of his assistant and, by extension, for Anne and himself. He couldn't explain the cause, it originated from too many fragmented influences, and the least of them was the ulcer he was building by rushing his lunch.

It required something out of the ordinary to distract him from his thoughts but a little incident occurred while he was eating which penetrated the blank wall of privacy he had let fall across his eyes. A few tables down the aisle from him sat two men, both were of the same physique - large but lean. It took a moment or two for the security man to take in the more subtle significance of his interest. He saw that although one had grey hair and the other brown, there was a similarity of feature that just might mean they were related. Such an occurrence, of adult twins in the same place, was sufficient alone to draw the security man's interest.

As he watched, they rose from the table and left quickly, the brown-haired man remonstrating with the other. Bailey quickly lost interest after their departure, having other things to think about. Besides, he couldn't know the same brown-haired man had been the one Davies had seen earlier, watching Bailey's departure with such keen interest.

Chapter Six

(23rd December: 1330 - 1700)

In the back of Bailey's mind since hearing of Davies's drinking, was the thought that he would find his assistant in the 'Trucker's Place.' After all, that was his favourite haunt. It was perhaps as well, therefore, that he didn't visit the security office until after lunch as it would not only have been the haste in which he'd eaten his meal that gave him his present indigestion, but also worry.

Davies was not in the room when he entered. From a check of the rounds book, it appeared he hadn't been back since he'd walked downstairs with Bailey. A glance around the room disputed this assumption, however, as the two bottles of whiskey were not to be seen. A smell of whiskey, which he traced to a cup, demonstrated the fact that the assistant security man had indeed broken his word, as the manager had said, and partaken of his Christmas stock.

Concern had been Bailey's main emotion as he had thought of Davies, over lunch. Now it was anger. To let the side down when they were already short-handed was criminal. He must find his assistant quickly and ensure the security of the MSA. To this end, he decided to combine a search for Davies with a belated rounds.

His first call, after making a tour of the complex, was at the 'Trucker's Place'.

'Not a sign,' answered Banjo, in response to Bailey's question. 'I've been looking out for him all day.'

'Thanks,' said the security man, surreptitiously checking that they weren't being overheard. 'Let me know if he comes in, won't you? He may have had a little too much to drink - and I'd appreciate it if you kept that to yourself.'

'Mum's the word.'

From the transport cafe he crossed to the motel, pausing only to let a gritting vehicle pass on its way to the motorway. As he watched, it took the curve of the slip road and switched on the amber flashing lights.

It had been his intention to go directly to Anne's room but as he passed below the ex-burly-man's room he was invested with a curiosity to see what had happened to the charred equipment. The windows of both rooms were boarded up which meant that the investigation had probably already taken place.

Quickly he ran up the stone stairway and noticed that a replacement hardboard door now filled the entrance. To hold it secure there was a hasp and staple held together with a cheap padlock. As with the previous lock, this proved unequal to Bailey's talents and he was soon heaving against the unsecured door.

Unfortunately, he was unable to open the door as it appeared to be jammed shut. As his heaving produced a dreadful din he soon gave up, fearing that the noise would bring people to investigate. Further, it would be embarrassing if it was learned that he had opened the padlock without a key. He therefore gave up and went down the stairs again. It was probably a wasted trip anyway, he reflected, and he dismissed the matter from his overcrowded mind.

The doubts, which had nagged at his brain while he'd been in the cafeteria, now returned. Unless he could find Davies before he drank himself into oblivion, he would be completely on his own. Not only would he then have to carry out covert actions without help, but the whole spectrum of his overt activities would be doubled - until his assistant was back in action. Such a workload would severely hamper undercover work and probably halt his bid for a successful conclusion in a few days' time. And, as he moved towards the girl's room, he had no doubts whatsoever that he could not afford the luxury of her presence any longer; principally because of the distraction it created, but also the burden she could become. The problem was; how was he to tell her?

'No, I haven't seen your assistant since about ten-thirty, when I went over to the complex,' she said. Then, noticing the concerned look on his face, added, 'Why do you ask, Ian? What's the matter?'

'I don't know. I just can't find him,' supplied Bailey, deciding that to omit a part of the truth couldn't harm his plans, and might even help them. 'He's been missing four hours now. But there is still the possibility that it's just because our paths haven't crossed.'

'But you're not happy,' she said, adding what Bailey hadn't said, but his tone had implied.

'No, I'm not happy at all. They agree with me that it could be connected with the beating we took yesterday evening,' he said, and 'they' was just another piece he had added, for colour. 'With only myself to look after the place - and I've got to sleep sometimes - the service station is going to be virtually wide open. If the gang we encountered last night should pay us another visit, they could clean the place out - stores, the shop, you name it.'

'But surely the police...'

'The police are overloaded already.'

'What about extra security men?'

Bailey shook his head. 'Not enough time apart from the big firms, and they are too expensive. No, I suppose Trufoods Limited would prefer to lose the stock and claim on insurance rather than pay their prices,' he lied.

'And you'll be left in the middle,' added the girl, then, realising she hadn't been very clear, she said, 'If you encounter them on your own you'll not stand a chance.' This last was said with a note of alarm, which gave Bailey an odd feeling of guilt.

'Not quite,' he said, quickly. 'The foreman you met last night, Braidwood, has offered his help - and that of his men. Apparently he did the same for your father.'

That seemed to calm her a little. It was then that he played his ace. 'With the sort of situation we might have here, it's no place for you.'

'But I haven't finished yet,' she cried, with sudden anger, her head whipping up to face his.

'Neither Braidwood nor I will have time to talk to you about your father, Anne. And I'm sure that, with us being so short-staffed in every area, the manager doesn't want you disrupting the running of his service station.' Bailey's words were delivered with a cold preciseness that was hard to ignore and he felt that at last he had got home to her the dangers - outside of his little charade - which genuinely accompanied her stay at the motel.

'All right. I see what you mean. I'll go,' she said, simply. 'But not until tonight. I saw the foreman earlier - though at a distance and I couldn't catch him. I'd like to have a word with him before I leave.'

Bailey felt it could serve no purpose to dispute her sighting of the foreman, knowing as he did that Braidwood had spent the morning at his Plant Depot, and so he kept quiet. He had other things to think about, anyway. He felt guilt that he had needed to mislead Anne, though he felt that his relief at her leaving the motel in safety more than compensated for this. Most of all, he had a sense of loss. He wanted to say he would see her again and knew that this also could serve no purpose other than cause complications. So he said nothing and left for the motel office.

'Seen Davies?' asked Bailey of the motel manager.

The manager looked a little puzzled. 'Davies? He's just gone round the back of the motel,' he said, the puzzlement carrying to his vocal chords. 'I thought you were with him.'

Bailey was already on his way out of the door while the manager was still speaking. Consequently, he didn't catch all of the man's reply and was soon to regret his haste.

The security man sprinted down the shorter wing of the building without seeing anyone. Then he turned the corner and gazed down the narrow strip of lawn that separated the motel from a thick belt of saplings, which provided a windbreak. In the semi-darkness, it was difficult to see any distance but he could just make out the shape of a man at the end of the building. As he approached, his thoughts changed from bewilderment to suspicion - and he lightened his step accordingly - for he could see that the figure was absorbed intently with some detail of the end window frame. Curious now as to what Davies was doing outside the room he had only just left, he crept closer to get a better look before disturbing him.

That was as far as he got. Suddenly he was feeling a similar pain to the one he had experienced at the flat, as something heavy hit his head. Then the semidarkness became full-darkness as he plunged into unconsciousness.

The next thing Bailey knew was that Anne seemed to be saying such nice things to him that it would only be a shame to wake up. That was the best of his slow return to consciousness. The rest of it wasn't anywhere near as good. For a start, it is never the case to resume consciousness and instantly revert to one-hundred per cent fitness. Instead, a great deal of disorientation accompanies the normal course of things and if the cause was a blow to the head, then there is usually the addition of a headache the size of Gibraltar - and a lump to match.

The soothing siren-like whisperings that Bailey had heard were not, unfortunately, among the general symptoms in such cases - unless the patient happens to be dreaming. Bailey soon found out that he wasn't. He also discovered that as soon as he revealed signs of life the endearments were quickly muted.

'What happened?' asked the security man, displaying a lack of originality.

'I don't know,' said Anne, relief in her voice.

In response to her uncooperative answer, Bailey would have liked to demand just why she didn't know, but the carefully framed question came out as a sigh.

'If you can manage to get to your feet,' continued the girl, 'I'll help you to your room.'

It was a long journey to the bed, upon which he finally flopped, and he reflected that no hangover he had ever known was as excruciatingly painful as the pain he felt in his head now. However, he did feel that several comparisons could be drawn between the two maladies.

He waited until the girl had finished dabbing at the broken skin, with a lotion she had unearthed from her luggage, before he got around to trying to speak again. His choice of question fell on the subject of the lotion: whether her reason for carrying it was solely for the treatment of clumsy security men. But he decided against voicing it - it was painful enough to concentrate on serious questions without inviting flippancy, and he certainly needed to ask some serious questions.

'How did you come to find me?' he asked, for his first effort.

'I heard a sound,' she answered, placing a dampened cloth on his forehead. 'A man shouted something.'

'Probably me when I was sandbagged,' offered Bailey, in explanation. 'Was that all?'

'I couldn't place which direction it came from but then someone knocked on the back window and, when I looked out, I could just see you laying on the grass. It gave me a bit of a shock. I thought you'd collapsed or something.'

'I had,' protested Bailey, in a rough voice. 'It was an assisted collapse.'

'Do you think that might be your sense of humour returning?' she asked, her tone serious still. 'Or are you concussed?' Like the security man, her levity was a relief valve for the tensions she felt.

She busied herself with the task of finding him some aspirin then, and rather than shout - and cause himself unnecessary pain - he waited until she had returned to his bedside before he spoke again. 'You've got to admire their manners, even though they are slightly imperfect,' he began. 'For instance, I find Davies fiddling with your window frame...'

'Davies? Window frame?'

'The very same,' he confirmed, but he paused then as if considering this. 'But anyway, I catch him at the window. When I am about to ask him what the bloody hell he's doing, someone hauls off and clobbers me one. Then he calls help by knocking on the window. How kind and considerate. We've only got to wean him off blackjacks and his training in good manners will be complete.'

'You *are* concussed,' decided Anne. 'But it does seem a bit odd.' She helped him to a sitting position then, and helped him to take the tablets.

'Very odd,' he agreed, refusing to lay down again. 'And I must thank you for being so alert, Anne. God knows how long I might have been out there before I was either found or froze to death.'

But the girl's concentration wasn't on his version of what might have been. She was worried about Bailey's health *now*. As he moved to a sitting position at the side of the bed, she protested. 'You can't go anywhere yet. You're not well enough,' she said. 'I'll call a doctor. You may have concussion.'

'What's a doctor know about concussion that I don't?' he said, not giving her a chance to answer. 'In the past two days I've spent enough time lying unconscious on the ground to become a world authority.'

'Well at least put a plaster over the cut,' she argued.

'No need. I'll put my hat over it. That's modern medicine - give it plenty of air,' he said, with a gaiety he didn't feel. Then, he added, 'That's a point, where is my hat?'

'It must still be outside,' said Anne.

With a complete absence of swaying or hesitation he rose to his feet and left the room. He had taken no more than a dozen steps around the corner, however, before he had to lean against the wall until the dizziness had passed. Then, only seconds later, he continued to the spot where he had been attacked, accomplishing the trip without mishap.

He found his hat and torch quite quickly but he didn't return immediately. Instead, he played the torch's beam onto the window frame and, during a careful inspection, he could see a pattern of holes leading to the window. The holes were in pairs as if formed by staples - but whatever the staples had held, had now gone.

On his return to the room the girl was waiting anxiously.

'Did you find it?' she asked, even though the hat was clearly visible in his hand.

The question wasn't worthy of a verbal answer so Bailey just nodded, which was a wrong move as it didn't do his head any good at all. 'Yes, thanks,' he said, relenting, but he knew her question had not been what she had really wanted to ask.

'I'm not going,' she blurted, and he knew this was what she had been building up to say.

Inside, Bailey felt tired. Surely, he thought, we don't have to go through all that again.

'You are going to need me,' she said, firmly, 'and I'm staying whether you like it or not.'

'All right, *stay*,' he said, and again the effort caused him more pain. However, it couldn't halt the sarcastic comment that frustration forced him to say, 'I'll try and make sure that if I'm ever clobbered again, it will be outside that window. Okay?'

He saw the hurt in her eyes and then he was grateful that the wince he made could be attributed to his head injury. 'I'm sorry, Anne,' he said, roughly. 'But seriously, be careful where you go if you leave this room.'

The girl nodded her head slowly and Bailey left.

The manager's secretary said nothing when Bailey went straight through to the inner office. Nor did the manager. Both were stunned at the change in the security man's face, which now bore the secondary symptoms of his injuries in that the skin lacked colour and the area beneath the eyes was smudged with grey.

'What happened?' exclaimed Hickson, as Bailey shut the door on the girl.

'I found Davies.'

'You found him?!'

Bailey was momentarily impressed by the force of Hickson's reaction, but the manager hadn't finished. 'He hit you?'

'No, but his friend did.'

'Explain.'

Bailey explained. He told the story as he remembered it, from leaving the manager's office before lunch to his return now, omitting only the detail of his conversation with Anne, and his inspection of the window-frame. When he had finished, the manager's reaction displayed all the warmth and tenderness he had built up for his staff over the preceding months. 'You know it's against company rules for staff to share accommodation with members of the opposite sex, don't you?' he said, gently.

'I don't give a damn about your company rules,' shouted an exasperated Bailey, thankful that the aspirins were working flat out. For a second he couldn't continue. He wanted to say that he'd got all sorts of problems to work out and could do without the manager's stupid observation, but he didn't. Instead, he said, 'The girl is the daughter of an ex-employee. She appears to have a morbid fascination for her father's memory. I have tried, gently, to get

141

her to leave for her own good but she doesn't want to go. Eventually, I shall persuade her. However, I am not going to physically throw her out, and neither will anyone else. I will do it my way, all right? We owe her father that consideration.'

Hickson nodded, impressed by the menace of Bailey's stilted speech. Then he reached for the telephone. 'I'll leave it to you,' he said, gravely. 'Now I'd better phone the police about Davies.'

'No.'

'Wha..?'

'Don't call the police,' said the security man. 'It's pointless dragging them out now, the thing's cold. I'll see them myself later, when I do rounds.'

Hickson replaced the receiver. 'We've still got to find Davies,' he counselled. 'And if he's gone bad - as seems the case - we've got to get you a replacement assistant, as well.'

'If Davies is still on the MSA, I'll find him,' said Bailey. 'Let's not jump to the conclusion he was part of the attack, either.'

'But you've just told me that, er, his friend, hit you...'

'It is a distinct possibility,' agreed the security man, 'but I don't see the motive behind the attack. It is therefore just as possible that a slightly intoxicated assistant security man was trying to carry-out rounds when I spotted him. He may have been leaning on the wall, for support.'

'But what about the man who attacked you?'

'I don't know, but it is possible that he not only hit me, he could have hit Davies, as well. Instead of looking for a security man who has gone bad, we may be searching for one who is injured.'

Bailey could see that Hickson was still worrying about the assailant. 'You mean to say that we have a madman running around who picks on security men?' queried the manager.

'Who knows? It could be connected with the attack yesterday. We will have to wait and see.'

Hickson leaned back in his chair and sighed. 'Whether you find Davies is bad, or you find him inebriated' he said, 'you will still need a replacement security man. Otherwise, you will be on duty alone for four days, which is just not on.'

'I have no intention of doing the whole trick alone,' explained Bailey. 'I will liaise with the police and see if we can arrange for them to carry out the odd patrol. The foreman, Braidwood, used to help out when my predecessor was in trouble. Doubtless, you knew that. I could prevail upon him to help me.'

Opposite Bailey, Hickson was shaking his head in disbelief. Bailey added one more qualification for his argument. 'If you take on a new security man - though where you'll get one at this time, I don't know - you saddle me with the problem of training him. It will mean my staying awake to take him on his rounds. I'll be dead on my feet whether you find someone else or not, and I prefer to depend on my own resources - with a little help from the police and Braidwood - rather than put up with that.'

The manager's head was shaking a little less vigorously now but that didn't mean he was coming round to Bailey's way of thinking, he could have been developing a headache. 'I don't like the idea of you using Braidwood. Police, yes - the road builders, *no.*'

'Why not?' persisted Bailey. 'They, like you and Trufoods, work for the same company - Hargreaves. They've always been of use to Simmonds in the past.'

'That's true,' agreed Hickson. Then he lowered his voice, as he said, 'But if you use them, it is unofficial. Got it? It's only your welfare I'm thinking of...' He broke off then, to answer the telephone.

Beyond his amazement at Hickson's concern for an employee it struck the security man that it had taken very little persuasion for the manager to agree to his suggestions. It suited Bailey to keep the hue-and-cry for Davies between himself and the police sergeant. It also suited him to take the full burden of security at the MSA rather than risk having a 'stooge' planted by the ungodly. That Hickson was so willing to accept such plans supposed that he had equally valid reasons for their employment. What nagged at the security man's brain was the notion that his agreement was not due entirely to the ideals of 'good business'.

After a short conversation, the manager slammed down the receiver. 'What a day,' he exclaimed. Then he put his head in his hands before slowly rubbing his eyes. Finally, he looked up at Bailey.

'Bad news?' prompted the security man, as the manager showed no sign of an explanation.

'Of a type,' replied Hickson, his voice tired. Then he shook his head. 'Of forty-two motorway service areas...Three, that's all they chose, but...'

'What is it? A bomb?'

'No. No, not a bomb,' replied the manager, a little clearer in his speech. 'But a bomb would have been quicker. No, it's the Anti-motorway League. They are carrying out sit-in demonstrations at three selected sites over the Christmas period. Head office were on to me all morning about it, just in case we were chosen. It seems that the league chose this time to protest as there is generally little else to entice news-coverage at Christmas, and that is the aim of the demonstration, publicity.'

He rose from his desk then and moved around to the door. 'It seems *we've* been chosen,' he continued, his hand on the doorknob. 'Ten anti-motorway demonstrators have just arrived in the cafeteria, but before you're tempted to throw them out, I must tell you that Head Office's policy is to allow them to stay unless they cause trouble. Therefore, we had better go along and preach goodwill to all men.'

'And find out what the bloody hell they're up to,' supplied Bailey.

'Exactly. After you.'

It was impossible to overlook the ten anti-motorway demonstrators, even in the brightly-lit cafeteria. Quiet as they were, bent over their coffee cups in whispering conclave, no passer-by failed to look their way and none but the most fleeting passer-by forgot to glance across to the three tables at less than one-minute intervals. Peaceful had been their watchword in formulating this demonstration and peaceful it would be. However, that wasn't to say it would be dull. They would advertise their presence - and cause - another way, and loudly, through their clothes.

The kaleidoscope of colour, which adorned the outfit of each member in the group, was formed of anti-motorway slogans and motifs. Had the whole vision of colour been converted into sound then there was no doubt that not one occupant of the cafeteria would have escaped permanent deafness following only minimal exposure.

It was towards this beacon that Hickson directed himself, with Bailey keeping a discreet distance behind.

'I'm the manager and I'd like to speak to the leader of your group,' said Hickson forcefully, his gaze sweeping the sea of colour before him.

'That'll be me,' said a resonant male voice, away outside the arc of the rainbow. 'Jeremy Inglefield.'

For a moment neither Hickson nor Bailey could see where the voice had come from. However, the man who rose to face the manager would have stood out in any group, and not because of his clothes. He stood some six-feet-four in height and his physique clearly demonstrated that he was an athlete. Bailey felt some surprise at the vision before him, in the first place because he had expected something of a dodderer for the leader of such an obscure protest group. Secondly, the man's unwavering glance, as he took in the two men before him, was indicative of someone who would always consider himself equal. Thirdly, and with more pronounced surprise, Bailey recognised him as the older one of the two men he had seen there at lunchtime.

In the time since then, the man had shown formidable restraint in not changing to the same colourful outfit as the other protesters. In the end, he had selected a token identification with them in the shape of a tee-shirt, etched garishly with a motorway road-sign crossed very boldly in red, most of which he managed to conceal beneath his parka.

In the next two minutes, Hickson was true to his company's word and completed introductions, of himself and Bailey, in a discreet and agreeable way. When they had finished covering such niceties as clause *what-do-you-call-it* of the Public Order Act, Bailey turned to leave for the office.

'Who let the circus in?' asked a voice which Bailey recognised.

'Hello, Larry,' he said tiredly, as he noticed the seated frame of the foreman at the table behind him. 'Working late, again?'

'As usual,' replied Braidwood. 'I hear young Graham is on another binge.'

'Another?'

'From what I hear,' he said, smiling. 'I was talking to some of the boys who saw him floating around this afternoon.'

'He'll be floating all right if I get my hands on him,' said Bailey with feeling. 'Any idea where he is now?'

The foreman shook his head. 'He's got a flat in Peterborough, though.'

'Yes, so I heard. I'll have to get someone to check that.' Then he remembered that Braidwood hadn't answered his question, and added, 'You said *another* binge, just then. Does he do this often?'

'Not often. I'd say more like very occasionally. Simmonds used to keep it out of the front office. He was good like that, treated him like a son.'

'But why now?' asked Bailey, and really it was to himself. 'No, don't tell me. It's Christmas.'

'A good enough reason for Graham, I should think,' said Braidwood. 'But he'll be back. Give him a couple of days. You'll see.'

'Which is just *great* when there are only the two of us to begin with on this duty,' protested the security man.

The foreman laughed loudly at this, but he soon got himself back under control. When he had his tone became serious, concerned.

'Hey, look,' he said. 'We're likely to be here for a couple more days. Me and the boys don't mind helping you out, if we can. I should think we know the ropes by now.'

Bailey smiled. 'Thanks, Larry, I'd appreciate that, very much. I'll give you a shout if I need you,' he said, and moved away towards the exit.

'You do that,' called Braidwood. 'You do that.'

Then he smiled again. From across the tables the anti-motorway leader was watching him.

Chapter Seven
(23rd December: 1700 - 1930)

In the walled transport yard of a chemical plant on the East Anglian coast, a string of security lamps cast a pale light on the gleaming trucks. Baldursens prided itself on its fine safety record and its adherence to every safety regulation on the carriage of toxic substances. Its fleet of purpose-built tankers bore testimony to this fact, each one marked correctly for the chemical it carried. Such expenditure, of tens of thousands of pounds on the safety aspect of their work, demonstrated their commitment to the public good. It was also the *minimum* commitment, by law.

Each one of the tanks was so constructed that it would withstand a sizeable impact in case of accident. The markings, posted on boards with coloured symbols, supplemented the wording made to warn the emergency services of its contents in the case of a spill. Such warning is essential if a corrosive or toxic waste spill is to be tackled effectively and in safety, if only to ensure that forewarned is forearmed.

Not all toxic waste is carried to such high standards of safety. Tankers may be unsuitable for a particular load, improperly marked and have no comprehensive breakdown of the formula copied

150

elsewhere. Or, it could be that proper cleaning hasn't been carried out between changes in types of waste - probably the most dangerous of the practices normally occurring. But none were a touch on what was happening in the corner of the yard that evening.

With the onshore breeze came a drop in temperature which drove all but those actually loading indoors. So it was that the driver of the flat-bed truck and the dispatch clerk were huddled in the office while the drums were rolled off the loading bay and onto the platform.

The dispatch clerk was a talkative type but the driver stuck to monosyllabic comment, bitten-off with a sullenness which would have disconcerted one less thick-skinned than the clerk. But it achieved the driver's intention and killed any drawn out conversation between the two.

While they waited for the loading to be completed the clerk made coffee for them both and then went to stand by the window to watch the loading. He had seen lorries and tankers loaded many times over the years so the loading of this particular lorry did not hold his interest. What kept him occupied was his speculation about the driver. He had met all sorts of truckers in his time, from the quiet types to the roughnecks and 'cowboys'. Placing Shughie was difficult for in the months he had been doing this run, the scot had kept very firmly to himself. He had put in more hours on the road than any other driver the clerk had known. It was a practice which was illegal on its own, but taken with the false documents he carried, and the stuff he was carrying, exceeding the allowed hours was a mere bagatelle.

Outside, something caused a metallic noise and the clerk's eyes swung round to see a drum wobbling with vibration after being dropped prematurely. For a number of seconds he held his breath, then he shuddered out a sigh as he thought of what might have happened had the drum breached, for he had a fair idea of what the drums contained. He had no knowledge of the chemistry involved, but he did know that the liquids poured into each fifty-gallon drum were too toxic for transport in the tankers. It had something to do with the corrosive effect on the lining of the tank; over one or two runs it would be barely noticeable but in continuous use it would soon eat its way through the lining. The cost of replacing tanks so used would be staggering, but the waste still had to be moved. That was where men like Shughie came onto the scene.

It was idiotic, really. After implementing the safety levels across their fleet of tankers, the chemical company ignored them completely with the most dangerous of their waste products. They would load them onto Shughie's truck - a far from suitable vehicle - and, without markings, he would transport them to their destination, a firm of chemical recyclers. There had never been an accident involving the 'cowboys' as long as the clerk could remember, but that was probably due to the fact that this was a motorway run. However, it could only be a matter of time.

And when an accident did occur it would be the driver's head on the block. The company's risk would be minimal. When challenged with responsibility they would merely proffer the contract drawn up between themselves and Shughie, which would contain a clause stating that he would provide the correct vehicle for transportation of the waste. The fact that he did not own a vehicle other than the twenty-year-old relic being loaded outside, would not be their problem. Liability would fall squarely on the scot.

The question the clerk asked himself now, was why do it? Why take the enormous risk? He knew something of the answer: money. The wad of banknotes which was still on the table - payment for his last run - explained some of it. He knew that the company would pay as much as ten times the going rate for the job, rather than be faced with the prohibitive cost of such regular tank replacements. Yes, money was one reason. It had been the case with many drivers before Shughie, too, but there was something else in the fiercely introverted scot which he couldn't fathom.

The tarpaulins were being lashed down now and the other clerk turned round to Shughie. 'It's ready,' he said, simply.

Shughie nodded, without looking his way, and upended the coffee cup. Then, scooping up the pile of banknotes, he rose to his feet and went through the door. He didn't even look at the load as he marched to the cab and climbed in.

Within a minute he was pushing the yellow-and-blue nose of the rig through the opened gates in the wall, and then he roared off into the night. Behind him, the gates were shut again, against prying eyes.

At about the same time that Shughie began his run, Bailey was slouched in an armchair. Under the harsh fluorescent lights of the security office the effect of the aspirins was already wearing off, and he debated whether to take some more or a hot bath as alternative treatment. He was also tired and seemed to be aching all over - even his feet had been rubbed to soreness by the gumboots he had worn earlier during rounds. He had believed them to be his size but found, all too painfully, that they were a little on the small side. In order that he could ease the pain slightly, he removed his present footwear - a pair of leather shoes - by swinging his legs onto the seat of another chair and prising off each shoe with a toe.

Feeling a little more comfortable now, he slouched lower in the chair and reverted to thinking about his assistant. 'Where are you, Graham?' he said to himself, but aloud. Blind drunk in some hole, he didn't wonder. Or perhaps he was involved in something more sinister. He reviewed these and other thoughts and the problems posed by Davies's disappearance; especially its effect on his work.

He stared ahead in deep thought, his eyes resting upon his shoes but not seeing them. His brain was mainly committed to solving the problems affecting his aims but, every so often, it was interrupted by the insistent conviction that his assistant would not have gone against his orders. Repeatedly this thought returned to nag him, but against all the evidence it was impossible, and he wondered if it wasn't just his ego which kept his belief alive.

As the thoughts whirled around and around inside his head he felt himself growing sleepy. He decided he must leave the office now if he wasn't to fall fully into sleep. Besides, he was achieving nothing by staying, as his tiredness was causing his thinking to become repetitive and stale.

It was then that he screwed his eyes shut to help clear away the lethargy he was experiencing. As he opened them again he saw his feet on the chair and the shoes in disarray where they had fallen next to them. It was then that he *saw* what he had been staring at for some minutes.

Since his initial tour with Davies, where he had trekked through the workings of the eastbound complex, the clay sticking to his shoes had dried out. With the knock they had received as he prised them off onto the seat, some of the clay had been dislodged from the angle between the sole and heel of one shoe. With it had come a plug of leather which Bailey could now see had once fitted snugly into a hole in the leading edge of the heel.

A closer inspection of the shoe, aided by a scissor-point, confirmed Bailey's growing suspicions, for he retrieved a short metal cylinder which he recognised as a homing device. It was activated by pressure, as when the person wearing the shoe put his weight on the heel. This produced a radio signal which was received as a 'bleep'. A monitoring station could be upwards of a mile away and still receive a good signal and if this station were equipped with direction-finding equipment it could tell in which direction the device lay. In a less accurate way it could also gauge the distance and, by comparing these two pieces of information with a map, arrive at a fair location for it.

With the realisation of what he had found came a flood of questions as well as answers. No longer was he tired, and the aches were half-forgotten in the excitement he felt at his discovery. Now he knew the reason behind the break-in at his flat: to plant the device in his shoes, and he would wager that not one item of footwear had escaped the treatment. It would also explain why he hadn't unearthed even the slightest clue outside those won solely through his clumsiness.

Then he thought of this clumsiness, and frowned. It didn't make sense to plant a device like this and still tail him, as the burly man had done. It didn't make sense, he suddenly realised, because he hadn't been wearing a pair of doctored shoes on those rounds. He had been wearing Simmonds's gumboots and the man must have heard him leave the room and followed him. Another thought chased this one, did that mean the burly man had operated the monitoring set? Bailey hadn't seen it when he visited the room, but then, he had been interrupted in the middle of his search. Did this mean that the devices were no longer operative, that the monitoring station was a charred lump of metal with the rest of the equipment in the burly man's room? Did the fact that the ungodly had gone to such trouble to keep tabs on him, mean that they knew his true identity and purpose, or did it simply indicate their need to keep an eye on an unknown security man?

He didn't know the answers to these questions but he decided that he would progress cautiously. He would replace the device in his shoe just in case the monitoring station was still in existence. With luck, he could use the knowledge to his advantage. Whether he was 'compromised', his *real* identity known, was impossible to know as yet. What he did know was that he would need to report that he had made contact.

With this in mind, he left the security office and went downstairs to the bank of payphones, feeling them to be more secure than using the MSA's own exchange. Within five minutes he had given his boss a rundown of the events to date and though he didn't say so, the inference that he was in need of help was indicated through his report.

When he had finished the monologue, Rider came straight to the point. 'I'd like to get as much support in there with you as possible, Ian. You don't need reminding of the problems that throws up.' Bailey knew exactly what he was referring to; the impossibility of an agent *blending* into the background of a small community - as essentially the staff of Benwick were - without suspicion. 'But we've been working on it, rest assured.'

Bailey's response was dismissive, 'How long have we got?'

'That's the point,' replied Rider. 'I was about to contact you. You've still got four days, as far as we know, but the timetable after that has drawn in a bit. The merchandise has to be delivered to the States by the first.'

'Jesus!'

'That's right, call on Him. We need all the help we can get.'

'But what if they delay their move?' asked Bailey.

'Then you've got problems,' returned his boss, conversationally. 'You'll have to force their hand. But as soon as you have it located, remember, hand it over to us and we'll be there in strength.'

'Anything on the witness?'

'Nothing. We'll keep on looking, but I don't hold out much hope,' said Rider.

Armed with plenty to think and worry about, Bailey left the payphone and headed for the main entrance and, although the snow was flurrying around him, he could see it wasn't yet sticking. He hadn't quite reached the glass doors when he saw the van drawn-up close to the pavement. In large letters down its side it proclaimed itself to be an outside broadcasting station for television.

Bailey continued on his way out through the doors and, heading in the direction of the motel, had actually passed the vehicle before his pace faltered and he turned around. A single idea, not yet fully formed, had provoked this action. Then he started back towards the van.

The driver of the vehicle was just climbing down from his cab as Bailey approached. 'I take it your team is here to cover the anti-motorway demonstration,' said the security man.

'I don't know, mate,' replied the man. 'I'm only the driver. They're all up there in the cafe, though.'

'Thanks,' called Bailey, and headed for the cafeteria.

The camera was sited well outside the cordoned area but so positioned that it pointed in that direction and provided background for the interviewer. Talking to a man with a microphone amid the din was the leader of the anti-motorway group, Inglefield.

As the security man approached the circle of activity, he could see that they were beyond the stage of practice shots and into the real interview. He paused then to ask one of the technicians a question, 'Is this live?'

'Recording,' was the response.

Bailey nodded and moved over to the interview and Inglefield. It was a move which brought swift reaction for not only had he interrupted the camera's field of view but stood *between* the camera and the interviewer.

'Can't you see we're shooting?' came the interviewer's scream. 'Get out of the way. I've got an interview to do an' a deadline to meet.'

'You're in charge here, I take it,' said Bailey, unabashed.

'Yeah. So what?'

'I'd like a word, in private,' said the security man, and when the interviewer showed reluctance to comply, he added, 'Now.'

The interviewer hesitated a half-second longer, swiftly interpreting Bailey's tone, before he turned to Inglefield and said, 'Excuse me a minute, please.' Then he rose and followed the security man a discreet distance away from the rest, calling, 'Take five, boys,' over his shoulder as he went.

'This is good, yeah?' he said.

'It depends what you call good,' responded Bailey. 'I want you to include something in your televised report.'

'Now, that *is* good,' said the interviewer and his emotions fought between impatience and anger.

'It concerns a murder in the past tense and several possible murders in the future tense,' said Bailey, seriously. 'There may even be one in the present tense, *if* you don't cooperate.'

'You trying to intimidate me?'

'No,' said Bailey, and smiled his reassurance, 'just my little joke,' except that his eyes didn't show any sign of humour.

'Murder, you say,' repeated the interviewer, savouring the word. 'You realise that the duty editor has the power to cut anything I send in.'

'I'll have to take that risk.'

'*Shoot*,' said the interviewer, and drew a notebook from his jacket pocket.

The crew had hardly resumed their rudely interrupted interview before a small trench-coated man sidled up to where the security man was watching the proceedings. Bailey had been aware of his presence for some time, expecting the man and his cassette-recorder to come over at any moment. It was this man, or someone in his line of business, who he had wanted to speak to in the first place and his approach to the television man had been the bait to get him interested.

Bailey had been in security for a long time and knew that wherever national television cameras go there is likely to be a sprinkling of regional or local radio-station reporters. The likelihood of gate-crashing a television interview successfully was remote and it wasn't altogether certain he could have succeeded with the radio man. However, by appearing to draw the more prestigious television reporter's interest, he was instantly newsworthy to the other, trench-coated figure.

'I only deal in sound,' said the little man, combining an apology with his introduction, 'and local at that. But I'd like to ask you what all that was about.'

'All what was about?'

The reporter smiled. 'Look, if little Lord Fauntleroy over there,' he gestured to where the interviewer was busily listening to Inglefield, 'writes anything in that notebook of his, it's news.'

'Okay,' said Bailey, 'Are you ready to roll?'

Five minutes later, the security man left the reporter and headed for the motel. It was 1930 hours and his story should be out over the local radio - the exact area he wanted - within the next hour. He was pleased with the way things had gone and he looked forward to the luxurious respite of a warm bath and a little sleep.

He wasn't to get his little sleep. As his gaze swept the cafeteria on his way out, he chanced to see Anne sat at a table shared by Braidwood and the anti-motorway group's leader. Intrigued though he was at such a gathering, he didn't halt his stride to go over to them. Instead, he decided his bath was more important, and then - in place of his nap - a visit to the Police Post.

Chapter Eight
(23rd/24th December: 1930 - 0700)

The light snowfall of the afternoon had ceased by the time Bailey emerged from the motel at 2100. Now, only a shiny wetness marked where the white flurry had alighted. If the snow alone had made no change in surface conditions the plummeting temperature had, and the formation of slippery ice almost caught out the security man more than once as he plodded to the Police Post.

The girl had not returned while he had been in the room. He reasoned that this was because his company was not of the best at present and, anyway, she could learn more about her father from Braidwood. It rankled all the same, especially as she was sharing her company with the anti-motorway man. Again, envy was one of the emotions he felt, together with jealousy and concern for her safety.

Inside the Police Post, it was warm and bright but, even though he shut the door noisily against the cold, the only acknowledgement of his presence was a nod in greeting from Sergeant Brennan, neither of the other two policemen altering the direction of their gaze by one degree. What held them in thrall was a small television, which was in the middle of showing a news report. No doubt they had learned of the TV crew's presence earlier, reflected Bailey, and were awaiting the item with interest.

The camera shot showed the US Secretary of State as he walked up the steps of some building. The building wasn't identified. The newsreader's voice-over informed the listener that this visit was in connection with the Middle East crisis, the US Secretary of State having been tasked with briefing European governments.

Then the screen flickered to the newsreader and a background photograph of a motorway service station. Bailey listened at least as intently as the others to what was said, including all fifteen seconds of the interview with Inglefield. But as even the interviewer wasn't shown or heard, the information given to him by the security man was not used. Bailey was not over-worried by this cut - whether by the interviewer or the editor - as he realised it had been at best a long shot. Now he could only hope that the material he had given the radio reporter would be used, even though it would only be transmitted to a limited audience.

While the two constables were engrossed in the rest of the news - not least the female newsreader - Bailey went over to the desk and spoke to Brennan. He first told him of Davies' disappearance and then gave his thoughts on the subject. This brought a reaction from all three, for intent as they had been on the television, the two policemen now switched their attention at Bailey's mention of Davies.

'D'you think we can have a word in private on the subject?' asked Bailey, unwilling to say what was really on his mind to such a large audience.

Brennan's expression echoed the interest he felt but he said nothing as he indicated the open door of the other room.

Once inside, with the door now shut, Bailey delved into his uniform top and produced a small folding card, which appeared very similar to a police warrant card.

'What bunch is this?' queried Brennan, inspecting the document.

'Never mind if you don't recognise it,' replied Bailey, retrieving it. 'Just believe that your Chief Constable is sufficiently impressed to verify my credentials. You can get him on this number...' From another concealed opening in the lining, he fetched a scrap of paper.

The sergeant pushed the proffered paper back. 'I'm sufficiently good judge of a man to know that you are someone a little more high-powered than the role you have adopted on Benwick would suggest,' he said. 'I've known since we first met. Now what is it you want?'

Bailey was impressed by the man's forthrightness. He needed an ally and Brennan seemed to be the man for the job. He knew however, that the sergeant was not the type of person to do things blindly and, if the security man wanted his help, he'd better explain his reasons.

'D'you remember the hijack which took place about a year ago? It was played down in the newspapers as that of a lightly-escorted truck, loaded with a consignment of scrap precious metals.'

'Lostbox, you mean?' asked Brennan, carefully. He was aware that the codeword had been given a security classification at the time.

'Exactly. Operation Lostbox. It happened at a place sixty miles from here at...'

'Brasford, near the A1,' put in the sergeant. 'I was one of the hundreds involved in the dragnet for the truck.'

'There were five trucks - all ten-tonners - each carrying six tons of gold bullion.'

'Blimey!'

'A lot of shiny metal and not a sign of it since then,' he persisted. 'Well, until a few days ago.'

'You know where it is?'

Bailey shook his head. 'Not quite, but I know where it might be. It's in this area.'

'Still in East Anglia?'

'Still in East Anglia - and somewhere under the motorway,' he confirmed.

'And your job is to locate it.'

'Correct.'

Brennan frowned. 'You've quite an area to search,' he said. 'What are you going to do, dig up the motorway?'

'I don't think we need to go to such lengths. I don't believe the gold is under the finished portion of the motorway.'

'Well, that narrows it down a bit,' said Brennan, turning to cast a glance at a large map on the wall which bore the superimposed route of the motorway, 'but how can you be certain?'

'I'm not certain,' sighed Bailey, 'but two facts persuade me to believe it. The first is the note that old man Simmonds wrote just before the accident.'

'Simmonds? He knew where it was? When did he write this note? Why didn't he tell me?'

'Hold on,' said the security man, at the sergeant's outburst. 'He wrote the note only seconds before the accident and while he was in the car.'

'How did you know this?'

'We found the note in his car after the murder.'

'But his car was burned out. The report says so,' he argued, and then Bailey's final word registered on his brain. 'Murder?'

'Murder,' confirmed Bailey. 'And his car wasn't burned out. It was the other one - the one that contained the two people. We amended the report so as to conceal the fact that Simmonds had the opportunity of passing on the information.'

'But murder. How do you know? The man is dead and so are the two occupants of the other car,' persisted Brennan.

Bailey sighed again and reflected that his choice of ally had certain drawbacks. 'Unless the two cars were doing some spectacular stock-car tactics -

behaviour which isn't normal in people of their age - *and* swopping paint-schemes halfway through...'

'Paint schemes? What has that to do with it?'

'The paintwork on Simmonds's car was maroon. That of the other car was green, according to the records. Somehow, yellow was added when each vehicle was dented. Therefore one assumes another vehicle was involved.'

Brennan nodded. 'Yes, all right, I'll buy that. But it could still be manslaughter.'

'Frankly, I'm not particularly worried whether it was either murder or manslaughter but no-one writes a hasty note on such a topic as Simmonds chose if it doesn't imply a connection with his demise.'

'And that was?'

'Pardon?'

'What did the note say?'

Bailey told him.

'The twenty-seventh is only four days away,' exclaimed the sergeant.

'Precisely. I've got four days to locate the bullion,' said the security man. 'Ready for the second reason?'

'Yes,' replied a puzzled Brennan. 'I'm not sure that the note on its own convinces me that the gold is located hereabouts, even though Eddie was a foreman with the construction company.' He was plainly thinking aloud now but Bailey didn't mind, he needed as much thought on the subject as possible.

'The second reason,' repeated Bailey, after a pause, 'is to do with the delay they seem to be experiencing in completing the motorway.'

'Yes, I've heard - very quietly, of course - that it has something to do with water problems. It's due to a high water table, they say.'

'They say,' repeated Bailey, without being offensive. 'What if that were just a cover to delay the motorway progressing beyond the point where the gold is buried?'

'You're telling me that the gold is under little more than some topsoil down by the end section?'

'I'm suggesting it. But it would explain why no progress has been made for several weeks.'

'And the problem in the boiler-house is just dressing?' queried Brennan, cynically.

'Why not? Flood a hole in the ground and call it seepage.'

'Hmm. Of course, it could be that foundation trouble really is the cause.'

'True. But I won't find the gold by discounting every idea I get, will I?'

'Sorry,' said Brennan, sincerely. 'I was merely trying to be objective. It does seem though that you have precious little to go on. It's quite possible the gold is nowhere near the motorway.'

They were silent for a few seconds as they reflected upon this fact.

'There is one other thing,' said Bailey. 'Well, a lot of things, actually.' Then he recounted some of the odd occurrences, which had happened since his arrival at the MSA. He skipped over the attack outside the main store, as Brennan already knew of this, but he told him of the attack behind the motel, and he included an account of the burly man's death, though he omitted to mention that he, himself, had started the fire. When he had included the flat break-in and tied everything together, Brennan's reaction was a little more pronounced. He had listened without interruption to what Bailey had to say but, though his expression was fixed for the most part, it became a chilly countenance when he heard of the attacks, and positively amazed at the true account of the burly man's death.

When the security man had finished, Brennan shook his head slowly. 'I'm surprised at your patience with my sniping earlier,' he said. 'I was trying to be the helpful policeman, I assure you.' He smiled then, slightly embarrassed. 'I discover that it's *you* who knows the score and, from what you've told me, I'm not even in the same league.'

Though he had stopped talking, Bailey refrained from rushing in to break the sergeant's train of thought, which seemed in imminent danger of verbal release. The pause was, however, short. 'You're right,' said Brennan, having arrived at the end of his difficult thoughts. 'Adding everything up, it would seem that someone is very wary of you - and thirty tons of gold would make anyone a little overprotective of it. Who do you suspect?'

'That's just it,' exclaimed Bailey, frustration in his voice. 'Everybody. I could even implicate you without much trouble. After all, gold has a very powerful effect on some people - thirty tons of the stuff could have the same effect on a crowd.'

'Thirty tons of gold,' said Brennan, savouring the sound. 'I just can't get over that. I can't comprehend its value.' He shook his head to indicate the impossibility of the task. Then, he added, 'Why were they shifting it?'

'You saw the news tonight?'

'Yes, of course, you were there,' replied Brennan, frowning.

'The US Secretary of State *is* here on account of a Middle East crisis, though not the one that most people would automatically think of. He's here to collect loans made to European countries in the form of gold.'

'I'm sorry, I don't follow,' said Brennan, the frown still in place.

'The Organisation of Petroleum Exporting Countries, or OPEC as we all know it, is becoming a little fed up with the US paying for its oil with a devaluing US dollar. As you may know, oil is traded in US dollars. With the US printing money rather than raising debt through the issue of treasury bonds – because no-one will buy the latter – the US dollar is becoming devalued quicker than OPEC can put up the prices to compensate. OPEC has threatened to insist upon payment in gold, which, though valued at historical highs, at least doesn't change with the volatility of the US dollar.

'Now the US probably won't have to physically move the gold to the OPEC countries but OPEC want to be assured that the US has the gold to pay them with – stick a note on to say it now belongs to OPEC. They want an audit.'

'But I thought that was the normal thing anyway - for each banknote in your pocket there is an amount of gold backing it up in some bank vault.'

'That was the theory, at least in part, say – in the case of the US dollar – 40 cents on the dollar. However, all the major currencies went off the Gold Standard many years ago. Currency is effectively backed by debt, borrowing, what the government of each country can sell in bonds,' responded the security man.

'The OPEC people believe that now, several years after they began stockpiling dollars in return for the oil shipped to the US, that it may have been devalued by the 'States printing more dollars than are covered by bonds. The West believe she does have sufficient reserves to back each dollar - and have said so - but OPEC wants an audit of the gold as a precursor to it insisting upon payment by the precious metal. That is why the man is running around Europe to hasten the return of US gold.'

'Now I'm with you.'

'Good. Now you'll understand that if a sizeable chunk of that gold should be lost it would be difficult to produce it from your country's small change. The gold I'm looking for is that which was on its way to the US from Britain. The US Secretary of State is trying to round up the loose change from other European countries as well as hasten the stuff already going back. You can imagine the embarrassment that a non-balancing set of books would cause when the Swiss go into Fort Knox. We're involved in a shell-game.'

Brennan nodded. 'When is the audit?'

'January the first.'

'Christ!'

'Seasonal, but not original,' said Bailey, remembering his own response to the news.

'And you're the only one looking. It's no job for one man on his own...'

Bailey smiled, but it wasn't a nice smile. 'We've thousands of people chasing many leads across the UK and near Europe. Unfortunately, even though we knew about the OPEC strategy over two years ago, the diplomatic boys reckoned they could make the problem go away. Again unfortunately, this began to send the people to sleep, who were tasked with investigating the gold theft – they were down to a team of twelve at one stage – and it is only in the past month that the diplomatic people have indicated they've failed and we've ramped up the search effort. I'm only following one lead and there are excellent reasons why I am only a team of one.'

They were silent for a moment or two, as the import of what Bailey had said sank in. What Bailey hadn't said was that the reason he was working alone was because, unless he and Rider were very much mistaken, flooding the area with operatives would have defeated the search and recovery effort. Such action would only ensure that the thieves would abandon their efforts and, with just a week to the start of the audit, that was something Bailey and his boss just could not risk. What he had told him was a plausible story about the OPEC situation, not complicated with the whole truth, but one that he hoped would achieve his one objective: to bring Brennan firmly on side.

'How can I help?' said the sergeant, at last.

'Thanks,' said Bailey, in acknowledgement. 'I need someone to carry out rounds of the MSA so that I can get at least some sleep. It would be just the occasional tour, but it will go a long way towards keeping me operational over the next few days.'

'I'll arrange that.'

'And to give me a lift later tonight.'

'In search of a pot of gold?'

'Something like that,' he replied. 'After all, they do call it the Golden Highway.'

When he had finished telling Brennan exactly what he wanted, he left. As his feet crunched over the thin ice covering the car park he reflected that he had told his new ally a great deal that was based on truth - though not all. He had taken the sergeant some way into his confidence but, although he believed he had chosen wisely, he still felt a little concerned that he may have chosen the wrong man. Several times as he crossed to the complex he shivered, a reaction that had nothing to do with the cold. It was a reaction he would experience many times before the night was out.

The calendar had barely flipped over to Christmas Eve when Bailey quietly let himself out of the motel room. He had heard the soft murmur of Anne's breathing through the dividing curtain when he awoke only minutes earlier. At least, he hoped it was Anne for he hadn't seen her since spotting her in the cafeteria, and hadn't noticed her return, as he had been asleep for the past two hours. However, unless the ungodly wore her particular scent, he did not doubt it was she and had therefore dressed in darkness and with a minimum of noise so as not to wake her.

He felt better now. The sleep, combined with his meal after leaving the Police Post - albeit merely sandwiches purchased from one of the foyer dispensers - had swept away his tiredness and lessened the pain in his head to no more than a sensation of fragility. Though not worn specifically for this reason, his three layers of clothing insulated him from the cold and added warmth to the excitement he felt in his stomach.

The light was meagre as usual, as he crossed the motel forecourt, which was as well, for he also wore the unseasonable footwear of black plimsolls, which - together with the bulky appearance of his clothes - might well have raised an eyebrow of any dedicated observer. It was in an attempt to allay the suspicions

175

of any such persons that the security man didn't immediately head for his rendezvous but first dawdled for fifteen-minutes-or-so on rounds. Satisfied that he was not being observed or followed, he then quickly contrived - by a circuitous route - to arrive at the rear of the Police Post and under the window of the inner room.

'Here's your radio,' said Brennan, in response to Bailey's light-tapping on the window, and he handed the security man a small radio not unlike one he had used before, but channelised to a different frequency. Like most in his 'trade', Bailey was suspicious of mobile phones, in the days when the signals from such devices are too readily intercepted, interpreted and tracked, by those with the requisite skills. Tonight, particularly, he did not want his movements or intentions known to any eavesdroppers.

'Are they ready?'

'When you are,' responded the sergeant.

'See you later,' said Bailey and moved away from the building.

He then made straight for the slip road, which led onto the motorway and was waiting there when the police Range Rover slid alongside.

During the fifteen-minute trip to their destination, little was said, beyond discussion of Bailey's instructions.

'I want you to stop by the barriers and then go about your normal business,' he said, removing the pale blue uniform that constituted the top layer of clothing. Then he put on his black balaclava, which, like the one-piece black woollen suit, would both keep him warm and camouflage his presence in the dark. Then he draped the strap of the radio over his shoulders in a secure bandolier style.

'What time do you expect to call us? What call-sign will you use?' asked the driver.

'I won't need a call-sign because I won't be speaking,' replied Bailey. 'We will use a system of clicks, each click representing a word or action.'

It was a simple code and he was confident the two policemen understood it by the time they arrived at the dropping-off point.

'This may take a couple of hours,' warned Bailey as a parting shot.

'We'll be waiting,' said the driver, through the open window. Then he dropped the lever into gear and the Range Rover shot off at speed.

It took Bailey several minutes for his eyes to become accustomed to the near total darkness but, when they had, he could just make out the shape of the materials dump in the distance. He judged that the camp would be beyond the clump of mounds to the left of the whole but he used this information only as a reference. His initial destination was the northern end of the dump, or to the right. Slowly at first, he took to the rough ground below the motorway and then quickened his pace, until he had covered the mile separating him from the dump in less than twenty minutes.

As he looked down from the peak of a mound, he could see the track below, which they had used on the tour. Following the broad line up the hill, he could see the spot where Joe had refused to go any further. Beyond this, and over the hill, Bailey could see it wind first to the left around the shoulder and then drop steeply to the flat plateau. Where it went from there the security man couldn't see as the shoulder of another mound hid it from this point and beyond the extremity of his vision.

It took a further twenty minutes to arrive at the plateau and, when he did, he was bathed in sweat for what had seemed a gentle undulation of mounds - from his recent vantage as well as that of the three-wheeler's cab - was an obstacle course for a man. Now he must not halt; not even for a minute as the wetness of his sweat could too easily become ice in the sub-zero temperature. Without pausing, he strode out along the uneven track.

Gradually he was aware that the track had straightened and that the surface underfoot had changed into that of a metalled road. Further investigation revealed that it was quite a narrow highway just wide enough to take two lanes of cars. To either side appeared to be a silvery expanse, which Bailey soon discovered - by the simple expedient of slipping on a patch of ice and falling in - was merely the frozen topping of a quagmire, at least four feet deep, very wet and very, very cold.

To be drenched to the skin in such cold conditions was probably, he realised, the worst thing that could have happened to him short of death. However, if he didn't get into dry clothes soon, he would probably die anyway from hypothermia. On top of this, he now had a waterlogged radio, which was most probably useless and so he switched it off.

He was tempted to turn back there and then but three things stopped him. He had come almost a mile along the narrow road already and was determined to find out what was at the end of it. His sodden suit, composed totally of close-knit wool as befitted the interior lining of a diving suit, would keep him warm enough to ward off exposure if he could manage to convert sufficient energy to heat, which meant keeping to a fairly fast pace. Lastly, he might not get another chance to reconnoitre this area and he wasn't going to get any degree of exposure for nothing. He therefore broke into a loping run, taking care to keep well away from the treacherous edge of the road.

It was almost another mile before he saw a dim shape loom into view over to his right. Quietly he advanced, slowing his pace until he was down to a fast walk. As he got nearer, he saw that the building was quite large and covered in corrugated-iron sheeting. Packed around it were numerous vehicles and machines but a corridor had been left to allow access to the massive double doors.

'Braidwood's Plant Depot?' thought Bailey, almost aloud.

He made a quick circuit of the building, trying to gain access and to discover whether anyone else was around. He drew a blank on both *outside*, but as he hadn't found any opening large enough to see inside, he couldn't be sure if he was alone. It was when he drew back some distance - to see if there were any skylights - that he discerned a row of three windows at one end of the building and fifteen feet from the ground.

Close to the wall at this point was the nearest of the vehicles, a huge dumper-truck. With extreme care on the slippery surfaces, Bailey climbed to the top of the cab and found that he could just see into the building's interior. What he saw was disappointing. Without light, he could only make out the object nearest to the window. It was a truck, a commonplace rigid flatbed, which had suffered some minor panel damage. Nothing else could be seen as all was near blackness, and only the truck's light paintwork made it visible.

He was still confident that he would find something of significance as he climbed down from the dumper and ran over to join the road again. He decided to go on for one more mile before turning back but he hadn't covered more than a quarter of that distance when he came upon a group of some dozen houses, which a sign announced as Grafton.

A cursory search of the village produced nothing of interest to him, but alerted several dogs, and so he went on along the road. He had travelled less than two hundred yards when he came to a T-junction with a wider road. It was then that the first shivers began and he decided that he must give up what he believed was fast becoming a wild-goose chase. He had been wrong in assuming that Joe's refusal to take the three-wheeler over the ridge was anything more sinister than a healthy respect for the danger of toppling the brute and getting them both killed. He would return to the construction camp and look around before making his way back to the motorway rendezvous position. With this in mind, and nursing his disappointment, he started back along the road, his pace slightly quicker than before.

Then, as he discerned the raised line of the embryo bridge in the distance ahead, something caught his attention. It was the lack of a mobile phone mast where he had seen one on his tour in the three-wheeler. At first, he thought he'd strayed off course and was in the wrong place. A short diversion told him why he couldn't see it; it was now a tangled mess of metal lying on its side, looking as if it had been trampled by a large beast. He hadn't seen the three-wheeler on his travels so far. He wondered whether it, too, was abroad this night, prowling the countryside, as he continued to lope along the track.

It was at this point that the effects of his beatings, tiredness and extreme cold conspired to cause him to make his most important mistake of his mission so far. He allowed himself to be persuaded that, as he had searched everywhere but the embryo bridge and found nothing, the significance of the bridge as the location of the gold was very high. Therefore, he should not go over there and risk leaving evidence of his visit. He would just wait until the ungodly made a move on the 27th and call in the troops to help him capture the whole gang in the act. He even had the coordinates on his mobile phone to guide them to the exact position. It was true that he had mitigating circumstances for not wanting to go the extra mile in his condition, but in not doing so, he put the success of the whole mission in jeopardy.

By 0245 hours, Bailey had negotiated the crisscross of tracks that lay over the materials dump like a net. The constant running had stopped his shivering but he knew he was now 'burning the candle at both ends' as he courted exhaustion in order to defy exposure. It wasn't that he found running a mere one-and-a-half miles a drain on his stamina, though admittedly the sodden garment he wore added a few pounds to the load he must carry; it was the task of generating enough heat to keep him alive, drawing heavily on his stores of burnable energy, that worried him. Soon he must stop running to preserve energy and, when he did, the shivering - his body's self-defence mechanism to protect its vital organs - would begin again and continue until the fire went out: one classic progression to death through exposure to cold.

To search all of the forty-odd caravans would have been impossible for him in his present state and not likely to be profitable anyway. Therefore, as he approached the construction camp he made almost straight for the beacon of light that shone from one of the modern office cabins. As he got nearer, he became more careful and noticed, from a temporary concealment, that the light was in another window of the office cabin he had visited on the tour.

Quickly, he moved to a position below the window, preparatory to sneaking a look into the office. His haste was unfortunately his undoing, for it made him careless. Had he paused to cast a glance over the ground by the window, before he moved towards it, he would have seen the curved piece of metal - a piece of debris - lying in his path.

The noise it made as he caught it with his right foot was shattering in the quiet of night. Such was its effect on the security man that he didn't pause to worry about the pain in his right ankle but dived towards the nearest concealment, beneath the jacked-up cabin.

His reactions were only marginally faster than those of the man who ran from the cabin, for Bailey was scarcely still where he lay before the man was outside. Then, for a second, the man stood still and only the swinging door made a sound. Through pain-filled eyes, the security man watched the figure slowly turn to the right. It was Joe, and in his hands was a rifle.

For two or three minutes - though it seemed much longer - Joe walked slowly around the cabin, his eyes probing the dark shapes of the other buildings. Then he concentrated his attention on the office hut itself, and began looking into the darkness beneath.

Bailey's brain raced as Joe approached the point along the cabin when he must see him. He calculated that so long as he didn't crawl under the hut he had a slight chance of remaining undetected. However, if he did crawl under then the security man should have the advantage in the confined space.

The seconds passed like minutes as Joe got nearer and nearer - the rifle held ready to fire at anything he saw beneath the hut.

'Come on, my beauty,' urged Bailey in thought, his nerves now stretched as he felt the return of his shivering.

Then suddenly his radio blared out in a cacophony of officialese as a police message came over. In comparison, the din caused by his striking the piece of metal earlier was nothing. An explosion of TNT could not have had a greater effect on the two men.

Bailey *knew* at that moment that it was the end for him. He saw Joe crouch lower with the rifle pointed unwaveringly at the centre of his pounding chest, only four feet away in the darkness.

Bailey waited for the shot. There was no time for anything else. He must just wait for death. But death did not come. Nor did injury, or even a near miss - for Joe had gone.

The security man had just time to glimpse the receding shape of the figure as it disappeared back into the cabin. Stunned though he was, Bailey was not prepared to await a repeat performance and was out from beneath the cabin before the noise of Joe's first footfall had penetrated the thin flooring. His instinct was to flee but with a super-human effort, he paused, just long enough to glance through the window, before he went hell for leather into the darkness towards the motorway.

It was only when he was some distance from the construction camp that the instinct to flee had waned sufficiently for him to reflect upon what he had just seen. His reflections, augmented by close scrutiny of the route back the way he had come, told him that he was unlikely to be pursued by Joe after all.

The image etched on Bailey's brain, in that very brief glance through the cabin's window had been of Joe, back towards him, as he fiddled with a desktop radio transceiver. That was all there had been to see. However, when he added the fact that his own radio was switched off - and had been since his accidental dunking - it required no great intelligence to realise that the reason for Joe's hasty retreat was to turn down the volume on his own set. Instead of nearly causing his death, the noise had possibly saved his life, or at the very least his discovery.

However, Bailey felt a shudder then, for he realised the significance of what Joe's monitoring of a police frequency *could* have had on him. This realisation had little to do with the obvious connection he had now established between those on the construction site and something very fishy indeed. The fundamental reason for the reaction was the thought of what might have happened had he now spoken into the radio rather than use the code he had invented.

As it was, he couldn't be sure the radio would work. Water and electricity do not mix and if there was just one hole for the water to get in... Well, they might find his frozen body when they got tired of waiting for the call and came to look for him, he reflected. He couldn't see himself managing to traipse back thirteen miles to the MSA in his current state. As he neared the barriers he switched on the radio, pressed the transmit switch four times - and prayed.

Five long seconds passed before he heard four equally spaced clicks in reply. Then all he could do was keep moving while he waited for them to pick him up - and hope they would be quick about it.

Whether the Range Rover had been waiting just over the horizon for his call, or had just happened to be at this end of its patrol area, Bailey didn't know. Nor did he care to ask. He did wonder, however, what another few minutes in the cold would have done to his health. He also soon dismissed the thought as academic.

On the way back, he had stripped off the woollen suit and wrapped a blanket about him, aided by the number two policeman. It was only when they could see the MSA in the distance that he was able to begin struggling into his uniform and replaced the sodden plimsolls. Even though the car's heater had been turned full on, Bailey had found it impossible to stop shivering and his brief message for Sergeant Brennan - to be relayed by the policeman in code - was said in staccato speech. Perhaps it was fortunate that the message was short - simply to the effect that the tour had been without success - for it required some effort to form the words.

When they arrived at the slip road that led onto the MSA, Bailey alighted and quickly scrambled into the cover of darkness. He had brushed off their entreaties to join them in the warmth of the Police Post, without explanations, as they could not know the danger risked by such an action. When the vehicle had disappeared from view, he moved from cover and headed for the motel.

It took him the better part of a minute to fit the key into the lock, so great was the shaking of his hands. His efforts to still the chattering of his teeth were all in vain, until he chose to open his mouth wide making it impossible for a molar fandango to occur and wake the girl.

With his eyes already accustomed to the darkness, he had no trouble in making out the shape of his bed and he moved over to it as quietly as he could. Then, again with some difficulty, he shrugged off his clothes and rolled between the covers.

There followed ten minutes when the shivering persisted unabated, but when he began to drift off into sleep he would be wakened - time and again - by the chattering of his teeth as his jaw muscles relaxed and shut together. In an effort to deaden the noise, he drew his head beneath the bedclothes and tried for sleep again. He was physically exhausted now, his body having given a lot in order to keep alive, and he believed that even the ungodly couldn't prevent him from sliding into a coma-like sleep. He was wrong, of course, because the human body can summon reserves which even the fittest man would not believe. However, he was only reacting to the stimulus of his brain, after all.

It was then that his beliefs were tested, for he now felt a hand press lightly against the covers close to his neck. Perhaps his reactions were a little slower than usual but this was due - at least in part - to what his other senses told him. Never before had he wrestled an assailant who wore the sort of perfume he could now smell, or even expensive cologne - and this was certainly an expensive fragrance, the one he'd detected earlier. They also didn't speak with a woman's voice - at least not in the beginning - or announce themselves to be Anne.

'What...?' he croaked, his teeth biting off the rest of the question.

'Shh,' was her reply, and Bailey felt her body press against his as she slid beneath the bedclothes. 'I decided that the only way I was going to get back to sleep was by stopping your teeth chattering. Meet your new hot-water bottle.'

He had already disproved his brain's persuasive message on sleep, and was now quite awake, and although a few more minutes would pass before he stopped shivering completely, he was to prove that the human body *does* have extraordinary reserves indeed.

Chapter Nine

(24th December: 0700 - 1500)

When Bailey awoke in response to the alarm at 0700, the girl was gone. He didn't get up immediately but gave in to the deadness he felt, a legacy of his ordeal, for some part of the night, at least.

He had lain in this semiconscious state for only a couple of minutes when he heard the door open and saw the girl doing a balancing act with coffee-cups and sandwiches.

'Feeling better?' she asked, smiling.

As he sat up in bed he winced, which was answer enough.

'Perhaps breakfast will help,' she suggested, and handed him the coffee.

'Thanks,' he said, and the way it came out could have been construed to mean gratitude for the coffee, her warmth-giving presence earlier, or what had followed.

'It isn't very nice out there,' she blustered, slightly embarrassed and anxious to get onto neutral ground.

'Snow?' he asked, and though he didn't show it, he also felt anxiety as he thought of the difficulties that a layer of snow would present in his search for the gold.

She nodded, unable to speak as she had just bitten into a sandwich, but she moved over to the window and, when she could, said, 'Here is your early morning weather report. The perfect weather for Christmas: lightly falling snow, which appears to be sticking. It'll be beautiful later when...'

Suddenly she froze, her eyes the only indication that she was still concentrating on something outside. Then, without explanation, she opened the door and ran out - the door slamming-to behind her.

Intrigued, Bailey got shakily from the bed and padded over to the window. It took a couple of seconds for the dizziness to clear when he got there, but he was still in time to see the girl approach a man who had obviously stopped in response to her call, as he was still in the process of turning to meet her.

He was a small stocky man, with unruly black hair, which fell untidily onto the collar of his donkey jacket. The animated discussion that the security man now witnessed, began as though it were the reunion of old friends, but Anne turned a little more agitated as it progressed. Gradually, the man fell silent and the girl's remonstrations seemed to be ignored. Finally, and with deliberation, the man shook his head, which was the signal for Anne to turn on her heels and march back to the motel.

By the time she got back Bailey was again in bed and resuming his breakfast. 'Irresistible urge for a snowball fight?' he asked, cheerfully.

191

The girl's face was closed and her eyes brooding. 'No. I've just seen my brother-in-law, Scot,' she said, distractedly, her mind elsewhere and her gaze focused on the middle distance.

'You seem worried, Anne. Can I help?' he asked, gently.

'No, no. A family problem, you understand.' Then she seemed to snap out of the trance. 'I'd prefer it, if it remained so.'

Bailey nodded. 'Okay.'

He though nothing more about it until after he had taken a rejuvenating bath, dressed in the crumpled uniform, and was halfway across the car park on his way to the Security Office. What prompted his renewed interest - and then only for a brief moment - was the sight he had of the stocky man away on the lorry park. He was balanced on the front bumper of a yellow-and-blue truck and was busy cleaning grime from the windscreen.

In the hour that followed his call at the Security Office, Bailey trudged around the MSA on his rounds. In the midst of the snowfall, cars punctured the whiteness with red and amber lights and their brakes squealed with the wetness as they shunted about the car park in blue clouds of exhaust fumes. Caught up in the rush - created by the need to arrive at the their destinations before the weather closed in on them - people scurried to and fro between their cars and the complex, gasping clouds of vapour as they went.

Even in the short period that he had been out on his beat Bailey noticed a slight increase in the wind force. Now the snow slanted at a more acute angle and he saw the beginnings of several snowdrifts as he returned to the main entrance of the complex, his rounds completed.

It was while he was brushing off the white blotches from his parka that he caught sight of Anne. It was her clothes that had drawn his eye, as he recognised at once the particular outfit she wore. Otherwise, he would doubtless have missed the fact that she was engaged in a heated telephone conversation, her head barely visible as she bent into the padded surround of the payphone booth. As he'd seen her mobile phone in the motel room, it struck him as odd that she was using the payphone, but he thought no more of it than that.

He saw this in one short glance but he didn't approach the booths. Instead, he remembered his promise to respect her privacy in the family matter - for he was sure that was what she was now discussing - and turned for the stairs and the warmth of his office. Had he bothered to prolong his glance in her direction he would have noticed queues forming at the payphones and the notice, deeper into the concourse, proclaiming that the problem with mobile phone reception was known and that it was being investigated.

The paperwork that went with the job of security man on Benwick was almost non-existent. Besides the rounds book, and the occasional incident report, there was nothing of an administrative nature for Bailey to do. It was hardly worth putting on the computer, a requirement of a Trufood operating procedure. In any case, it soon became apparent when he tried to access it, that the online application for event recording was 'down', as was all internet access.

Consequently, soon after his return to the Security Office he took to staring through the window at the white landscape beyond. For ten minutes-or-so his brain was the only part of him doing any real work, as he slouched in the armchair. It wasn't the mundane, which occupied his thoughts; such was unlikely to cause the frown he wore. His mental activity concerned something far more serious: the change of plan demanded by the heavy snowfall.

The word *if* figured a lot in the most optimistic of his thoughts. *If* the snowfall wasn't too heavy, *if* a period of milder weather persisted, then in the three full days now left he could still see his original plan employed. For that matter, *if* played a great part in the pessimistic thoughts, which passed through his mind - and depressing they were, too. If the heavy snow continued for much longer, it could do nothing but help the ungodly by concealing the cache right up until the day of recovery. Of course, once they had disturbed the site - and disinterred the gold - the resultant mess would be like a beacon for any air search, but it wouldn't be much use to the authorities if the gold were already out of the area.

There was now a definite need for a change in tactics. No longer could he depend on the plan of reconnoitring the area during the days up until the twenty-seventh, hoping to pick up enough information to pinpoint the site. The landscape would soon have a sameness about it, which would present a formidable barrier to further search. He would need to be more forceful and take the initiative.

How he was to go about this, he hadn't decided. He fully realised the hazards of overplaying his hand, knowing that the most damage he could do was to alert the ungodly who would disappear into the woodwork and leave the recovery to a later date. Although he could expect them to be a little disheartened at the upset to their plans, it hardly compared with the severe repercussions likely to occur on the international money markets, which the resultant shortfall in bullion would bring. He needed a softly-softly approach, one that would not scare off the gang.

To arrive at a plan that would locate the gold as well as avoid such pitfalls as he'd considered would be extremely difficult. Bailey was tempted to believe that a foolproof plan didn't exist. Just how fervently held was this belief could be estimated from the result of several minute's thought, when he crashed a fist onto the table in frustration. This emotional gesture did two things, however. First, it broke him out of the dream world where all plans are perfect. Secondly, it convinced him that his plan would need to be less than foolproof, but practical.

Back to thinking in practical terms, he decided on an extension of the original plan, but instead of concentrating on searching out the gold himself - and merely keeping a lookout for the ungodly - he would change his priorities. He would concentrate his efforts in selecting a member of the gang who would lead him to the gold on the day of the recovery. The hit-and-miss quality of the plan occasioned him the oddest feeling of unease but he decided he really had no alternative. The problem that faced him now was that of deciding who was a member of the ungodly.

Outside, the passing of another gritter - with its amber beacons flashing - distracted his attention. The landscape had begun to lose its landmarks already, the white snow softening the edges of things and masking the more distant prominences. Only on the car and lorry parks below did it seem to have been disturbed, crisscrossed with black lines where tyres had gouged a furrow. Even here, there were islands of white where the more long-standing vehicles - such as his own - were still clothed in unblemished whiteness. Over on the lorry park things weren't much different but there hadn't been the same amount of usage since the snowing had begun. Bailey could see only a few tracks left by lorries, one set of them belonging to the yellow-and-blue truck, which was slowly edging out from behind the Scammell.

Braidwood's 'brute' stood forlorn under the canopy of snow, the almost flat tyres adding to its derelict appearance. Surrounded by an area of snow that was marked only by the scuff of feet - the foreman's, decided Bailey - the broken vehicle affected the security man with something of its isolation. His response was to physically shudder and withdraw his attention to the problem he now faced.

One by one, he went through the list of people he had met since his arrival at the MSA. He reasoned that to canvas the hundred or so people who ran Benwick would be impossible in the time available. Neither would it be desirable to strike up an acquaintance with everyone, which such a survey required. The idea was frankly preposterous. He must stick to monitoring those he had got to know quite well, for it was also logical that the ungodly would watch him better if the watcher knew and spoke to him thereby getting to know his habits and movements.

This presented him with a much shorter list, but which was still too long. He rapidly discounted Lela and Joyce, the girl receptionist, and Anne. He also dismissed those of the kitchen and cafeteria staffs, who he had got to know on his rounds, as well as those who ran the shop. That he should dismiss the participation of any woman in the plot was a decision based on the premise that, as the hijack had occurred before the MSA was built, none of the women would have been around. Bailey felt it was very unlikely that anyone would have been recruited to the gang *after* the hijack, if only for security reasons.

There were four names on the list, which he arrived at for his final selection. Three of them were employed in the Hargreaves group of companies and Bailey considered that link important; Simmonds had known about the gold and had been employed in both construction of the motorway and security on Benwick. If, Bailey reasoned, Hargreaves had allowed other re-appointments from construction companies to Benwick then it was possible that one of his other suspects, Hickson, had known of the crime. By stepping into the shoes left by Simmonds at the construction site, Braidwood must be suspect and, because he had known Simmonds as a father-figure, Bailey included the wayward Davies. The fourth member may also have had some involvement with the crime, though Bailey had no way yet of knowing. But he did know that, for reasons not yet fully formed, he did not trust the anti-motorway leader, Inglefield.

Repeatedly he ran through the list of names. As each name came around his hyper-suspicious mind found ways of making each one into a greater villain than his predecessor in the list. It was headache-forming work; such was the welter of real or imagined words and actions he ascribed to each one over the preceding two days. Every nuance was analysed until it became distorted and useless. Then he would start again.

It was with no small relief, therefore, that he reached to answer the ringing telephone.

'I heard about your predecessor on the radio last night,' announced the man's voice, when he had made certain he was talking to the security man.

'Yes,' encouraged Bailey, sensing nervousness in the man's tone.

'I think I've got some information for you about it - the accident, I mean, in which your predecessor was killed. Except it wasn't an accident.'

'How do you mean?' queried the security man, his interest growing.

'You realise if this gets out it may ruin my marriage,' said the voice. 'I shouldn't want that.'

'Naturally,' said Bailey, not knowing what he was driving at, 'but I don't understand what you mean.'

'Promise me you won't call me for any investigation. I can't risk it.'

'I promise,' said the security man solemnly, ready to promise the Earth now and worry about the consequences later.

The man paused and Bailey could imagine him wrestling with his conscience, but it wasn't for long, and having come to a decision his voice became clear and business-like. 'I was on the motorway at the time of the...incident. I was returning with a girlfriend who, incidentally, was asleep throughout and knows nothing of it. I shouldn't have even been on the motorway - you see, my wife thinks I was in Kent at the time...'

'I understand,' prompted Bailey, interested in nothing but what the man had seen. 'Go on.'

The man, who added the information that he was a representative salesman, spent the next three minutes relating what had happened, which gave the security man a glow of satisfaction as it confirmed what he had believed all along. In addition, he felt a surging excitement when the rep got around to describing the vehicle that had caused the damage. Yellow-and-blue, or possibly black, he had said, and Bailey felt the bits of jig sawed information snap into place in his mind.

He remembered the incident that he had attended on his first night at the MSA. He remembered the witnesses' description of the rogue truck that had caused the accident. Yellow-and-black had been the consensus with regard to its colour scheme. Another thought occurred to him. 'You didn't happen to notice the number plate did you?' he asked.

''Fraid not, chum. I was too busy being terrified,' was the response.

Bailey repeated it: 'VDR...'

'No.'

'Doesn't ring a bell?'

The pause at the other end was short. 'Sorry, couldn't tell you whether it was or not.'

The security man decided he was nit picking anyway and had far more important business elsewhere as he remembered where he had recently seen a truck fitting the description.

'You've been very helpful,' he said, rising from his seat. 'A telephone number would be useful - say at work. It would be treated in the utmost confidence.'

It took precious seconds to persuade the man to part with the information but Bailey felt it was important that he have the means to corroborate the authenticity of his informant.

'Incidentally, I tried the mobile number first,' said the caller. 'Got a non-availability message. Thought you might like to know.'

Bailey was not listening. His mind was on other things. He rang off and ran from the room.

As he took the stairs, three at a time he reflected that he was playing a long shot for there was little likelihood of the truck still being on the MSA. He was counting on the driver having taken it to the fuelling point and still being there, or only just off the service area.

He nearly bowled over a youth as he ran to his car but he saw as he shot a glance back that the figure was still standing upright. The car started first time and after switching on the wiper blades and rear screen demister he depressed the clutch and flung the stubby lever towards second gear, mindful of the snow on the asphalt of the car park. As he let out the clutch, he felt for the adhesion before the car's V8 could spin the wheels. Nothing happened.

The tachometer blipped up to three or four thousand revs each time he attempted to select second, second, third - and even an unproductive first. It was some indication of his keenness to be moving that he should bother with the last but soon he realised that he would be going nowhere for some time.

'What a time for the clutch to go,' he said aloud, seething with frustration, which got physical release as he banged the steering wheel with both palms. Though he had said it, he didn't really believe that the clutch had gone from any normal malfunction. It was too pat, and an obvious advantage to immobilise him, thereby cutting down his area of operations. After all, the ungodly didn't know that he had the cooperation of those at the Police Post, he hoped.

There was no point rushing now so he slowly released the bonnet catch and got out of the car. As a double-check he swept his gaze around the MSA in case the yellow-and-blue truck was still around. The result confirmed his suspicions, however, for he could see no sign of the vehicle amid the falling snow.

It took him less than five minutes to discover the cause of the car's immobility, for tracing the power-train soon found him on his knees in the soft snow as he inspected the transmission tunnel - where the propeller shaft had once been.

He reached for his mobile phone, to get assistance from the Police Post, but belatedly discovered what many already knew, finally understanding Anne's use of the payphone, when he failed to get a signal. Unfortunately, he couldn't know that the loss of signal was not accidental or due to the weather, nor was the lack of internet connectivity. He was tempted to throw the mobile away, such was his frustration, but reason intervened as he realised it still contained the GPS coordinates for the embryo bridge, which might be needed if the dismal weather continued.

Three minutes after leaving the car - at precisely 1000 - he was back in the Security Office. He slumped into the armchair and stared out of the window. It was thinking time again.

He now had a fifth contender for his list, Anne's brother-in-law, Scot. This was an obvious choice, as it seemed certain he had driven his truck to cause at least two collisions - both ending in deaths. Though the security man didn't yet know the reason for the second incident, the first implicated Scot as a member of the ungodly because Simmonds had been bumped off to safeguard the location of the gold. Which was great news for Bailey, reflected the security man, morosely, when the man had left the MSA and might yet elude the police. After all, he decided, the police had known his registration for many hours now and hadn't apprehended him even when he was on the MSA. Gloomily, Bailey was aware for perhaps the hundredth time that he faced an uphill struggle to even fathom out who was involved, never mind locate the gold.

He tried repeatedly to get back to the previous list of four names, realising that it was highly improbable that, even if they traced him, the police would be able to monitor Scot until the recovery date, but his thoughts would keep returning to a promising contact who had slipped through his fingers. No matter how he tried, the promise afforded by an identified member of the gang, proved by his involvement in the two motorway incidents, could not be driven from his mind.

Then he thought of Anne. He remembered her involvement with the man, and a lot more things, which had soon formed in his suspicions the notion that she may even be a sixth name for his list. He remembered again her insistence to stay. For what? To keep in contact with Scot? To pass messages to him? When questioned she had been evasive, or at least unconvincing in her replies. When asked what the problem was with her brother-in-law, she had replied that it was a family problem! Bailey didn't doubt that patricide was indeed a family affair.

He remembered she had spoken with Braidwood a lot too, and with another member of Bailey's little clan, Inglefield. He didn't wonder that she might have had meetings with Hickson or Davies. With the way his mind was functioning, he could imagine anything, but he reasoned that he could be just as wrong as right. Lastly, he realised that she had been in very close contact with one other person - mainly at his own instigation - and that person was himself.

It was with a sinking feeling that he thought of the possible ulterior motive for her presence in the motel room. After the burly man's death - and the end of the radio direction-finding equipment - surveillance had appeared to be non-existent until he had happened upon the man at the rear of the motel who he now suspected had been trying to fix a bug. The girl had pleaded with him to be allowed to stay at that juncture, which brought him to the conclusion that she had been planted to keep an eye on him. He didn't know what other explanation there could be.

Perhaps it was his ego that prevented ready acceptance of her guilt. He had to agree that the facts fitted closely enough to suggest her collusion with the ungodly. Possibly, the fact that he had developed feelings for the girl had affected his judgement. It was time for recriminations against himself as he scolded his ego for letting her stay, against his better judgement. Now he may have a Mata Hari to deal with - and against all his hopes, too, as he had seen something of a long-term relationship between them.

However, it was done. Bailey was chosen for such jobs as much for his ruthlessness as for his inventiveness under pressure. He must deal with the girl but his inner feelings allowed just one alteration from the rules: to be absolutely certain of her involvement he would put her to the test.

The nature of the test came to him in a flash. He reflected upon it and checked it out for weaknesses but was finally satisfied that although it maybe lacked subtlety, it had a sort of charm that was apt in the circumstances. It would require just one telephone call but, as he doubted the security of his office phone - going as it did through the main switchboard in the manager's office - he went down to use one of the payphones in the foyer.

The tramp of sodden footwear had left a slushy mess on the floor of the foyer, which seemed to be increasing despite the efforts of two cleaners. By the bank of payphones, a number of people had congregated to wait for a free booth, and Bailey added himself to their number.

In the fifteen minutes he waited, he had the opportunity to polish up the details of what he would say. He also picked up quite a lot of information from his surroundings, notably from the telephone users. He learned much about conditions on the motorway from what he couldn't avoid overhearing - the anxiety they felt having raised their voices a little higher than normal in both pitch and volume. It seemed that the road surface was now treacherous in places, though many gritting vehicles had been seen. Some reported that they would be late, others that they were turning back. A few weren't lucky enough to have a choice as they were reporting the breakdown of their vehicles and calling for help. A number of callers were finding some difficulty in the use of such ancient technology: clearly, to some brought up on mobile phones, texting and twitter, it was a new skill. Fortunately, the presence of a Christmas spirit meant others were keen to help.

As the minutes ticked by and the stories became repetitive he took to watching the comings and goings through the foyer. At one stage, he saw the anti-motorway leader, Inglefield, descend the stairs and walk over towards him.

'Queue here for your contact with civilisation,' greeted Bailey.

Inglefield smiled. 'How long's the wait?'

Bailey told him how long he had been waiting and they spoke for a minute or two before Inglefield decided to come back later. Watching the man returning up the steps, Bailey decided that he was the oddest campaigner he had ever known: most would have made capital out of the situation, boring all they met. Cynical observations - like motorways having brought one thing more efficient than the old trunk roads; *three* lanes of desolation in winter blizzards instead of one - were more to be expected from his particular faction. It was very odd behaviour, and Bailey made a special note that no matter who he chose to follow to the gold, he would keep an eye on Inglefield for as long as he remained at the MSA.

'Hello, *darlink*,' said a voice beside him. 'In another world are we?'

Bailey almost started at the interruption to his thoughts, then turned and saw it was Lela. 'You're a bit early,' he said, smiling in response to her friendliness. 'Keen to get to work, I expect,' he mused, still grinning.

Lela made a face. 'Not at all. I start early - and I leave early. It is Christmas Eve and I have many things to do.'

The security man nodded at the glass doors and the opaqueness beyond. 'I hope you manage to get out,' he said. 'It doesn't look too good.'

'Do not worry, *darlink*,' she replied, the sureness of tone confirmed when she squeezed his arm with a gloved hand. 'I have seen much worse than this in my life.'

Then she move away and Bailey remembered Braidwood's account of her wartime experience. Her slight limp, which he noticed now as she made for the stairs, enhanced an already vivid picture of her wartime role thrown up in his imagination.

'Happy Christmas, Lela,' he said under his breath.

Within seconds of completing his very brief telephone call, Bailey was trudging through the snow of the car park on his way to the motel. If his test was to be conclusively for or against her involvement with the ungodly, he must be there to gauge her immediate reaction. All the same, he wasn't quite prepared for the reaction he got.

He had hardly touched the door when it opened and the girl threw her arms around him, at the same time drawing him into the room. As she embraced him, he felt her whole frame trembling.

'Hey, steady,' he said, gently but firmly pushing her out to arm's length. 'What's the matter?'

'The phone,' she sobbed, finding great difficulty in speaking. 'It ...it... There was a voice. Horrible.' Her eyes glistened with tears, hurt seen clearly in the deeply-etched frown.

Bailey was already convinced of her innocence. He felt revulsion at his work, but he knew he must make absolutely sure and that was why he pressed on. 'Who was it?'

The girl tried to say something but gave up and merely shook her head.

'What was the voice like? What did it say?'

'He said I should stay away from you or - like you - I would end up dead.'

'And the voice?' he said, adding an edge of urgency to his voice now. The detached, professional part of his make-up was still able to see that her response was within the scope of a very good actress, though doubt was already dispersing this probability.

'I don't know,' she sobbed, confused. 'It was hazy.'

It was time for the final part of the test. It was the part that Bailey relished even less than causing the pain he had already, because it meant she might very well hate him.

'What did it sound like?' he asked, shaking her gently. 'Like this?' He imitated the sounds he had made over the phone which, although not having the sterility of electronics or the use of his handkerchief as in the original, were such a fair representation that she responded immediately.

'Yes,' she cried, eyes wide with recognition. 'Yes, it was just like that. I...' In a second her expression had changed from the relief of a shared experience to one of abject sorrow tinged with incredulity as she realised he, of all people, had tricked her - and in a particularly cruel way.

For long seconds she just looked at him, the pain in her eyes very real. She didn't have to say what was in her mind for in silence her expression was quite loud enough in asking: *why*? The model's poise was gone now, as she stood flatfooted and forlorn, the blotchy make-up revealing the truth behind it. Moreover, Bailey saw a little girl, confused and very hurt.

He dragged her to him then, almost smothering her with the force of his embrace and he spoke many words, which tried to explain and apologise at the same time. However, he knew that nothing he had said - or could say - would represent exactly what he meant. Then he released her, an inch-or-so.

It was some time before she stopped snuffling and coughing quietly, and trying to use her handkerchief without letting go of him. She had heard every word Bailey had uttered and most of it made sense. In explaining his actions, he had had recourse to recount a lot that he wouldn't otherwise have disclosed.

'I can't believe, Shughie - that's what everyone calls Scot - could do these things you claim,' she said, at last. 'Yes, he does step outside the law, I believe, and that is bad enough. But I know the real reason isn't greed and I'm sure he couldn't do *that*.' She couldn't quite bring herself to label her brother-in-law a murderer.

'The evidence is conclusive,' cautioned Bailey, feeling the strangeness of a situation where one moment all was hysterical crying and next, cool reasoned conversation. Then, people react in different ways, he reflected. Odd though her behaviour was, he saw no reason to continue suspecting her of anything illegal.

'Only minutes ago you had conclusive proof involving *me*,' she said quietly, but the warning was clear. 'Do you really believe you were right in my case?'

Bailey nodded acceptance of the logic in what she said. He smiled at her, too, but it was only a mask to hide what his true thoughts were for he still believed that Shughie had to be a murderer. The silence dragged on for a few seconds in which time Bailey tried to phrase his doubts in such a way as to avoid further emotion on her part.

However, the girl saved him from the task for she suddenly pulled away and crossed the room to her bed. Then, she reached under the pillow and withdrew the crumpled envelope. Without explanation, she handed it to him.

It was an anguished letter, written by Simmonds to both his daughters but the envelope was addressed to Anne. He had tried to say in a few lines what hadn't been said over many years. In a desperate attempt at reconciliation - spread over several pages - he seemed to have been preparing them for something. That something took up both sides of the last two pages.

In a clearly nervous frame of mind, he had written of his plan to blow the gaff on a big job. He had said that he would very likely go to prison for it, but he didn't mind. All sorts of pressures had been brought to bear in order to force him to keep silent - even the threat of reporting Shughie's antics to the police. However, he couldn't stay silent when hundreds of people might die.

The letter, he explained, was a warning that even though he was a rogue - and maybe deserving of his daughters' displeasure - what frightened him more than threats or prison was that they should grow to hate him. He hoped, also, that they would not suffer by his actions, and that - quite simply - he was sorry.

It was a moving letter that was difficult to decipher because of the haste in which it had been written. A glance at the postmark explained something of this as it showed the letter had been posted the day before the incident. As he handed it back to the girl, he noticed she was crying again.

When he had put his arm around her, she brushed the tears away with her handkerchief and looked up at him. 'We've been a pair of bitches,' she said weakly, 'and I was the worst.'

'No, you aren't the unfeeling person you think you are,' he said gently. 'You're talking about a person of the past - and what happened in the past. It's better left in the past, too. Does your sister know of this letter?'

Anne shook her head. 'No. I decided there was something I must do before I saw her. She's not strong enough to take it.'

Suddenly Bailey straightened in reaction to both the girl's words and a thought that had just crossed his mind. 'Tell me if I'm wrong,' he said, 'but I believe you came to the MSA to discover what you could about the job your father was about to expose.'

'That's right,' she answered. Then her jaw tightened and she said, 'I was going to find out as much of my father's activities as possible - legal and illegal - and then go to the police with the letter.'

'Then we are more or less after the same thing,' declared Bailey, and gave her a squeeze. 'Hello, partner.'

Anne managed a smile.

Having recognised their shared objective, they could only feel happier in each other's company now. As they talked, all ill-feeling at Bailey's ruse evaporated from Anne's thoughts, to be replaced with what she had felt since arriving at Benwick - that she felt secure with this man and wanted to stay as close to him as possible, whether in pursuit of her planned objective to track down her father's killers, or for her own happiness.

Discarding his more pressing duty of investigating his five remaining suspects, Bailey relaxed in the girl's company. He was almost mesmerised by the warmth and strength of the radiations from her and felt there was only one way to dissipate the unbearable maelstrom of feelings he was experiencing.

Such was her response that they were soon laying on the girl's bed, naked and very involved in making love. It wasn't the same act as that which had followed Bailey's trip to the construction site; this was premeditated by both parties. It was a gentler, more sensitive coupling, tempered yet enhanced by their admittance - in thought if not yet confirmed in speech - of the stronger commitment they now shared.

Chapter Ten

(24th December: 1500 - 1700)

For two hours they lay in each other's arms, neither wanting to break away. Occasionally they would lapse into sleep only to be wakened again by a movement of one or the other or the noise of the wind rattling the windows. The noise from outside had been steadily increasing throughout the late morning and early afternoon, but each time they shrugged it out of their minimal awareness.

It was the telephone, which finally broke the spell. Bailey had to lean over the girl to pick up the receiver and as he did - switching on the bedside light as he did so - the girl could see the expression on his face. To her, the voice at the other end was mere gibberish and, after looking to Bailey for enlightenment, she was sure he was hearing nothing more intelligible. Then his expression changed into a tight mask and, after an acknowledgement, he replaced the receiver.

'What was that all about?' she asked, watching as the security man pulled on his clothes.

'The manager,' he threw over his shoulder. 'Someone reckons he's gone missing.'

'Hickson? Missing?' she asked, sharing the surprise he felt.

215

'Precisely. How can they say he's gone missing? He could be away visiting.'

Anne nodded, but said nothing.

'Anyway, I'm going over to see what's happening,' he continued, shrugging into his parka. 'Don't leave your room while I'm away - until I let you know things are all right.'

'Yes, *sir*,' she returned, sitting up and cracking off a smart salute.

For a split second, Bailey took in the sight of her bare torso and was torn between leaving and staying. Then he sighed his reluctance most expressively, before opening the door on the swirling snow and stepping outside.

It took him considerably longer than normal to cross the four-hundred yards to the complex owing to the blizzard, which met him face on. Although it was barely three in the afternoon, it was already darkening, the falling snow now grey. On the ground, it was six-inches deep and large drifts were forming against anything that didn't move.

It was Joyce, Lela's friend, who had made the hysterical telephone call, and Bailey was still wondering at the intensity of her emotion during the conversation as he climbed the stairs of the staff entrance. He found her, white-faced and only just in control of herself, as he entered the manager's office. She was crouched in the chair behind the desk staring straight ahead, her only activity drawing deeply on the cigarette she held.

As he approached the desk, he cast a glance sideways through the open door of the manager's living-quarters, and what he saw swayed him towards belief in the woman's claim that Hickson had left.

'All gone,' she confirmed without looking up and there was intensity in her closed expression.

Bailey didn't comment but instead went through into the other room. He hadn't been inside the manager's living quarters before and he didn't need to have done, to know that no-one lived there anymore. The shelves and tops of the wooden furniture were now bare, only dustless shapes showing where ornaments had once stood. The wardrobe - doors wide open - was bare of clothes except for a belt and a tie. The way that these lay at the bottom suggested that the move had been somewhat rushed as they were both of high-quality, yet strewn as if mislaid.

'How did you come to find this?' he asked when he returned to the manager's office.

'I noticed his car was missing.'

'And you came up here on the strength of *that*?'

Joyce said nothing, but the troubled expression she wore told of another reason for her action. Bailey saw this but at first thought he had misread it. Then he decided to try it, anyway. 'You weren't involved with Hickson, were you?' he asked carefully.

Joyce nodded, and as she looked at him, the tears welled up in her eyes. 'Yes. Brian and I have been involved - as you put it - for some months now.'

Bailey groaned, inwardly. Here he was, with three days to go in the final scene of an incident that promised worldwide chaos on the money-markets if he failed, and he was beset with domestic problems, one of which may have frightened off a prime suspect. He was wearying under the burden of what he considered trivial problems and it said much for the extent of this weariness that he overlooked the possibility that Hickson's running out wasn't the *result* of his domestic problems, but simply the cause.

'Perhaps you'd better tell me the whole story. Then I might be able to do something about it,' he said gently.

'There's not much to tell,' she replied, brushing away a stray tear. 'I met him when the service station opened and we got to grow fond of each other. We're both single and there shouldn't have been any problem. But we never lived openly together. He didn't want it known that he was involved with one of the staff, as he reckoned it was bad for discipline. I agreed with him to some extent, but he took it too far at times and would ignore me when he went through the restaurant on his rounds. Naturally, nobody knew about us - apart from Lela, that is.'

Bailey remembered the scene he had witnessed when leaving the restaurant on the first night on the MSA. He told Joyce about it.

'Yes,' she confirmed, 'I remember it. He's been like that for the last fortnight. I've never known him to be so bad-mannered. It seemed as if he was trying to cut himself off from me - as if he wanted to call a halt but wasn't man enough to say so decently.'

'You've no idea why?'

'None. I've wracked my brains to discover a cause but all I come up with is little things. You might know what he's like by now and understand when I say he was almost fanatical about this place. I did occasionally say that he loved it more than me, I know, but surely that was only self-defence for his ignoring me in public.'

Bailey couldn't give her the reassuring answer she needed. He didn't know the manager well enough - perhaps if he had he would have been able to clear or condemn him of involvement in the gold hijack. It was almost academic now because the man had run out - not only on the woman - but also on Bailey's rapidly shortening list of suspects.

He looked back towards the outer office, then back to Joyce. 'Where's the girl?'

Joyce shook her head slowly. 'I know what you're thinking, but I don't believe he would run out on me for another woman, especially her. I've thought a lot of bad thoughts about him while I've been sat here, but I don't think running off with his daughter - in the way you think - was one of them.'

'The girl was his daughter?'

'By a previous marriage.'

'Where was she today? Did she go with him?'

'Day off,' she said, simply. 'Christmas with mum.'

Bailey thought about this for a moment, for the first time seeing the similarity between father and daughter. Why he had run, was the uppermost thought in his mind, at that moment. That, and wondering whether Joyce was indeed the spurned mistress she seemed to be, or just following Hickson's orders.

'What prompted you to come to the flat?' he asked.

'I told you - his car...'

'What's so suspicious about a man's car not being in the car park? He must use it sometimes.'

'But he rarely did, he lived here almost like a hermit,' she insisted. 'I told you he was almost married to the place, didn't I, and if he was going anywhere he would always tell me.'

'Except that he hasn't been telling you anything in the past two weeks, has he?'

'No.'

'So while he was away you thought you'd take a look around to see if there was anyone else in his life, yes?'

Joyce nodded, and her shoulders shook as the sobs came again.

Bailey believed her now. He believed her not just for the tears or obvious hurt she displayed, but because her story made sense. It was untidy enough to be real and, seeing what Hickson had done to this woman, he became of the notion that he would very much like to interview the manager.

The security man spent some minutes comforting the woman and then advised her to go back to work, as that would take her mind off things - at least with Lela around it would, he reflected. In any case, as the weather outside was atrocious, and she was in no fit state to drive on the treacherous roads, there was no other advice he could give.

When she left he moved around the desk to sit in the chair she had just vacated. Then he leant on the desk and cradled his head in his hands. Though his thoughts then were on the domestic distractions he was facing, he spent only seconds reviewing his conversation with Joyce. His main concern was the other, more personal situation with Anne and he cursed himself for being such a fool as to get involved with her during this critical mission. It was no defence to know that he couldn't help himself; that it wasn't some meaningless affair. He told himself his involvement with her was very, very unprofessional and placed both of them and the mission in danger. He just hoped the ungodly knew nothing of his feelings for her because he didn't know how he would choose between the mission and Anne should such a choice be forced upon him.

He was still sat at the desk, his thoughts having moved on to bemoaning the loss of another member of his list, when he heard the door of the outer office opening. 'More interruptions,' he thought, as he saw the squat figure of Lela come round the doorjamb. How he could possibly concentrate on the problem of selecting the most promising of the two remaining - in situ - suspects, with the constant distractions he was suffering, he didn't know.

The truth was that he had already exhausted the time available for the luxury of quiet and peaceful reflection. Events were taking over. From now on, he would have to think on his feet, as he would not have time to pause. This wasn't *quite* true, for he managed a little more thought in the moments he remained seated at the desk.

'Yes, Lela?' he prompted, tiredly.

Lela smiled, and pulled her hands from behind her back. 'I brought you this,' she said, cheerfully, and Bailey found himself staring into the muzzle of an automatic pistol.

For a moment he didn't speak, which is understandable when you realise that it was around thirty-odd years since she had probably used such a weapon. However, his mind had the opportunity that the silence afforded to surmise on an enlargement of his list of only two names - Braidwood and Inglefield - by contemplating the addition of a third, Lela.

Then she lowered the barrel and Bailey sighed aloud.

'Aren't you going to ask me where I found it?' she asked.

'Found it?' repeated the security man, stupidly. Then, collecting his wits, he added, 'Where?'

'In the cafeteria, underneath one of the tables,' she explained. 'I was helping out because one of the women hasn't turned up. It was under the table used by that big man.'

'Big man? The foreman, Braidwood?' he asked, keeping an eye on the barrel of the gun which seemed to waver in his direction with each change of emphasis in her speech.

'No, not *Larry*,' she responded, managing exaggerated emphasis in the disclaimer. 'It was the other man, the one with the funny tee-shirt. He is something against the road, I think.'

'Inglefield?'

'Yes, that's the one,' she confirmed. Then she smiled mischievously, as he had seen her do on the night of his arrival. 'It was not *quite* on the floor - it was in his bag.'

'You've told no-one of this?' asked Bailey, unable to fully appreciate her little joke while she waved the automatic around.

'No-one but you.'

'Not even Joyce?'

'Not even my poor friend, Joyce,' she answered. 'What do you think he used it for?'

'Protection, no doubt,' he replied, gravely. 'against wicked old ladies. Thanks for bringing it to me.'

Lela giggled. 'I must go back now, it's so busy.'

She laid the gun on the desk, and Bailey sighed again. 'They make you nervous?' she asked.

'Only when other people are holding them.'

'Ah, yes, I know what you mean. I was once in a business like yours,' she said, suddenly serious.

Bailey tried to hide his surprise at her comment under an attempt at humour. 'Oh, which motorway service station would that be?'

Lela returned to giggling. 'Very good, Mister Bailey, but I recognise in you something of my contemporaries in the last war, you know?'

Bailey didn't reply immediately for he didn't know what to say. Fortunately, he was spared the need to say anything, as the telephone rang out on the manager's desk. As he reached towards it, Lela turned on her heel and, only pausing at the door long enough to wave, disappeared into the outer office.

It was a weary-sounding maintenance foreman at the other end.

'Could you *please* tell the manager when he gets back that one of the hoppers is playing up and I'm unable to keep on top of the gritting schedule because of it.' The foreman's voice was pitched high with tension. 'I've tried clearing it but we haven't the men to do a proper job.'

'Would it help if I came down and gave a hand?' offered Bailey.

'I'd certainly be grateful for all the help I can get. I'm busy rounding up volunteers at the moment for that job,' he responded. 'Listen, I'd appreciate it if you could call through to the Linton crowd and ask them to try and cover our eastbound section. For some reason the phone has gone as well.'

Bailey glanced at the window and the now blackness of the night. Blackness, that is, except for the grey of large snowflakes wafting past the window. The snowfall seemed to him to be getting heavier.

'What's the number?'

The foreman told him, and Bailey rang off.

He moved directly to the switchboard in the outer office and then dialled the outside number. Three times he tried but each time the result was the same - nothing. No dialling tone, no engaged tone, or even a disconnected tone - just nothing whatsoever. The switchboard was completely dead.

His suspicions raised, he moved over to the table upon which stood the switchboard and pulled it away from the wall. Then he searched in his pockets for a penknife to unscrew the plate on the wall into which fed the thick cable from the switchboard. He soon found the penknife wasn't necessary, however, as he only had to touch the back-plate for it to fall away to the floor, exposing a confusion of multi-coloured wires, which must have been ripped from the terminals with great force.

'Now what was the reason for this, Hickson?' asked the security man, aloud. To stop a call coming in, he wondered, or a call going out? Or was it just for annoyance value? He could surmise all day, and with as little result, but that wouldn't make the important call to Linton.

Fortunately, and as proved by the foreman's call to the manager's office, the internal system was still functioning, so Bailey used it to contact the Police Post. Brennan answered.

'Got a problem,' announced Bailey.

'*You've* got a problem? Everybody's got a problem,' returned the sergeant. 'I've got a problem, too. I haven't been home since yesterday and there doesn't seem any likelihood of it in the near future.'

'Bad as that.'

'Worse. But what's your problem?'

Bailey told him about the manager's disappearance and the foreman's plea for assistance. He also told him about the switchboard - but not about Inglefield's gun, as he suspected that that would entail just too much police assistance at a time when he wanted things done quietly.

'Well, of course we've got a separate outside line so I'll try them on that. If that doesn't work though it may be some time before I can get a patrol car to Linton. It's just pandemonium out there!'

Bailey felt a growing tension as he picked his way between the vehicles, the noise of car-radios blaring carols, and the blurry figures which he encountered on the car park. He was on his way to the maintenance compound and rapidly becoming a snowman in the process. The feeling that he was being hemmed in seemed to accompany him, growing stronger as he added the likely consequences of first the hopper defect, the loss of communications with Linton, the awful weather conditions, and the resulting effect of isolating the MSA.

Added to the odd occurrences that had happened of late, he felt that a whole world of activity was taking place outside of his understanding. After Davies' disappearance had come that of Hickson, having left an empty flat, an unhappy mistress and an unserviceable switchboard. On top of these events, he'd been handed a gun that had been found in the possession of a supposedly *peaceful* demonstrator. The only drop of comfort that he felt as he slushed up the slight rise was that he could now feel the gun in his parka pocket.

The compound yard was better lit than most areas of the MSA as it was bracketed by two large floodlights each shining down from towers some twenty-five feet high. Even so, the attenuating influence of the heavy snowfall was such that only a dim glow reached the areas of activity. The nearest hopper was one such area, encircled by heavily insulated figures who cajoled the gritting vehicles into the right position beneath the funnel, while another man operated the simple trap-door mechanism. Then the *whoosh* of loose material could be heard, as it fell into the waiting vehicle's bin below.

Bailey saw all this as he moved over to the large shed. Once inside he made straight for the foreman's office and - while the foreman was busy giving instructions to another man - warmed his hands on the butane heater. 'Just get them over there and I'll be out in a minute,' he heard him say, and then the man left.

'Hello again,' greeted the foreman. Then he rubbed his eyes. 'What a day.'

Bailey explained that there might be some difficulty getting the message through to Linton, but didn't mention the sabotaged switchboard in his story.

'We'll just have to hope they can stretch their fleet to cover our section,' said the foreman. Then he shook his head. 'It's just what I needed in conditions like this - I don't think. Just when we are on three ounce spread, the hopper goes out of action.'

'How long does it take to use up a full hopper-load?'

'Depends on the spread. We had two full hoppers of forty tons each at midnight, which at the rate we've been using the stuff should have lasted us a full day, at least. But with number two going out almost two hours ago, I've lost its last fifteen tons. That means number one will be due for a top-up very shortly - bloody well impossible in these conditions, as I don't want to have the loader collide with the hopper and put that one out of action as well.

'No, the sensible thing to do is to reduce the spread to quarter ounce - behind the snowploughs,' he said, mainly for his own benefit, as he thought out his tactics aloud.

'Will that be sufficient?' asked the security man, sympathising with the foreman.

'Bloody well hope so, but I doubt it,' he returned, with feeling. 'You see, the heavy spread helps flatten the snow by acting as an abrasive under the wheels of following vehicles. Unless fresh snow comes along the grit provides good friction for wheels to grip on. Quarter-ounce, on the other hand, is for light snow only but by reaming off the top few inches of snow with the snowplough we can artificially create the light snow conditions and tackle it with quarter-ounce.'

The foreman smiled then, but it wasn't a humorous smile. 'The problem then can be likened to burning a candle at both ends. Because the snowplough slows down the gritting-vehicle, it can treat only a much shorter stretch of carriageway. By the time he has arrived at the end of the section it is deep snow again at the beginning. Eventually, if the snowing lasts long enough we could end up with our vehicles stranded.'

'Not to mention the vehicles behind them,' provided Bailey.

'That too,' agreed the foreman, his expression quizzical, as if this was a secondary concern.

Bailey got to his feet. 'Which means it's quite important to get that hopper working again.'

The foreman nodded. 'We're just about to have another go at clearing it,' he said, lifting a duffle-coat from a hook on the back of the door.

'I'll give you a hand,' said Bailey.

The two men soon joined several others who were crouched in the lee of a gritting-vehicle that had been parked underneath the defective hopper. Soon a rope had been attached to the large metal handle of the trap-door mechanism and the men were strung out along the rope, ready to take a purchase.

For a quarter of an hour, the ten men tried various ways of applying their full weight in unison. Bit by bit a trickle would descend but there was no sign of freeing the trap-door completely.

Then someone clambered to a position atop the vehicle from where he could see into the hopper. 'It looks like there's a log stuck in there,' he shouted, above the wind.

Bailey was the second man up. It did indeed look like a thin piece of wood at first but, as his eyes became more accustomed to the darkness, he saw the dull glint of something reflecting at the end. His brain completed the picture for him. He saw that it was an arm - the glinting object at the end being a large ring - and he knew he had found Davies.

Bailey was in a cold fury over his discovery, but his thinning veneer of professionalism held his emotions in check. Beyond his natural regret that his young assistant should have been murdered - and he would entertain no other view on the death - he felt a rage that it had occurred at all. It seemed to be a personal insult to him that the ungodly should feel they could go about their unlawful business without regard for his presence - whether his true role were understood or not.

He was sorely tempted to react violently when next he saw either of the remaining suspects still on the MSA - Inglefield and Braidwood. He felt the need to rid himself of his frustration through violence meted out to them, but he knew there was far more at stake than could be gained from personal gratification. Instead, he promised himself that the time would come when he could play by their rules.

He informed the Police Post of his find, using the foreman's telephone to do so. Then he took no further part in the initial investigation but headed back through the blizzard towards the complex, with the intention of making a few discreet inquiries there.

As he trudged through the snow he got to wondering how his assistant's body had come to be in the hopper. It was unlikely that he'd been killed there, it seemed to Bailey, but Davies must have been placed in the hopper during the night, as it would be too risky during daylight. The maintenance foreman had already told him that the hoppers were full at midnight, so it would have to have been sometime before then. But where had Davies been between going missing and ending up in the compound? Had he been killed immediately Bailey left the MSA, on his tour of the construction site in the morning? If so, where had his body lain until it was dark enough to move him in secrecy? And, most important, *why* had he been killed?

There were many questions, and very few - if any - reasonably logical answers. One possible answer was to the question of where the body had been kept between death and transfer to the hopper. Bailey remembered the burned-out room in the motel, and noticing that something heavy prevented him opening the door. He had visited the room in the afternoon of the same day that Davies had disappeared. Then he remembered something else; his visit had been before he had caught Davies outside the window of his motel room. If so, Davies could not have been in the gutted room. Unless, he reflected, the man outside the window had been someone else dressed in his assistant's uniform.

At the same time that such confusing thoughts had joined others buzzing around his head, Bailey found himself at a point along the half-hidden track where he could turn right for the complex, or left for the motel. By visiting the room again, he might find some answers, he decided, and so he turned left.

He had to wade through a waist-high drift of virgin snow in order to climb the lower steps to the room, which at least proved that no-one had been that way for some considerable time. At the door, he again worked on the lock and pushed the door gently. Without resistance, the door swung back on its hinges and Bailey's penlight probed the charred interior of the room.

There were many footmarks by the door, which was to be expected, as the firemen had needed to investigate and make sure the fire was truly out. It seemed that, although the weight behind the door had been removed, there was nothing else to find of interest to him, but he scratched away in the wet ashes, anyway.

Then he heard the noise. It was nothing more than the scuffing of a shoe on the stair but Bailey froze as if petrified. With his anger at Davies's death simmering beneath the surface, he was in a killing mood and he flattened himself against the nearest wall to wait.

The door opened slowly but hadn't travelled for more than a quarter of its radius before Bailey's hand shot out and dragged the figure towards him. At the same time, he held the pencil-flash in the first of his other hand and shone it in the interloper's eyes. With the man temporarily stunned, the security man released his grip and raised his hand to strike.

The motel manager flew back in terror against the wall. He sensed, correctly, that severe injury was but a millisecond away and he broke into very fast talking. He had probably said all there was to say before Bailey lowered his fist, but he repeated it a little more slowly just the same.

'The police want you,' he said, gasping from nervousness. 'They asked me to tell you. I saw you pass the office window and came up to tell you.'

'What's it about?'

'I don't know. They just want you on the phone.'

'Lead the way.'

As they entered the office, the light hurt Bailey's eyes and he temporarily shielded them against the glare. Then he saw the red smudge on the manager's coat. 'What happened there?' he asked, directing the man's attention to the spot with a glance.

The still-shaking manager looked down and his eyes opened wide. When he was sure he wasn't injured he looked back at Bailey and his eyes opened wider. 'Your hands,' he directed. 'It's off your hands. You've injured them.'

Bailey had already reached for the telephone as the manager spoke and saw the red blotches mixed with the black charcoal that covered his fingers. Leaving the telephone where it lay, he wiped his hands with a handkerchief and discovered that although the red was blood and the black was from the floor of the room above, he hadn't been cut. It did tell him one thing. There had been a body behind the door, as he had suspected. Without comment, he reached for the phone again.

'Brennan here,' said the voice, when Bailey had announced his presence. 'We just got a message from a patrol car. They say they've got our manager. He's still on the motorway and his car has broken down.'

'Good,' said the security man, and there was something in his tone that wasn't very pleasant. 'Are they bringing him back?'

''Fraid not. It's not one of our patrol cars - it belongs to the neighbouring force, which covers the westerly stretch. Besides, they've enough on their plates without running a chauffeur service.'

'It's important I interview the man as soon as possible,' said Bailey, picking his words carefully in the presence of the motel manager.

'I thought so,' replied the sergeant. 'That's why I've cut short the rest period of one of my patrols to take you to him - he won't be going anywhere for a while, I should think.'

'Excellent! I'm on my way,' said Bailey, and slammed down the receiver. If Hickson could have known what was in his thoughts at that moment, he reflected, not even the snow would have prevented him crawling away from the motorway, and the impending interview.

The security man didn't bother with the subterfuge he had used before, of meeting the patrol car out on the motorway. Instead, he went straight over to the Police Post and joined them there, the fall of snow being so dense as to effectively screen him from observation by anyone more than a few yards away.

The conditions out on the motorway were truly horrendous, Bailey was amazed, and impressed at the expert way the driver handled the Range Rover to keep them going in a straight line. Even though the security man was impatient to see the manager - and hoped that the policemen wouldn't interfere when he found him - they had to stop several times to give advice to stranded motorists, and although the reported position of their destination was only twelve miles from Benwick the journey took three-quarters of an hour.

When they arrived, neither the manager nor his car could be seen. What was more, the snow on the hard shoulder was undisturbed at that spot and, even though they carried on for a few hundred yards, it was obvious the manager's car hadn't broken down there.

'There couldn't be any mistake in the position, could there?' asked Bailey, feeling a sudden unease.

'They don't make mistakes like that - nor do we,' responded the driver.

'Could you check?'

'Of course,' said the driver, 'but I know the outcome already.'

It occurred to Bailey that unless he was very much mistaken, so did he.

Bailey recognised Brennan's voice over the radio as the sergeant replied to their query. He also detected a note of bewilderment. 'I've just been onto their controller by phone,' he explained, 'and they insist that none of their cars reported such an occurrence or reported it to us. I don't know what's happened but I've asked him to check with each patrol as they go in for rest periods.'

As the driver acknowledged and reported that they were returning, Bailey felt like telling Brennan not to waste his time. He now knew who had radioed-in with the report. He had remembered his nocturnal visit to the construction site and the snapshot image of the interior of the office cabin. Joe had used the radio there to transmit a bogus report, Bailey was now certain. But why? To get him off the MSA? How could they know that the security man would go? They couldn't, surely. Bailey was convinced the hoax had been enacted for just that reason and he was now very anxious to get back.

The return journey took longer as the Range Rover was barely a match for the conditions they met. Their progress was painfully slow and Bailey grew more and more impatient. Once or twice, he was tempted to urge the driver to increase speed but knew it would do no good; the man was already driving the vehicle to the limits of its road holding abilities. Instead, he stared impotently at the thousands of white dots, which floated to meet them and mentally urged the vehicle to go faster than fifteen miles per hour.

They got back to the MSA a few minutes before 1700, after they had picked up some stranded drivers. Hardly had they drawn to a halt outside the Police Post than Bailey had jumped out and begun marching towards the complex.

Once there he stamped the caked snow from his feet and moved over to the bank of pay-phones. There was no queue anymore and he hadn't reached them before he knew why; on each telephone had been placed a notice, which said, quite plainly 'Out of Order'.

Without hesitation, he turned back to the entrance and retraced his steps to the Police Post. His finding the pay-phones out of use had strengthened a suspicion he had held for the last half hour. What Brennan told him on his arrival added confirmation to it. In the last few hours - since the snow had threatened to block the motorway - other forms of communication had begun to fail. The switchboard had been sabotaged so that outside calls could not be made, the pay-phones were out of order for probably the same reason, and the sergeant had just told him that his radio was no longer working - and neither was his telephone to the operations room. For whatever reason, someone had assisted the weather in severing all links between Benwick and the outside world.

Chapter Eleven

(24th December: 1700 - 1800)

The Range Rover that had brought Bailey back to the MSA was one of the last vehicles to leave the motorway, for although several four-wheel-drive police cars still prowled the snowbound carriageways with great difficulty, few other vehicles were equipped to operate in such conditions.

Out on the motorway very little moved apart from the swirling snow. Most cars had long since lurched off to more hospitable surroundings, before the worsening weather was complicated by darkness.

A few drivers, however, had ignored the warnings and now sat immobile and isolated in their vehicles. Some of them ran their car engines to have use of the heater but even this afforded only temporary respite for the snow soon formed in deep drifts, which all but cocooned them, and prevented use of the engine because of the attendant dangers from exhaust fumes.

Then their only contact with the outside world was the rumble and vibration they experienced as a truck passed by. At such times, their worries were heightened as they wondered if the next truck they heard would be the one that hit them.

By 1700 this risk, at least, was very much reduced as there was only one truck which still battled on through the grey blur along the motorway, and it was driven by Shughie.

He was very tired now. Too many hours at the wheel in too short a period had taken their toll. Now he needed to call upon all his experience in order to keep awake. That was why the heater was switched off and the windows wound fully down, the icy wind meant to hold off sleep through sheer discomfort. He also took to exaggerating his watchfulness of the road ahead, darting glances in different directions and out to different ranges so as to avoid staring himself into a sleep-inducing trance. And, why also, he was singing.

Shughie sang everything and anything in the most unmusical tones. Even the fluctuation of engine note, caused by the differing degrees of adhesion beneath the truck wheels as icy patches were encountered, had something pleasantly lilting about it. But it didn't matter, nobody was listening and his own interest was concentrated solely on remembering the words, the better to keep him alert.

It was odd, therefore, that in quick time he should stop all activity and take to staring out into the maelstrom of snowflakes beyond the windscreen. Quite suddenly, he was mentally elsewhere, prompted to reverie by the realisation that this was his very last trip and that in a few hours he would be sharing Christmas with his wife.

His thoughts then went beyond this and he remembered the sole reason behind the 'cowboy' career he had pursued over so many months. As the truck trundled on with less and less supervision in the dangerous conditions, Shughie was once again in the consultant's office listening to the verdict on his wife's health.

'Two years. Perhaps, three. There is simply nothing we can do.'

The scot had been stunned at the finality of the doctor's words. He had almost missed the rest, so uncomprehending was he that there was no hope for his wife. The man's words, almost an afterthought, had then drifted through the haze and into Shughie's consciousness.

'At least, not this side of the Atlantic. There is a team... Oh, but what's the use?'

'What team?' Shughie had demanded, sensing that he might have been shown, if not thrown, the life-belt that might save Linda.

'They're exorbitantly expensive,' the consultant had insisted, hurriedly, realising his mistake. 'They're the best, and therefore their time must inevitably be expensive.' With this addition, he had hoped to undo some of the damage he had caused by voicing the afterthought. It wasn't that he entertained doubts in the ability of the team he had spoken of, but he knew full well that the man before him could not possibly afford to use them.

'How expensive?'

The consultant had told him, adding a thousand pounds in order that he might dash the husband's hopes quickly instead of have him suffer the anguish of unassailable dreams.

'I'll get it somehow,' Shughie had promised, and even though the consultant had heard such brave - if empty - declarations often in the past, he had been sufficiently impressed by the glint of determination in the man's eyes to feel distinctly uneasy.

This was how Shughie had read the interview and had been determined nevertheless to raise the money for the operation. He had never doubted he would achieve his aim and now the date was fixed - and had been for the last three months - when he and his wife would fly out to the 'States and her operation.

However, the bid almost ended right there on the motorway. It was only some sixth sense, keeping ceaseless watch for danger, which alerted him to the fact that something was wrong.

Perhaps it had been a change in engine note or the slightly vague feeling of the steering when the wheels touch ice. Whatever it was, it brought him abruptly to terrified wakefulness as he strove to grasp the significance of the alarm. In the gloom ahead, he could just discern a string of vehicles, which had parked where the hard shoulder should have been. Then he felt the steering and noticed there was no response - he was slewing straight towards them and only a hundred yards now separated them.

It was then that he felt the cold fear in his belly. It wasn't fear for himself or even for those who might be languishing in the cars he was fast approaching. His fear was based on the subject of his efforts over the past year - the saving of his wife's life - and the terrible irony that the accident looming ahead could wreak. Another segment of his brain was cool efficiency, however, issuing crisp directives based on experience, which his body converted into skilful operation of the truck's controls.

Deftly he checked, prodded and cajoled the truck at the slightest sensation of adhesion. Inch by inch the front came right, in the direction of safety, but it was not enough. The ice was patchy and no sooner had he found a touch of response than it was lost again. Still, he battled on.

With fifty feet to go he judged he would miss the rearmost vehicles but it was certain now that he must collide with the rest in a glancing blow which offered no hope for the lives of those waiting inside.

There was no time now for even spoken prayers, not that Shughie knew how to pray. But he did have the time to shout out a mental plea that he might achieve the impossible and avoid the cars. Though he didn't think of it at the time, he would have been surprised to know that in the last milliseconds before collision it was not his wife that he was pleading for - or even his own life - but for those complete strangers facing imminent death.

Whatever construction he might later put on the events that followed, the facts were plain. Having travelled over the patchy ice, which had formed by the sloughing action of colliding cars, his offside wheels fell into the thin band of scraped road that had been the trail of one such vehicle. The result was immediate and positive: control returned as the wheels touched something to adhere to and the truck passed the last car by the width of a snowflake.

It would take many minutes for Shughie to fall back into the kind of dangerous trance, which had contributed to his near-accident, but he was taking no chances. He immediately resumed his tuneless singing and exaggerated watchfulness - and reflected upon his luck.

In the confined space of the cold and dripping cavern, the two men struggled tiredly with the last box. From the meagre light of a single low-wattage lamp, they picked their way through the ankle-deep water over the uneven ground, while ahead shone the vertical beam of light, guiding them to the entrance like a beacon.

Above the rough-hewn entry hole stood the man who had supervised the recovery of many other boxes over the past few days. As on the other occasions in the boiler house, Braidwood's expression was frozen into seriousness but now he managed a wry smile as he saw the last of the small heavy boxes come into view at the bottom of the hole.

It had been a difficult period for them but at last they had completed the recovery, two days ahead of schedule and despite the pressures of the past few days. Within the hour they would be away from the service area. He could afford to relax slightly now, even though he had a lot to do before they took off. In consequence, he allowed himself the luxury of reverie and reflected upon the reasons for rushing into the recovery operation instead of waiting until the planned date, a date itself forced upon them because of the risk of discovery prompted by the Department of Transport's completion inspection.

Simmonds's death had brought unexpected problems - or rather, problem, in the shape of his replacement. Bailey had not been the dodderer of a security man in search of the easy life that they had anticipated. Young, intelligent and, with a past which had indicated involvement as a professional security man, it could be assumed he possessed a highly sensitive antenna for unusual occurrences.

They had decided to watch him from the start. Andy and Joe had managed to plant tracker devices in his footwear when they had visited his flat. With this, it was expected they would be able to monitor him, and therefore plan their recovery sessions for when he was at a safe distance from the boiler house. However, they had experienced their first close shave on the very afternoon of his arrival when he had stumbled on the ill-concealed cavern. Only Braidwood's quick thinking had saved a possible compromise when he made the hoax call to the security office and provided the distraction outside the main store.

The foreman watched the other two men operate the portable hoist as he thought of this, the racket of the chains penetrating his reverie. As they toiled, he saw the box jolt upwards in millimetric steps. Outside, the pump still chattered, covering the sound they made.

Andy's death had been quite a serious blow, he reflected, for not only had the fire robbed them of the means of tracking the devices in Bailey's shoes - and therefore removing their ability to locate his position blind - but it had jangled the nerves of his men too. They had nursed the jitters ever since learning of the burly man's death, as was so obviously demonstrated when Davies had stumbled upon them at work in the hole. In their nervousness, they had hit him a little too hard.

Without electronic aids, he had been forced to rely on the use of distraction, whether by ruse or otherwise. He had stumbled upon the first opportunity for such when he overheard Brennan agree to take the security man out to the scene of an emergency. For Braidwood it had been a simple task to arrange an incident on the motorway and, indeed, he had employed the same means as had accomplished the ex-security man's demise

He had been fortunate to previously arrange a tour of the construction site and had been able to spend the next morning in the boilerhouse while the security man had enjoyed a trip in Joe's capable hands. In truth, Kingston had believed the foreman to be in the plant depot, which - passed on to Bailey - served the purpose of distracting attention from his preoccupation with the boiler house.

His final ruse had been carried out only two hours ago. A hoax police report transmitted by Joe at the construction camp had sent Bailey in pursuit of the manager, whom the inconsolable Joyce had revealed was anxious to interview Hickson. It had given him the time to finish the job and means of getting rid of Bailey permanently, for in the prevailing weather, he could not believe the Range Rover would make it back to the service area.

It had been a distraction, Braidwood conceded, having Bailey around during this critical period of their activities. After Andy's death, Joe had wanted to kill the security man there and then. Wiser heads had prevailed: distracting on wild-goose chases, beating up or rendering the security man unconscious, were 'acceptable' if they were to keep their activities in the area of speculation. After all, Bailey had not indicated in any of his activities or conversations that he was convinced the gold was in this area, or that he had any real grasp on what was going on. Running interference against the security man's activities meant they could control him to some extent. Killing him would have alerted the authorities that he was on to something and the troops would have arrived mob-handed to ruin the recovery. No, Braidwood decided, they had been right not to kill the security man.

His reverie was noisily interrupted by the whirr of chain, flashing through the ratchet, signalling the lowering of the box to the floor near his feet. It was time for work and he stooped to check the contents of the box - four squat bars. Then as with so many before, it was placed in a purpose-built crate, which sat on a low, two-wheeled battery trailer. With a glance, he indicated for the trailer to be moved and two men bent to the task of trundling the contraption out into the snow.

They didn't all leave immediately. Braidwood checked his watch and discovered that he was two minutes ahead of schedule. Although all the gold was now recovered, he saw no reason to signpost the position of his recent covert activity and put the remaining two men to the task of removing clues. The hoist was unceremoniously dropped into the hole as with a number of other tools and, while this was going on, he thought out his next move.

The weather had become a great motivator in deciding the exact completion time of his amended recovery schedule. It had offered the tempting prospect of allowing them to leave the service area without chance of physical pursuit. In order to prevent the outside world knowing of their activities - remote though the chance was - he had had his men sever all lines of communication and, as added insurance, they were now busy in the lorry and car parks immobilising any vehicles that might be capable of pursuit in spite of the conditions out there.

However, the genius that had helped the Top Man plan the operation from its inception was not satisfied with even these precautions against interference, he had other things to do before he could leave and, glancing at his watch, he found the time had arrived when he should leave the boiler house for the last time.

'All clear,' said one of the two men remaining.

'Good,' responded Braidwood, pulling up the collar of his heavy coat. 'You stay here. You know what to do. Give me five minutes.'

The man nodded and reached behind one of the electrical cabinets and operated a valve. Immediately, they heard the rush of water.

Then Braidwood turned to the other man and beckoned him to follow, and they moved out into the snow.

Out on the car park a lone figure was assuming the proportions and appearance of a snowman, albeit a very large one. He had been fiddling industriously with the offside rear wheel of the car for some minutes, ever since he had tired of crouching in the lee of the sheltering bulk.

The car did not belong to him, nor was there anything wrong with the wheel, but this did not seem to concern him noticeably and no-one had appeared on the scene to broaden the issue in any way. The machine's usefulness to him was merely that of an alibi as, from its convenient location close to the complex's main doors, he could monitor the comings-and-goings around that position without drawing attention to himself. In particular, he was watching the door of the boiler house - and had been doing so since Braidwood had entered.

When the foreman reappeared with the other figure, the man stayed where he was without sign of moving, his only indication of having seen them being the muttering of a few words under his breath, 'Four out - one remaining.'

Then he bent again forward again to his imaginary task.

At precisely the same time as Braidwood was leaving the boiler house, Bailey was struggling through the snow of the lorry park. His destination was the motel where, having the uneasiest of feelings about what was happening on the MSA, he meant to reassure himself of the girl's safety.

The most direct route to the motel was by way of the road, which ran along the high hedge, but the drifts of snow thereabouts made that way impassable. An alternative was the network of narrow paths that connected the Police Post with the complex, each formed by the tramp of many feet as travellers sought help from the police in contacting their friends and relations.

The path he now trod was also being used by several other people both ahead of him and behind, the whole like some lost platoon weaving its way across no-man's-land. So narrow was the flattened surface that it was impossible to pass-by the slower pedestrians without moving off into the more difficult terrain and so the speed of the column was dictated by those in front.

Immediately ahead of Bailey were a woman and her son, the mother so wrapped up that only her voice - busy exhorting the boy to move faster as she pulled on his arm - was indication of her sex. The boy was also talkative, his dalliance caused through his insistence on commenting upon everything he saw. Glancing briefly behind her, she addressed Bailey. 'I'm very sorry,' she said. 'Car mad. He's a pest, airing his opinions on everything. I blame his dad.'

Presently the thin path took them past the Scammell and they slowed even more as the boy gazed upon the dim outline of Braidwood's 'brute.'

'Cor, it's a Contractor,' exclaimed the boy, exhibiting a knowledge, which surprised the security man out of his meditation. 'It carries up to thirty ton of ballast when it's pulling a full load...' Whatever other observations he had wished to make were cut off when his mother won the tug-of-war, which had existed temporarily, as with a mighty heave she dragged him off along the path.

Beyond the Scammell the woman bore left across a patch of ploughed snow while Bailey continued directly ahead. Had the vehicle not just been mentioned by name he would not have been prompted to throw a backward glance at the Scammell before it faded into the distance. As yet, it was a seemingly unconscious reflex to look at the subject of the boy's interest but Bailey became aware that something had been triggered deeper in his brain by what he had said.

Even at a distance of ten yards, the tractor's outlines were vague, its white mantle blending with the white background. Only the lower section could be distinguished as it sat on the black tyres. Then Bailey looked briefly at the smudge of movement to its right and saw two men struggling with the familiar battery trailer as they strove to haul it to the truck.

Having turned back in the direction of the motel, Bailey had taken only a few steps before his pace began to falter, slowed by the onslaught of several provocative thoughts upon his brain. Swiftly, the thoughts produced a scenario linked by association. They were also linked by alliteration, noted the security man, all springing from the letter B: ballast, battery-trailer, boiler-house, Braidwood, bullion and even, 'brute'. Although Bailey did not attach any significance to this convenient similarity, or his own name, the words did throw up a picture of what might have been happening on the Benwick MSA.

Though he knew that the facts fitted together like the pieces of a jigsaw puzzle, he prayed inwardly that he was wrong. Such was the strength of the apprehension, which assailed him then that he knew he must prove or disprove his doubts immediately. That was why he turned abruptly left and headed for the boiler house and possible answers.

As he stumbled across the rough snow, his mind was so preoccupied with the matter at hand that he completely forgot the original reason for his trek through the snow: to visit and ensure the girl's safety. Which was a shame: not only for his own peace of mind, but for the girl, as well. What is more, he could have foiled an abduction and stalled the plans of the ungodly had he gone to the motel instead of the boiler house and he might - just might - have prevented the loss of more lives.

As it was, he gave no thought for the girl's welfare in all the time he was plodding towards the boiler house. Nor did he see the two figures who, themselves exclusively occupied with getting to their destination, passed by him in the murk, separated by little more than fifteen yards.

Within seconds, Braidwood and the man he had brought with him from the boiler house were passing through the hole in the hedge on their way to the motel - and the girl's room.

The man didn't notice Bailey's presence immediately, being intent on the task allotted to him of regulating the rush of water into the hole. When he did look up it was too late. Far too slowly, he reached for the bulge in his pocket, which told the security man all he needed to know. Before the man's hand had even reached his pocket, the security man was pointing the gun at his midriff.

'No,' said Bailey simply, and the man moved his hands carefully away from his sides.

Being careful to keep the man in his sights at all times, the security man moved closer to the hole. As he approached, he became aware for the first time of the noise of water rushing into the void and soon could see beyond the lip and to the end of the buried pipe that jutted from the side of the hole in a jet.

'Right hand,' he announced. 'Turn it off.'

The man hesitated just long enough to see Bailey raise the barrel of the gun an inch-or-so, which gave the man a nasty feeling of tunnel vision. Then he was turning the valve as fast as the one-handed operation would allow.

In a few seconds, the water had ceased flowing completely and Bailey moved closer to the rim of the hole and fell down on his haunches, the better to see the extent of the excavations. What he saw confirmed his worst suspicions. It wasn't the hole, or the fact that it stretched away into a dark tunnel, which proved that the gold had been here. It wasn't the hoist, still protruding from the water like the mast of a sunken ship, or the various tools they had used. It was the ultimate seal of proof for him, the discarded box, which had once carried four gold bars. It lay, half-concealed, beneath a mess of chain but recognisable from the description given him by Rider.

He was too late. Of all the thoughts and frustrations he then felt, this fact was predominant among them, but at least he now knew where the gold was. It would be up to him, one man - instead of the army Rider had promised - to halt the escape of Braidwood - and he knew without the slightest shadow of doubt that Braidwood was the man he must stop.

Still on his haunches, he noticed a slight movement in the man stood by the wall. By levelling his gun in a purposeful manner, he acknowledged and halted further movement. It was then that he heard the sound behind him.

It was Bailey's turn to be caught out for, when he turned and looked towards the door, he was facing a large man in whose hand was a gun, and it was pointing directly at him. There was no way that Bailey could move his own gun through a hundred-and-eighty degrees before the man killed him. Therefore, he lowered the barrel of the gun in acceptance of this distasteful fact.

When he looked up again he saw that the man had removed the hood of his duffle-coat revealing his face. It was Inglefield, the anti-motorway man. But Bailey had no time to ponder this turn of events as he was fully occupied with being amazed at what the newcomer was doing. Having lowered his gun, the security man had plainly accepted defeat, but now he watched as Inglefield raised the barrel of his gun, by the merest millimetre, and fired.

The dull 'plop' sound was odd in the large room but what amazed Bailey was that he had heard it at all. By all the signs, he should have been en-flight to the far wall, carried by the bullet from Inglefield's gun. Instead, he heard a muffled sound behind him and turned to see the workman sliding slowly down the wall, a gun hanging awkwardly from the index finger of his right hand. Then, very slowly, he pitched forward and toppled into the hole.

'Rider decided you needed someone to keep an eye on your back,' said Inglefield, putting his gun away. 'As usual he was right.'

'The real name is Grant,' he continued. 'The real Inglefield took a holiday on our advice before he arrived here yesterday.'

'Grant? Miller's bunch?'

'Correct. A bit of departmental liaison between your boss and mine,' said the man Bailey still saw as Inglefield. 'Rider's been looking for a way to provide back up for you. When he discovered that a man called Inglefield, who looked not too unlike me, would be visiting this place he talked Miller into spoiling my Christmas.'

'I'm certainly glad you're here, believe me. I can do with the help,' said Bailey, standing up, his legs feeling oddly weak. 'Your gun, I believe.'

Inglefield refused the proffered gun. 'I wondered where it had got to, but it's yours. I brought a spare just in case you needed one. When did you take it from my bag?'

'*I* didn't, it was Lela. She brought it to me this afternoon.'

The newcomer frowned at that. 'That's funny, I didn't think she was the kind. I wrapped it well against prying eyes, too.'

Bailey hadn't the time to continue speculation on the subject for more urgent problems awaited him, the most important of which was that of stopping the Scammell.

'The gold is in the Scammell. You know that, don't you,' said Bailey.

'I wasn't sure. I got the general idea that something was up. With you away on the motorway, I just watched Braidwood. He's been very busy this past twenty-four hours, responded Inglefield. 'I was watching this place just now and saw him leave. I was waiting for the last man to leave when you entered.'

'Braidwood was here? Just?'

'You must have passed him in the darkness.'

Bailey went over to the hole then, and looked down at the body, which was partly visible in the shallow water. 'We'd better tidy-up here and get after them,' he said, with urgency.

Within two minutes they were heading for the door.

It wasn't fair, of course. Although in the past Bailey had never paid much heed to the uncertainties of chance, he did so now as he contemplated his run of bad luck. Increasingly during the past three days, he had felt that luck was against him and what he had found in the boiler house didn't alter this view by any substantial amount. Admittedly, to have found an ally at all was to be counted as a plus, but knowing the formidable task facing them to stop the gold being moved, this hardly cancelled out the potential minuses. It just wasn't fair, therefore, that the two men should get no further than a dozen paces into the darkness outside before they were forcibly halted.

Silhouetted as they were, against the backlight from the boiler house, the element of surprised lay with those already out there. The two men had only sufficient time to realise that they were outnumbered before their assailants fell upon them, and then they were being bustled back into the light to fetch up mere inches from the edge of the hole.

There were five of them - three of them very obviously armed - forming a line that cut off escape through the door. One of the two men not carrying guns in their hands was Braidwood. The other was a small round man who was conservatively and expensively dressed. Bailey recognised the face from a photograph shown him during his brief. It was Hargreaves, top man of Hargreaves Construction and sundry other companies.

'Well, well. Bailey and Inglefield,' announced Braidwood. His tone, though surprised, had a certain arrogance about it that Bailey hadn't noticed before. This was a different person to the easy-going foreman he had known; he was intoxicated by his success in getting the gold out undetected and he made sure his satisfaction showed.

The small round man spoke then. 'Bailey?' he asked. 'The man who has been such a nuisance? You said he was still out on the motorway.'

'So he should be,' responded Braidwood, a frown momentarily creasing his brow. 'But, no matter. What is important now is why he and Inglefield should be lurking in the boiler house.'

Bailey shook his head. 'I don't know what the hell you're talking about,' he said, exasperation in his voice. 'I should be asking what you're up to. You know what I'm doing - it's obvious what I'm doing - I'm the security man around here and I am obliged to make the occasional rounds.'

'Of course,' said the foreman, but the sneer that accompanied his words removed their meaning and replaced it with disbelief. 'And Inglefield decided to join you for a walk. That it?'

'No, not exactly. I don't know if you've noticed but there's a blizzard blowing out there and we've already had one casualty - an old lady who slipped and fell. Mister Inglefield kindly offered to accompany me on rounds so as to help out if someone else should suffer the same fate.' As he spoke, Bailey indicated Inglefield whose nodding head lent conviction to the lie.

'Very quick thinking, Bailey,' said Braidwood, his tone congratulatory, 'but not good enough. I happen to know that your story is a complete fabrication.' Then he glanced quickly about the room. 'Where's my man?'

'What man?'

'The man I left here ten minutes ago,' he said, his voice rising with impatience.

'There was no-one here when we arrived,' said Bailey, stone-faced.

For a moment, Braidwood just stood there, surveying Bailey's face for a hint to confirm or deny his story. Then he suddenly jerked round. 'Gerry, Steve. Search the room,' he ordered.

This is it, thought Bailey. It was only a matter of seconds before they found out he was lying and both he and Inglefield could look forward to nothing else but a quick death. Unless, he reflected, they were to try and fight back. Miraculously, they hadn't been searched after being pushed into the room.

The security man could see the slight swell behind the sleeve of Inglefield's jacket where his ally's gun still lay in the pocket. The way that Inglefield's arm was held so straight, concealing the bulge from those in front of him told Bailey that he was well aware of its availability. His own gun was better concealed by the thickness of quilting which covered the pockets of his parka, but it would be more difficult for him to reach the weapon in a hurry - which was a shame, for speed was an absolute requirement if they were to stand any chance at all.

A glance, surreptitiously directed towards Inglefield, told Bailey he was ready and the security man began to 'fix' in his mind the positions of those people who were now busy behind him. A supposedly innocent glance over his shoulder in response to a noise, revealed to him that Braidwood was peering into the darkness of the tunnel. Taking a chance, the security man prolonged his gaze in that area to check the positions of the other two men. It was a mistake. The foreman caught his eye and Bailey thought he detected suspicion in his look. Then Braidwood began to rise from his haunches, a look of interest on his face.

Bailey thought fast. 'Look, will you tell me what the hell is going on?' he demanded. 'Guns and threats. What have I done?'

Although Braidwood didn't answer the outburst, it had at least achieved its objective by allaying the foreman's suspicions temporarily. Bailey sighed mentally then and tried to carry on with his preparations, hasty and impromptu as they must be.

He got no further, however, for Hargreaves broke the silence and the security man's train of thought by speaking to Braidwood. 'The time, Braidwood,' he reminded. 'It is getting on.'

Braidwood's response was immediate. 'Gerry? Steve?' he called.

'Nothing,' replied one, and Bailey saw the other - who had edged into his view - shake his head meaningfully.

In order to disguise his relief at these reports, Bailey turned again to Braidwood and gave a forceful repetition of the words he had last used.

'Pure as the driven snow, eh?' said Braidwood, his cheek muscles working. 'Well, I'm not easily fooled. I'm going to kill you Bailey, unless you tell us just who you really are.'

'I don't know what you're talking about,' replied the security man, having no trouble affecting an hysterical pitch in his voice. 'You know who I am.'

Braidwood sighed then and fetched a gun from his pocket, which he raised so that the barrel was pressed against Inglefield's head. 'Ten seconds, Bailey. Then I pull the trigger,' he said, his voice calm but with an underlying menace about it. 'I repeat, who are you?'

Probably he stood no chance at all, but Bailey - having almost used his gun moments ago - was about to try and get it now in a most useless gesture of help for the man he had only just met as a fellow agent. His action must surely result in his own death from the guns of the other men even though he would have the satisfaction of getting the man who had frustrated his plans to locate the gold in time. But at what cost? The rest of the gang would simply run with the bullion as if nothing had happened, as if people like Bailey, Inglefield and even Braidwood hadn't existed. It would accomplish precisely nothing for Bailey to pull the trigger of the gun in his pocket - except to cause at least these three deaths. But he didn't think of it like that. At that precise moment, he thought of very little at all. For some part of a second he was insane and Braidwood's death would be the first - and most certainly the only - outward manifestation of it.

But it didn't happen. Long before Braidwood's ten seconds were up, the thin voice of Hargreaves was intruding in the private battle developing between Braidwood and Bailey.

'Wait,' he said, simply. 'You seem to have information that I am not privileged to. That hasn't been our policy in the past, has it? So you tell me first, Braidwood, and then *I* decide what we do with them.'

Braidwood's gun didn't waver. For a second he didn't react to Hargreaves words in any way that the others could see. Then he spoke, his anger showing in his tone. 'Everything we know about them indicates they are not the people they seem to be. Their working together now does nothing but convince me of this.'

'Explain how you come to this conclusion,' said Hargreaves. 'We are short of time, but explain. We must be sure in what we think about these men. It may quite easily affect our plans. I don't need to tell you how much there is at stake.'

Braidwood withdrew two paces at that, lowering the gun to his side. 'Of course,' he said, reason returning. 'I should have thought it out. We must make sure.'

'Be as quick as you can,' urged the small man, 'this blizzard won't last forever.'

'You know a lot about Bailey already, so I'll tell you what we have learned about Inglefield,' began the foreman.

'More make-belief?' queried Inglefield.

Braidwood didn't rise to the jibe. 'Inglefield,' he said, 'came under our closer scrutiny because he just happened to be behind the motel when Bailey surprised Gerry and Steve. It was he who gave the alarm and prevented Gerry from doing a proper job on his friend.'

Bailey's glance took in the two men who had just helped the foreman search the room and he could see the similarity between the slight frame of Steve and that of poor Davies. It would be Steve who had impersonated his assistant and had been attaching the listening device when Bailey had approached from behind. Only a brief glance at the heavier man was sufficient to tell him that, of the two, it was Gerry who had dealt him the knockout blow and, of course, it had been Inglefield who had shouted - raising the alarm - and tapped on the window to distract Anne's attention.

'Prompted by this,' continued Braidwood, 'and the fact that, unobtrusive though he was, he seemed to be watching Bailey's movements with far too much interest, we searched his belongings. In his bag we found a gun.'

The foreman paused to look at Inglefield, then. 'Rather a startling change of weapon for an anti-motorway demonstrator, isn't it?' The gun, in place of the placard and sit-in usually encountered at peaceful rallies.'

'It's a violent world we live in,' returned Inglefield. 'Self-protection must be...'

'Don't waste our time!' The words were spat out by Braidwood, cutting off those mumbled by Inglefield.

Inglefield was impassive.

'So what did we do?' continued Braidwood, regaining his calm. 'We sought to use the find to our advantage. It could do no harm, and a lot of good, for someone to find the gun and turn it over to the security man. It would serve the purpose of distracting Bailey from any interest he may have directed our way and also sow the seed of suspicion in his mind as to what Inglefield might be up to. And so, this afternoon, one of my men managed to approach the bag again and exposed the gun for Lela to see as she cleared the tables.'

'How did you know she would bring it to me?' asked Bailey.

'With the manager gone, who else?' responded Braidwood.

Bailey nodded. 'For once you have used fact instead of conjecture,' he said, but Braidwood would not be put off.

'And what did you do when she brought the gun to you, eh?' he asked. 'Run to the police? Challenge him as to what he was doing carrying a gun around on *your* patch? Keep well clear, perhaps?' He paused, waiting for Bailey's answer. 'Which of these?' he prompted. 'And what of the gun?'

Bailey said nothing.

'Search him,' ordered Braidwood, and Gerry moved over to Bailey. 'And while you are at it, Inglefield, too.'

There was nothing the two men could do and soon Gerry had removed both guns and returned to his place.

'Curiouser and curiouser,' said Braidwood, theatrically. 'Any answer yet, Bailey?'

'You seem to know all the answers - or think you do,' responded the security man. 'You tell me.'

For a second Braidwood was silent. Then he turned to Bailey and stared at him as before, trying to read the answer in his face. Even though the security man's expression gave nothing away, the foreman arrived at his decision. 'I believe you challenged him and found he was working towards the same end - to halt the movement of the gold, once it was located. This may be inaccurate, but it doesn't matter, the indisputable fact is that you were both found in here, carrying guns, and we still don't know where our man has gone. By association with our mystery man here,' he gestured to indicate Inglefield, 'you must be involved in his game.'

It wasn't a conclusive argument by any means but, in the boiler house with time running out it was good enough. Whether this version would be accepted by all depended upon Hargreaves' decision, and he seemed to be hesitating.

Suddenly Braidwood swung round to face him. 'Whatever they are, they are too dangerous to live.'

'Yes. Their lack of cooperation, even to speak for their own lives, would suggest allegiance to some sort of mutual agency,' said the small man. 'I agree. Shoot them, and let's get out of here.'

If his foolhardy plan of some minutes ago had taught Bailey anything, it was that he must not be willing to throw his life away in a desperate action. The luck may not have been running for him of late, but his action before had been against the worst possible odds. Where the threat of the gun would have failed, even had it still been available to him, was in giving the gang only one possible response - to shoot. Now, with that decision already planted in their minds he must allow them the chance to change their minds through a more subtle approach. Even so, it had more chance of success than his earlier plan.

'That would be a most stupid action on your part,' he said, trying to maintain a tone of confidence in his voice. 'Not at all the businesslike approach I should have expected from you, Mister Hargreaves.'

His use of the term *businesslike* had been a piece of quick thinking, for he remembered Hickson's insistence on the need for a businesslike approach to all things and assumed that this piece of wisdom had sprung from Hargreaves' mind. It had the required effect: both men turned to look Bailey's way, having been about to head for the door.

'In response to what?' queried the small man, his eyes narrowing.

'Let us look at your score to date,' began Bailey. 'Murder charges for the deaths of your ex-security man, an elderly couple and one other person in a separate incident.' He purposely omitted Davies' death. 'With luck you should get those reduced to manslaughter because of the difficulty in proving the case of murder - always assuming the law could stick the charges on you in the first place. Then there are various other charges to do with the hijack itself, and the subsequent theft. All-in-all, nothing that would have you in prison for more than ten years with remission, wouldn't you say? Again, assuming you were caught.'

'Go on,' said Hargreaves, aware that the security man had a knowledge not expected of him.

'But if you were to murder two treasury agents the sentence is death,' he said quietly.

'Treasury agents?' It was Braidwood's turn. 'You want us to believe you are treasury agents? You have proof?'

'Oh, I think I can convince you of my identity,' responded Bailey. 'For instance, we first grew suspicious of the Hargreaves setup when he seemed to be delaying completion of the motorway, which he put about as being due to lack of funds. This sparked interest in one of our boys who believed that if the gold were buried under the motorway it would be almost undetectable, and a possible reason why we had been unsuccessful in our very widespread search. On the strength of this simple hunch, he began - if you'll excuse the pun - to dig a little deeper into your affairs.'

The security man watched Hargreaves very closely for confirmation that what he was saying was privileged information hardly likely to be available from any other source. No confirmation came, however, so he went on. 'He discovered that one of your companies had won the contract to build and run this MSA - and with a sum of money which was far in excess of the nearest bidder. This knowledge, added to his suspicions, was strong enough for us to take action. It was a shame though that he missed - as we all did - the real reason for your determination to build at this spot. Instead, we spent our time pursuing the idea that the motorway hadn't been completed because the gold was somewhere under the more convenient unfinished portion awaiting recovery, believing the MSA to be your way of ensuring continued presence in the area should things go wrong on the motorway.'

There was now an odd expression on Hargreaves' face but it was unreadable. As a businessman - as hard headed as they come - he could be depended upon to hide from his face what was going on in his mind, but he responded to the security man's next words. 'The problem was that you might sit on the bullion for months or even years - and the gold was already overdue for delivery to its rightful owners. We needed to force your hand without frightening you away. We brought pressure to bear using the financial constraints that had you genuinely embarrassed - forcing you to recover the gold quickly to save your empire. Then we needed only to be in the area at the time. It almost worked.'

Braidwood looked over to Hargreaves who responded with an almost imperceptible nod. Then he looked back at the two men as if seeing them for the first time. 'Treasury agents,' he said, thinking aloud.

'That's right,' confirmed Bailey, 'and if you kill us there is absolutely nowhere you can hide before our men find you. At most, you would have a week. No court case, no mercy, just elimination. All your trouble in getting all that gold to your distributors would have been for nothing, an entire waste of time.'

'He's bluffing.'

'Make no mistake, as soon as it is learned that the gold has been recovered and is on its way to your secret destination, there will be the biggest dragnet the world has seen for a long time. I don't dispute that, but then you knew that anyway. If caught you face a prison sentence with freedom at the end of it. If you kill us, our own secret law is enforced and you won't live to see any of the gold transferred into negotiables of your choice. You - and your crew - will be dead.'

'What a charming, if histrionic, plea for your life,' sneered Braidwood but he didn't have time to dwell upon this opinion for Hargreaves motioned him over to a quiet conference in the corner.

While this was in progress Bailey's mind raced over what he had said and tried to detect a weakness in his argument. He could find nothing obviously wrong with his reasoning except that he could not - contrary to what he had said - guarantee that justice would be meted out within the deadline. But this was mere detail. He knew - as every man in the various sub-departments that specialised in his kind of work knew - that the death of an agent seldom ended with the killer living to enter court.

As he mulled over this he glanced over to Inglefield. What he saw was disconcerting, for the man was grimacing in a manner that could be interpreted as an instruction for Bailey to look behind him. What he saw when he complied almost stopped his heart there and then, and even when it took on a more regular rhythm again he felt sure it was only a temporary resumption - before Braidwood had his cronies stop it permanently. There, on the surface of the water in the hole, was a patch of the lightest pink.

Hardly had he returned his gaze to cover the conference in the corner than Braidwood turned back to them and spoke. 'Against my better judgement you may be more use to us in life than in death,' he said, and there was no ignoring the contempt in his face.

'You see, Mister Hargreaves is a compassionate man. He has decided that you will help some of my men to control the crowd that will be on the MSA when we leave shortly. We fully realise that there is a danger of other agents being in the vicinity and shouldn't like to, er, jeopardise their lives, too. You understand?'

'You're so kind,' said Bailey, trying to match Braidwood's sarcasm but failing in his relief to be alive - short though the respite might be. 'But how do you control three- or four-hundred people?'

'By bringing them all together in the same place.'

'Impossible. They would smell a rat a mile off. You'd need an army to round up even the docile ones amongst them.'

Braidwood raised a hand. 'That is *our* problem. Your work begins when they are all in the cafeteria. You will impress on the staff to prevent the others going outside - with the manager away you are the natural successor.'

'What if they refuse?'

'You will be the first to die?'

'What if I refuse?' he asked, believing it a formality to ask, the answer being obvious, but he was wrong.

'I told you, Mister Hargreaves is a compassionate man. He understands love and such things. So, if you refuse - the girl dies,' said Braidwood, smiling oddly.

That truly got Bailey's attention. 'Bastards,' he spat out. 'Where is she?'

'She's safe and will remain so unless you do not comply with our instructions.'

'Let's go and get it over with,' said the security man.

Braidwood nodded. 'But one more thing. The hole. Turn on the water,' he ordered, and Gerry crossed to the valve and began turning it. Then it got noisier as the water rushed into the hole, but not so noisy that it could hope to drown out the cry of astonishment that came from Gerry.

They all turned in unison to follow his gaze, which was directed at something in the hole. Churned by the force of water from the hose, the muddy water was now growing redder as the blood from the dead man's body - pinioned beneath the weight of the hoist - percolated in bright clouds to the surface.

Braidwood's rage was such that he very nearly clubbed Bailey to death. As he rained the blows about the security man's head this rage was Bailey's ally for it meant that the blows were not focused on one spot but mostly missed and hit his shoulders. In the event, he endured the attack without grave injury until he heard Hargreaves's thin tones. Then the blows stopped.

When he rose groggily to his feet, aided by Inglefield, it was to see Braidwood being restrained by Gerry. Then he heard Hargreaves again. 'We leave now. It is late, and there is much to do,' he said.

His expression twitching as he fought to regain control, Braidwood took seemingly endless seconds to arrive at a calmness which meant he could be released. Then Bailey and Inglefield were ushered into the very much cooler atmosphere outside, the empty boiler house echoing to the noise of the rushing water.

As they went, Bailey reflected - through his pain - that although he had suffered a run of bad luck over the past three days, he had reason to be grateful, for he continued to be smiled upon by fate.

Chapter Twelve

(24th December: 1800 - 1830)

Braidwood's flair for engineering situations had been no less in evidence as he achieved his aim to gather everyone into the cafeteria. It was a simple ruse which brought about this 'impossible' chore: first he had severed the electricity supply and then, with his men acting the role of helpers rather than enforcers, implored every person on the MSA to join the others in the cafeteria to conserve warmth for as long as possible. What hadn't been explained - though no-one had raised the subject - was that the choice of venues could have been bettered, for even the warmth from all two-hundred-or-so bodies would go nowhere towards maintaining the temperature in such a large hall.

However, the ruse had worked. Now, as the stragglers entered the cafeteria, they were drawn by the strong attraction of companionship and warmth that the bustling crowd engendered.

There was also light. Four battery-operated spot-lamps, which dazzled the eye with their sharp light, shone out from the four corners of the room, each attended by one of the men who had been involved in escorting the weary travellers. What was not noticed in the hubbub and confusion was that one spot-lamp was trained solely on a group of men at the front who stayed close together, or that, as the entrance door was closed after the last person, it was locked by one of the four men. Nor could anyone but the inanimate group know that beneath the capacious storm-capes of the other three strategically placed men, were instantly available sub-machine guns.

At a signal from one of the men, Bailey rose to his feet. He was amazed at the speed at which the operation had been carried out. Consulting his watch, he found that no more than fifteen minutes had elapsed since he and Inglefield had been dragged out of the boiler house. Now, at a few minutes past 1800 he must carry out his part of the deal that had bought him his life.

He did not need to shout for attention, he merely walked to a place midway between two of the guards, against the temporary divider that separated restaurant and cafeteria, and turned to face the crowd. Perhaps it was the sight of the cuts on his face received from the beating at Braidwood's hands that brought the hush, or the need they felt to be coaxed through this terrible night. As he looked in their direction, half blinded by the spotlight played upon him by the guard near the door, he felt sorry for those of the latter category; they were about to suffer another jolt.

'The staff around here know me as the security man,' he began. 'We *have* got a manager but he is unavailable at present. That makes me the person in charge of the service area.'

For a second he paused, trying to arrange the words in his mind so that they would come out without melodrama. 'I'm afraid the fact that we are stranded here in the middle of winter, without heating or proper lighting is not the sum of our troubles. There is something else.

'There has been a crime committed here entailing the theft of millions of pounds worth of gold bullion. I should not worry you with this but the perpetrators of this crime believe there are people among you who would try to stop them leaving shortly. You may get some idea of their determination not to have anyone pursue them when I say that there are three guards in this room who are armed and who will shoot if they have to, to prevent anyone leaving this room.'

The first indication of the tension among the crowd came with the nervous cry of a young child. There followed a more general reaction, which had those nearest the three men - who were now brandishing their guns - shrinking back to leave large areas of unoccupied space in front of them. Then the noise level rose quickly as people voiced their consternation to each other. 'There is no cause for alarm if we do as we're told,' said Bailey, his voice necessarily raised to overcome the noise.

When the hubbub had subsided again, he continued. 'Those are the facts. Additionally, I have to warn anyone who would try to leave that they do not only run the risk of being shot, but that they will endanger the life of a girl - a hostage they have

277

taken with them. I have been informed that her life is in the balance. Only you can save her by staying here. *Please* have the patience to keep calm for an hour-or so. Then, when these men have gone, we will try to do something about conditions around here. Thank you.'

In the general silence that followed, Bailey resumed his position in the middle of the crowd. He had no difficulty finding his place for the spot-lamp was still trained on the group of people he had come to know, Inglefield, Banjo, Brennan and the other policemen. Around them were the packed faces of less-readily recognised staff and finally complete strangers. This grouping of the most dangerous people into the middle of the crowd was no accident, for it not only ensured that all were easily monitored, it made escape almost impossible. In addition, if anyone of them was foolhardy enough to try to run for it, he only had to look around him to know that he wouldn't only be laying his own life on the line, but those near him as well from the indiscriminate accuracy of a spray of machine-gun bullets.

For some moments, he just sat there oblivious to the murmuring around him as people exchanged opinions. Gradually, such comment grew into a subdued buzz and all the time the guards watched for the slightest unusual movement, especially by those in the centre. Occasionally, a sniping comment would rise above the rest. It was a woman's voice, despising, hard. However, the gunmen did not respond except to wave the barrels of their guns a little more positively.

'We've got to do *something*,' insisted Inglefield at last, breaking the silence that had reigned among the central group for some moments.

'I'm open to any suggestion,' invited Bailey. 'But not one that risks the lives of bystanders - or that of the girl.'

Though this remark plunged them back into silence, Bailey became aware that the manager of the Trucker's Place was seemingly experiencing some mental struggle. This manifested itself visually by the grimace he wore, occasionally punctuated by the opening of his mouth as if wanting to speak but left stillborn as if he repeatedly forgot his lines.

'What is it, Banjo? You look ill,' said Bailey.

'It's no time for joking, Mister Bailey. I've just been thinking about this girl.'

'Yes?'

'What does she look like?'

Bailey told him, his tones clipped as he strove to drive out the fear he felt for her memory.

'No, that's not her,' said Banjo, after a few seconds deliberation and he would have lapsed into silence but for Inglefield's insistence that he explain his train of thought.

'This was a different girl. She'd been in the cafe for about an hour before they began clearing us out,' he said, and began twisting his head round to look at the sea of faces behind him. But he didn't find what he was looking for. 'Kicked up a right old fuss, she did. Didn't want to leave, see. I don't see her here, though.

'She'll be here, all right,' said Bailey, his interest waning rapidly since learning that it hadn't been Anne in the Trucker's Place. 'They wouldn't miss anyone.'

As he searched and probed for weaknesses in the setup that might allow him to pursue the gang, it occurred to him that there was still something puzzling. One question was uppermost in Bailey's mind. 'Did they leave the water running in the boiler house?' he asked, directing the question to Inglefield.

Inglefield thought for a moment. 'I think they did,' he said, slowly.

'Hm. What's the betting the electricity wasn't just switched off, it was shorted-out as the water level rose to touch the cabinets?'

'But why? It surely isn't an essential part of their plan to deprive the service area of electricity *permanently*?'

I don't know. But I have been wondering why he showed up at the boiler house when the gold had already been recovered - and he believed I was still on the motorway.'

'Forgot something, perhaps?'

Bailey shook his head, which hurt. 'It's only a hunch, but I believe the man you shot had been given instructions to flood the hole and leave the water running. Braidwood was prompted to return when the electricity hadn't failed within a specified time limit.'

'You mean he intended to collect everyone together even before he suspected there might be agents around?'

Bailey nodded, which hurt a little less. 'Or, he was making absolutely sure that no-one could contact the outside world for some hours.'

'Which he must naturally ensure. Otherwise...' But Inglefield could think of no natural reason.

'Otherwise not only does he not get a head start, but,' put in the security man, 'he has no time to transfer the gold to a less conspicuous vehicle - or vehicles - for a speedier and more secure journey to whatever destination he has decided.'

It was Inglefield's turn to nod. 'Sounds logical,' he said.

'But just one other thing,' said Bailey. 'If he has gone to such lengths to ensure that no-one follows him, how does he expect his men to get away?' He nodded then, to indicate the guards.

'He must have left one vehicle in an operational state,' replied the other agent.

'Which one? That's the question,' added Bailey, and then he got an idea. 'Ask Sergeant Brennan if his cars are still operational.'

Inglefield turned away from Bailey and, leaning across Banjo, spent some moments conversing with the policeman. Then he turned back to Bailey. 'He's not sure, but when they stormed the police post, the gang had one member who was carrying the bits from under the engine compartments of his vehicles. As I say, he's not sure but he doesn't recollect seeing him tampering with the Range Rover.'

'And if you've got to go out in this weather, that's the car you need,' said Bailey, thinking aloud. 'So we probably know now how they intend to get away. Perhaps we've discovered an unexpected weak point in Braidwood's precautions. Who knows? At least now we have something to aim for.'

He had had to raise his voice slightly to ensure that Inglefield heard the latter half of his words for with the growing background murmurings and increased outburst of the woman's voice it was quite difficult to hold a conversation. It was Lela who had been sniping at the guards as was made obvious when she struggled to her feet.

She would probably have remained seated and continued throwing her criticisms at the guard for the rest of the night, but in response to a more than usually cutting remark one of the guards, standing near the restaurant divider, had been stupid enough to react by telling her to shut up. It was this that had prompted her physical reaction.

No sooner had she got to her feet than she began inching forward, the stream of words she directed at him fragmented by emotion. 'You *peegs*. You have no regard for the goodness of Christmas. You are evil men who would make these people miserable by waging war against them. You will suffer very much, I assure you. God does not forget this...'

She broke off then as, like everyone else, she heard the growl of the Scammell's engine as it burst into life outside. For a second she was silent as the note first waned and then grew. But she didn't stay quiet for long. She was no fool and realised that the only serviceable vehicle was about to move off leaving hundreds of people to a miserable night as the temperature in the room cooled. This incensed her even more and she continued all the stronger with her tirade, at the same time inching towards the man who had foolishly told her to be quiet.

With this noisy background, the attention of the crowd was not easily distracted but it was another of the senses, which finally drew all heads to look at the window, which gave onto the coastbound stretch of motorway. At first, many people didn't recognise just what they had seen. Against all the odds it seemed someone was approaching the service area along the motorway, the flickering light, which played against the interior of the cafeteria, growing brighter all the time.

A murmur different in tone from either that of the Scammell's labouring engine or that of Lela's rantings came from the crowd as they speculated in hope, on the identity of whoever was braving the blizzard.

A word, faint and indistinct seemed to be passing around the lips of the deeper voices of the truckers. 'Showy' was what it sounded like but then Bailey heard it again, louder this time, as someone's voice was raised more confidently than the rest. 'Shughie,' it said. 'It could only be Shughie.'

Sensing the growing excitement, exacerbated by Lela's high-pitched voice, the gunmen grew nervous and began shouting for the crowd to be quiet. This only incensed the polish woman the more, and she approached to hit the nearest gunman.

His attention divided now by a combination of Lela's antics, the growing unrest within the crowd, the rising volume of the Scammell's engine and the strong light from the road below, he was near to panic. With a shove, he knocked Lela several feet back towards the crowd where she collapsed on the floor. Then he raised the gun, wide-eyed at the crowd's response to his action.

Then he fell through the floor.

More correctly, there was a nerve-wrenching scream of metal on concrete followed by a tremendous thud, which vibrated the building. Simultaneously with this, the light from the motorway went out and there was a rending screech as part of the cafeteria floor collapsed, taking the two guards nearest the restaurant with it.

Two hundred people saw the next danger as it approached. Between the edge of the crowd and the newly-formed gash, the floor canted wildly and Lela, out there alone, began to slide along the shiny tiles, away from the shocked faces.

Bailey and Inglefield were the first to react, and very quickly indeed. They might have got to her in time but, confused and frightened at the loss of his allies, the third gunman - standing by the entrance to the kitchen - loosed off a couple of shots at the two men. Both missed and then the gun jammed but the delay as they hesitated prevented them grabbing Lela before she had reached the edge.

As Bailey watched helplessly, a sidelong glance detected several of the crowd descending on the lone gunman, who was still struggling, if briefly, with his gun.

Lela didn't scream; she made no sound at all. Nor did she disappear from view. Like some speechless puppet she simply slid on her stomach feet first towards the abyss and then jolted to a stop, all but her top half having disappeared from view. Her face contorting with pain and her eyes opened wide from the shock.

Then they heard the screaming. At first, impossibly, it seemed to be coming from Lela, but then they knew it was from below. A number of shots followed shortly, and bits of ceiling fluttered down out of sight into the hole.

While this was going on Bailey and Inglefield had inched along the inclined floor. Together they managed to lift Lela from the impaling length of reinforcing rod exposed by the floor's collapse, and that had halted her slide by sticking in her stomach. It was while they were dragging her to a safer place that they cringed back involuntarily at the heat of flames, which erupted then through the jagged hole, licking at the decor.

As suddenly as they had appeared the flames were gone, at the same time ending the spasmodic gunfire below. But the effect on the crowd was more prolonged. Now over the initial paralysing shock of the collapse they could respond to the stimulus of instinct. The woosh of flames had been all that was required to cause a human stampede.

Only the efforts of Sergeant Brennan's men and a few of the truckers averted serious injury among the crowd through trampling. The same could not be said for the remaining gunman, however, for quite a few people had passed, fear-stricken, over his still frame before the rush of people was slowed to a halt at the far wall.

Lela was still alive. A collection of people, most claiming membership of the medical fraternity, had gravitated towards the place where Bailey and Inglefield had brought her. Within seconds, both men knew they were superfluous to requirements, and Inglefield turned to the security man. 'We'd better get a move on,' he said.

Bailey shook his head. '*I* had better get a move on,' he corrected, his face bleak. 'You had better help out here. Brennan is going to have his hands full.'

The security man had hardly crossed the threshold into the kitchen before he had reason to pause. In the corner lay a crumpled body, the only identifying feature being the large cape, which was twisted untidily around the torso.

'Don't worry about him,' said a voice behind him, which Bailey recognised as belonging to Brennan. 'We'll put him somewhere out of sight of women and children.'

'Dead?' asked the security man, turning to face the sergeant, knowing his question was only a formality.

Brennan nodded. 'You'd better be going,' he urged, and then indicated another policeman who was standing some feet away but paying heed to what the two men said. 'Seeing you are determined to give chase, you may as well have someone along who knows how to handle a Range Rover in these conditions.'

Bailey smiled, but it was a grim smile. 'Thanks,' he said, and indicated for the driver to follow him as he headed for the door.

By the time the truck had stopped slewing over the compacted snow and come to a halt against the central barrier, it was some yards beyond the concourse. Shaken, Shughie hesitated before climbing down from the cab to inspect the damage to his rig, as he tried to work out what had caused the incident.

His approach along the motorway had absorbed all concentration until suddenly he was confronted by another set of headlights - *and on the same carriageway*. There had been no time for anything but reflexive action and automatically he had swung the wheel to avoid the oncoming vehicle. As he had done so, he imagined the other driver had taken the same action, thankfully in the right direction. It was just a shame therefore that there just wasn't enough space for the two heavy vehicles to slide past each other at forty-five degrees to the normal line. Moreover, sliding was the operative word; from the moment they had swung the wheels they were both out of control.

Shughie had heard the first collision as the other truck hit the nearest wall of the complex that supported the concourse. Then he felt the jarring as his truck's rear hit the tail of the other vehicle and then heard the rumble as his load broke free and fell off the platform. After that, there was nothing he could do but wait for the truck to stop.

However, the shocks weren't over when it had finally come to rest. For when he looked back at the concourse, after climbing shakily to the snow-covered ground, he saw that a great gash had appeared in the underside of the concourse where part of it floor hung down at a crazy angle. Beneath this, part of the supporting wall was missing, critically weakened by the tunnelling and water-damage in the boiler house. To complete the scene through the half-light and blizzard he could see that the other vehicle had continued after the collision and by the light of its receding tail-lights, he could make out the spread of drums – his truck's load - across the snowbound highway. Then he saw something else.

It seemed incredible, but there was something moving among the spilled cargo. It was a human figure, too, which slowly rose to his feet clawing his face with one hand as if trying to rub something from his eyes. In his other hand, he held a stick that he waved vaguely about him.

Spellbound, Shughie watched as the man let out the most horrible screams and then the stick began flashing red flame, and once he heard the noise he knew it was some sort of machine-gun. Hardly had he realised this than one of the drums erupted in a great gout of flame which shot vertically to touch the gash in the floor of the concourse. Below, a sea of fire seemed to spread to the lonely figure and suddenly it collapsed, the screams and gunfire ceasing immediately.

Shughie felt ill. The urge to retch was almost as strong as that which impelled him to get himself and his truck away from the spreading flames. Without hesitation, he scrambled back into the cab. The hot engine fired first time and, having great difficulty fighting the urge to rush he gently coaxed the truck backwards before turning the wheel and changing gear to bring it back onto the highway where, a short distance further on he stopped the vehicle and allowed the reaction of what he had seen overwhelm him.

Bailey's hopes of pursuit lasted precisely as long as it took for him and the constable to reach the Police

Post. Even before they could fully discern the outline of each vehicle, they knew the last means of transport had been taken from them.

The Range Rover, or what was left of it, was lying on its side with a great dent along its length. Behind it, in some confusion, were the other police cars, which had been further immobilised when the Range Rover had been hurled among them.

So no weak link had existed in Braidwood's planning after all, reflected Bailey, the bitterness welling up inside him. Braidwood had never intended for the guards to escape and the deep furrows in the snow indicated how he had ensured this, by having the Scammell ram the Range Rover.

'We might get something out of the other cars,' suggested the constable, having to raise his voice above the blizzard's roar to make himself heard.

Bailey was about to vent his wrath on the unsuspecting policeman when he managed to stop himself; it would do no good to take it out on him, besides, it was a good idea. 'Yes, perhaps we should get one of them working again. Slow time though, just to get help. We've had it as far as chasing them is concerned.' The security man's voice trailed off and he banged his clenched fist on the tortured metal of the Range Rover's rear door, before turning away.

Then he heard it.

It was the growl of a truck engine and it seemed to be quite close. He peered into the direction of the noise - the motorway - but could see nothing through the darkness and falling snow. Then he saw the lights as, like the rotating beam from a lighthouse, they swung round, increasing in brightness until he had to shield his eyes against the glare.

Without pausing, the truck moved slowly past the two men along the tracks so recently made by the Scammell - but in the other direction. As it passed Bailey broke out of the spell that had paralysed him since he had heard the first muffled roar of the engine, for he had seen something that provoked a recurrence of emotion. The emotion was hatred, as he recognised the vehicle by its yellow-and-blue paintwork.

In the absence of Braidwood or any of his gang, Bailey saw the driver as the only focussing point for his fury. It didn't matter that Anne had spoken on Shughie's behalf; such talk could not fully erase his suspicion that the scot had murdered his predecessor and at least three other people. The thoughts provoked him into a shambling run along the slippery surface of the road and, although he couldn't hope to keep up with the truck, he was only feet away when the truck stopped and the door of the cab swung open.

Without trying to halt his momentum, the security man launched himself upwards to grab at the arm that had pushed the door to the full extent of its travel. The result was a flurry of arms and legs as both men crashed to the ground, their fall only marginally cushioned by the snow.

Such was the force of Bailey's angry attack that Shughie had little chance to put up a struggle. The security man would surely have killed the man but for the intervention of the constable, and only when he heard a woman's voice, and one, which he seemed vaguely to recognise, did he halt his attempts to strangle Shughie and resist the policeman's efforts at separation. Nevertheless, he still maintained his grip on Shughie's neck.

'Please don't hurt him,' she cried.

Bailey was unsympathetic. 'Give me one good reason why I shouldn't strangle the murderer,' he gasped, his breath laboured from his exertions.

'Because whatever he is, my husband is not a murderer!'

There were few, non-physical, influences that could have halted Bailey so totally but the woman had found one. His relaxation of his grip on Shughie allowed the man to speak.

'Linda?' he called, spluttering at the re-opening of his breathing system. 'Is that you, Linda?' Then he got to his feet and went over to his wife as the security man released him completely.

'What in God's name? Why...?' he continued, reaching for her.

But Shughie wasn't the only one with questions to ask. 'Anne's sister?' asked Bailey. 'What are you doing here?'

'I've come to ask my husband to come home,' she said, close to tears. 'I need him.'

For the first time Bailey was aware of her appearance. He could see a lot that was Anne in her facial features, which didn't help his nerves, knowing as he did the danger she was in. Otherwise, there was little about her figure that could be likened to the other woman. Perhaps it was the way she clutched her coat with bony hands, which made her appear so thin. He couldn't know, but he did know that her appearance did not tally with that of someone in the best of health.

'Where's Anne?' she asked. 'She phoned to tell me she was here.'

'I'm afraid she isn't here,' replied Bailey. 'She was taken from here just now - as a hostage.'

Both the woman and Shughie reacted strongly to this, their eyes showing both surprise and fear. He gave them a very brief explanation.

'You say my husband is a murderer. How do you know? Have you proof?'

'Yes, I have proof,' replied Bailey, 'I have certain proof that this vehicle has killed at least four people.'

'I don't believe Scot would kill anyone,' she said.

The security man began to get irritated at her doubting of his word. To substantiate his claim he moved around to the front of the vehicle and began scraping the snow from the number plate. As he did so, he spoke to the others, their having followed him round. 'The killer truck's number was VDR something-or-other,' he explained. 'It was seen by a number of witnesses. As you see this one's number is...'

'MUP...,' supplied the constable.

The revelation didn't provide conclusive proof that the vehicle was not the killer truck but it gave Bailey pause to allow for doubt, especially when he remembered something from his trip to the Plant Depot. 'Where were you and your vehicle at two o'clock this morning?'

'I was in digs in Leicester,' replied Shughie. 'I can prove it if you phone them.'

Again, it wasn't conclusive evidence as it depended on the honesty of those at the 'digs'. But on a snowbound MSA, with no time for further investigation - if he was to have any chance of catching the Scammell - it would have to do for the present. And he told them so.

'I'm going after them,' he said, finally. 'I'll be using this truck.' He turned to the constable. 'Take care of these two until I get back.'

The policeman nodded and made to escort the couple away.

But Shughie dodged the constable's guiding hand. 'You wouldn't get more than a mile out there before you're bogged down in the snow,' he said to Bailey. 'I know. I've just driven forty miles in it.'

'So what do you suggest I do?'

'Anne is family,' replied the scot, by way of explaining what his answer would be 'you'll need me to do the driving - if Anne's to stand a chance.'

Bailey knew that was the only practical answer. He knew he was probably no match for the conditions out there and - like himself - he doubted whether there was a police driver who could do as good a job as the man who had battled his way through so many miles of snowbound carriageway already.

'Your wife?'

'My wife can wait a while more,' he said, and turned an inquiring look at the woman.

She nodded.

'Then we'd best away,' said Shughie.

Chapter Thirteen
(24th December: 1830 - 1930)

Out of the chaos Bailey had left at the MSA had come some semblance of order, mainly due to the organisational abilities of Inglefield and Brennan. Foregoing the space of the cafeteria - which was also somewhat open to the elements - for somewhere cosier, most of the two-hundred victims of Benwick's day of difficulty were now ensconced in the manager's quarters.

Inglefield had been busy. As Brennan had herded the people into the two larger rooms, the agent had led parties in search of blankets, lighting and equipment and the makings of warm drinks. The shop had been the obvious target for torches and batteries as well as other items in a carefully controlled raid. The blankets had come from the motel and use had been made of the kitchen for sustenance.

Once settled into some sort of comfort their situation was found to be less stark than first thought. By allowing controlled use of the entrance door for ventilation, and rotating the use of torches for light, it was a reasonably comfortable haven; the Christmas decorations adding colour and glitter as they reflected in the torch-beams.

Lela was the main focus of concern and was worrying the people who attended her. She had been unconscious throughout the time it had taken to carry her from the cafeteria to the manager's bedroom but, as Inglefield paid his first visit to her side since his forays in search of provisions, she began to stir, her mouth moving as she tried to speak. At first, her words were inaudible but soon she could be heard as she simultaneously began to raise herself onto one elbow.

Ignoring the entreaties for her to lie still and so conserve her strength, she stopped moving when she'd reached a half-sitting position. Her eyes, now fully open, took in the strange scene before her. Perhaps it was the sight of all those people gathered together in the eerie light, which prompted her next words, but her obvious delirium must have been partly responsible.

'Why no carols?' she cried, in a frail yet carrying voice. 'Is it not Christmas? Why do they not sing carols at Christmas?'

For a moment she looked puzzled, strangely confused that she should be tired from so little effort but she remained propped on the support of her right elbow and continued to look questioningly at the sea of faces. Then, while all those who could do so continued to watch her, they heard a weak child's voice begin to sing.

It lasted for just long enough for all eyes to find the singer, the small boy who had shown such interest in the Scammell earlier. Then a woman's voice, his mother, carried on where he had left off which gave him the confidence to continue. Immediately another voice joined in, and then another, until the words could be heard clearly. '...all is bright,' sung an increasing number of voices, which grew louder by the second. 'Round yon virgin, mother and child...'

Unnoticed by the majority of those who could have seen, Lela lay down again, a smile on her face.

'She doesn't hear them,' said the young man who had been attending her, to Inglefield. He had had to raise his voice slightly even though he was only inches from the agent, in order that he should make himself heard. 'She doesn't hear them singing,' he insisted.

Perhaps the scene had had an effect even on Inglefield for he turned to the man and, keeping his tone private, said; 'No matter, Doctor. Even if Lela doesn't hear them singing, it will do *them* nothing but good.'

Having been so closely interested in the welfare of his patient, the young doctor had not been aware of what had been going on around him. Now he looked up at the sight of women and children, policemen and truckers, and made a late start in feeling the emotion of the moment.

Out on the motorway there was no let-up in the terrible conditions and as Bailey braced himself in response to the occasional, sickening lurch, his only comfort was to know that those in the Scammell suffered the same retardant effect on their progress.

It was when he thought of this that he became even more fearful for Anne's safety. It seemed odd, but if he and Shughie managed to force Braidwood into a corner of any sort, it would mean the girl's life was in very grave danger. In addition, if the Scammell managed to get clear away, there was no telling what Braidwood would do to the girl to prevent her helping the authorities. As the truck tentatively negotiated the hazardous surface of the motorway, Bailey reflected upon the problem that faced him with some trepidation, to say the least.

It might have helped if he could have devoted his mind solely to the problem, to finding the safest course of action to ensure both the safety of the girl and the recovery of the gold, but he also had to make sure that Shughie stayed awake by engaging him in conversation. In the first half hour of the nightmare, they had covered the Scot's version of what had happened beneath the concourse and even what he had been doing on the motorway in those conditions in the first place. In the course of the conversation Bailey learned of a side to the man's character that was decent - as decent as any that would allow an already lethal weapon, the truck, to become many times more dangerous by carrying unsafe and highly volatile loads.

However, at that very minute, when the scot was applying all his expertise to accomplish Bailey's plans, he was not prepared to upset his own conscience by examining it too closely. Instead, the security man continued to bend slightly forward in his seat, his brain willing the truck to go faster as he became aware that, for the first time since Braidwood had dashed his hopes of a later recovery operation, he was in with a chance of accomplishing his mission - *if* the Scammell could be located in time.

'You going to tell me what happens when we catch up with them?' Shughie called, above the considerable engine noise.

Bailey collected his thoughts. 'There's little we can do to physically stop them,' he began. 'Our job is to follow them until either we run out of petrol, or *they* stop for any reason whatsoever. Then we find the nearest telephone.'

'And what if they move off while we're hunting this telephone?'

'We can take that as a near certainty,' responded the security man, indicating that the possibility had already occurred to him, 'unless they run out of fuel. Assuming otherwise, as long as we get to a phone reasonably quickly they will be trapped before they can leave the area or unload the bullion.'

Shughie nodded. 'Who's going to do the trapping?'

'Friends of mine,' said Bailey, his answer deliberately vague. 'Anyway, don't you think you're running a little too far ahead? We don't even know if we can catch them yet.'

Shughie grinned; the first time Bailey or anyone else had seen him do so for many months. 'If the truck holds out we'll make it all right,' he said, firmly. Then, interpreting Bailey's silence as hiding doubt, he explained. 'The Scammell will have to go slower than us because she's carrying a heavy snowplough up front. That wide sweep you can see is the result, and the high mound of snow she's leaving to one side tells me she is pushing against quite a bit of resistance.'

He turned to face the security man then. 'You see, although the snowplough makes it easier going for both of us, *we* can go that much faster.'

Bailey was not as confident as the scot: the way his luck was running of late - and it vaguely surprised him that he now paid heed to the existence of luck - too many things could go wrong. At least the chase was on, and at better terms than at any time since he had learned the gold was being moved prematurely. He had to be thankful for a second chance.

With nothing to do but try to foresee the difficulties ahead, and keep Shughie awake at the same time, he tried to combine the two. 'You've been around the motorway for some months now,' he began, 'who do you see among Braidwood's clan that is a particular menace to us?'

'You mean his heavies?'

'That sort of person,' he prompted, nodding to help his meaning through the noise.

Shughie spent some moments in thought before answering. 'I'll tell you what I'll do,' he responded, finally. 'I'll run through all the characters I know who worked with him and let you decide who is dangerous.' With that, he spent the next five minutes remembering a list of some twenty people, adding their descriptions and types of employment. Beyond knowing that Braidwood and Hargreaves were in the Scammell's large cab, Bailey hadn't a clue as to any others and so, apart from giving him an insight into the type of person associating with Braidwood, the list provided information that was merely academic.

There was one character, however, who interested the security man more than the rest. Shughie's description of the man fitted the one that Bailey had of the gunman he had last seen as a crumpled heap by the kitchen entrance to the cafeteria. 'A bit of a driver is Don,' said Shughie. 'Went in for the big rig races over in America for a few years. Then he took to driving for Hargreaves. Competent, too. He'd be the man to drive the escape car you spoke of - the Range Rover.'

'He's dead,' said Bailey. 'He was one of the gunmen holding everyone hostage in the cafeteria back there. He got trampled in the stampede.'

Shughie said nothing, and Bailey took the silence to be him concentrating on the driving, and perhaps a little quiet reflection upon one he hadn't liked, but whose abilities the scot had respected as a driver.

'You should know that he was doing his best to pin all this on you,' said Bailey. 'At least, that's what Mr Crane told me.'

'Banjo,' said Shughie. Then he nodded. 'He's a decent guy. He tells it as it is.'

Bailey was thinking: could it have been Don who had driven the killer truck in the two motorway incidents? He tied the evidence of the truck in the Plant Depot, and the number plate, together. It was a possibility, the security man reflected, and he said so to the scot.

'Change of suspect, eh?' smirked Shughie. 'But seriously, such shenanigans would be…would have been…no problem for a driver with the experience Don had. But why leave him on Benwick? Just to nobble the getaway car? It doesn't make sense.'

'Except that Don had perhaps provided the incentive for the others to stay,' replied Bailey. 'With Hargreaves's favourite driver left behind with them, the other gunmen would feel confident that they could get safely away from the MSA. As for throwing Don to the wolves, how better to be rid of a member of the gang who had outlived his usefulness? It saves on the share-out too.'

'Perhaps,' commented the scot, uncommitted in his opinion.

A thought occurred to the security man then. 'Perhaps Braidwood would have done better to keep Don to drive the Scammell,' he said. 'I should have thought he could have at least depended upon him to keep to the right carriageway.'

'When they left the service area you mean,' confirmed Shughie. 'Ah, well, you see that was just bad luck, my happening along. He probably decided that this carriageway was the better cleared of snow - probably knew it for certain if your story is correct - and as he didn't expect to be meeting any other vehicles on a night like this, he would make better progress. My happening along was just bad luck for him.'

'And good luck for us.'

Shughie didn't seem to hear him for he suddenly switched off the headlights leaving only the sidelights to illuminate a small area to the front of the vehicle. Bailey didn't comment on this madness but instead watched as the scot brought the truck's speed down.

After a few seconds, Shughie looked over from his peering into the murk ahead. 'I've seen the lights,' he said, in as excited a voice as he would ever manage. Far from impressed that the scot had seemingly reformed - as inferred by his outburst - Bailey wondered if the man had cracked. But he got no further with his speculation for an explanation came next. 'I saw the Scammell's tail lights.'

Bailey peered into, to him, a perfectly innocuous scene no different from that which had registered on his brain many times in the preceding minutes - if, until very recently, better illuminated. However, trusting in the driver's vision, he allowed the possibility that there might indeed be something out there other than snow.

'So they will know we're following them,' he decided, aloud.

'Yes, but I'm trying to give the impression that we're some way behind and, with a bit of luck, they'll soon believe we've stopped.'

'How's that?'

'By switching to sidelights as they passed around that bend ahead,' he answered, but Bailey still couldn't see anything beyond the wall of swirling snow. Again, he let it pass, for the scot was talking. 'They may believe that we're further away. In other words, falling behind.'

For some minutes, they continued in silence, their speed increasing slowly as Shughie's eyes became more accustomed to the minimal illumination afforded by the sidelights. Then he switched off the lights altogether, without reducing speed.

'Now we should be totally invisible to them,' he said, by way of explaining his act.

'Even if we happen to be blind ourselves,' mused the security man nervously, unused - like many road-users - to travelling at night without lights. Gradually, however, he began to make out a lot of detail, which hadn't been visible even with the headlights on. He saw the hummocks of snow to each side and the proof of Shughie's explanation: that the carriageway upon which they drove was by far the more navigable of the two.

Over the next ten minutes, Shughie increased speed to the very brink of sticking-point, sometimes dropping back as abruptly as he could to avoid a skid. But this perseverance paid off as he could soon announce to Bailey, 'There she is, no more than half a mile ahead. Surely you can see her now.'

This time the security man could see the twin red tail-lights, and out of injured pride, said so. Almost immediately, after he had spoken, however, the lights moved quickly right and then dipped down out of sight. 'They're turning off for the construction site,' he cried.

Shughie nodded. 'Here goes,' he said, warningly. 'From now on we're strangers in *their* territory.

As their vehicle approached the spot where the Scammell had turned off, Bailey was frantically trying to remember the layout of the construction site. He remembered that the track cut straight through the middle of the cluster of caravans and then divided - to the left, for the track that paralleled the motorway, and right towards the materials dump. He was vaguely aware that he had also seen two or three subsidiary tracks, which separated the rows of caravans and huts on the right-hand side.

When they dipped down onto the track, their problems really began. The vehicle was already out of sight and Shughie had no alternative but to use the powerful headlights - thereby announcing their presence - in order to pick out the hazards of the rough terrain. The first probing flash of the powerful beams told Bailey two things: that the snow's camouflaging effect disorientated him as to the layout of the site, which required several seconds study for him to overcome, and that the vehicle was just passing behind two caravans, some distance ahead of them.

'Guide me,' shouted Shughie, when Bailey announced that he had spotted the Scammell. 'I'm going to need all my concentration just to keep this bloody thing moving.'

'You're okay as you are, for the moment,' supplied the security man, switching his gaze from their surroundings to where he had seen Braidwood's vehicle. But the Scammell wasn't there anymore. Quickly he glanced to either side of the spot but still he couldn't see it. Then he began a slower survey, following the curve of the vehicle's track where it curved behind the snowed-in caravans.

'Fifty yards to a right-hander,' warned the security man, when he saw the track curve as anticipated. By following the track he saw it disappear down the third, and last, clearing which ran through this section of the 'village'.

The truck's engine note rose frantically in pitch as they turned onto the long strait taken by the Scammell, the wheels slipping in the rut made by the other vehicle. Bailey didn't notice this at first as his eyes still peered into the snow and darkness in search of the Scammell.

Then three things happened at once.

Shughie was the first to distract Bailey's attention for he began swearing at the truck, trying to get it to move, and revving the engine noisily to back up his entreaties. Then a hole appeared in the door window on the security man's side of the cab, followed by another that splintered the windscreen in front of Shughie, caused by a high-velocity bullet, which audibly announced its passing, a millisecond later, at the more leisurely speed of sound.

Even though the truck's temporary immobility was a great blow to their progress, and the fact that they were under fire was somewhat dangerous, the third occurrence was vastly more terrifying and effective in halting the truck's progress - *permanently*.

Sharing the same moment as the other two, the incident began with the direction of two very powerful lights, which illuminated the cab's interior as if it were noon on a summery day. Next came the roar of engine noise, which vastly swamped that of their truck. Silhouetted against the light, Shughie just had time to shout an unnecessary warning before the Scammell hit the truck somewhere behind the cab on his side, and the world began to revolve rather sickeningly for the two occupants.

It also went rather darker than at any time that night for, as the cab rolled over, the electrics failed and with the truck coming to rest with the side nearest Bailey on the ground, he found that he was literally blind.

Shaken but able to move, he checked himself for injury and was bemused to find that although he couldn't find the wound, he felt the wetness of blood around his head. As he was in no pain, he was prepared to write off the blood as merely the reopening of an 'old' head would and began extricating himself from the safety harness.

It was as he moved that he became aware of Shughie's presence a little closer than expected. The scot was suspended from his harness, with one of his feet almost brushing Bailey's face. Except that it wasn't a foot, it was an arm: Shughie was suspended upside down.

Vainly the security man tried to wake him, at the same time checking for injuries. It was as he did this that he discovered why he hadn't been able to match the blood with a wound, for the injury belonged to Shughie, a massive gash on the side of his head.

With something of a struggle Bailey managed to turn Shughie the right way up, having found that he was still breathing. Then he tentatively climbed to the jagged hole, which was the window of the driver's door. Carefully, mindful of the danger of continued sniping - if not ramming by the Scammell - he poked his head clear of the window.

In a split second, he had ducked back inside for he had sighted the Scammell, stopped, some twenty yards away. At the precise moment he had looked out, the cab door was being opened. But that hadn't been the cause of his reflexive action to seek concealment, that was due to his sighting of Joe - plainly visible as he stood below the door of the cab - in whose hands was a high-powered rifle.

As he crouched in the cab, wondering without optimism on his next move - if any - he heard the deepening growl of the Scammell's engine, which shortly began to fade. 'So they're on their way,' he said to himself, but aloud. What could he do now, he wondered? After falling for the same trick that he and Shughie had played on Braidwood, he didn't deserve any more chances even had they been handed to him. He realised now, too late, that the Scammell had disappeared on them because it had switched off its lights and circled round to catch them when the truck tried to take the difficult bend. Whoever had been driving the Scammell had already experienced difficulty there as Bailey and Shughie had seen by the deep ruts the Scammell had caused; it had been the obvious place for the ramming. And, of course, that was where it had occurred.

It was finished, Bailey knew. He tried not to think of the girl's predicament, taking his mind off his dejection by struggling with the still unconscious Shughie as he strove to haul him to the upper door. His mind went on ahead to his actions, once he had got the scot to a haven. He would try to locate the means to communicate to Rider what had happened; perhaps he would be lucky: they might even stop Braidwood if he got word to his boss before they had chance to leave the area. *Perhaps, might, if;* words for converting the realities of life into dreams. But they were also the words of hope.

Bailey knew there was hope yet, if Joe hadn't smashed the radio and severed the telephone lines.

However, that brought another thought, and one that instilled fear in the security man. He realised, perhaps too late, that he had been guilty of making an assumption, which could have terrible repercussions on his personal safety. He had automatically assumed that when the Scammell left, Joe had gone with it. Perhaps he was still there, outside, the cab door having been closing, not opening to let him in, when the security man had glanced over to it.

He heard the noise: the clank of something against metal, a boot perhaps, as it sought a foothold on the upturned truck. Frantically, he propped Shughie between the seats and began the search for a weapon, any weapon, which would offer him some chance of defending himself. Nothing.

As the noise got louder and he could now even hear breathing, he knew that his life was really in his own hands, and that he must be just a bit quicker than Joe: he must somehow get to the man's throat with his hands.

There was minimal light through the hole in the starred glass but even so, he could make out the shadow as it moved across the opening. Then he heard the breathing even louder, interspersed with sobs. Then he sighed, his pent-up nerves relaxing so much that he almost slipped from his footholds.

'Ian,' she cried, for it was Anne - a frail-voiced Anne, but undoubtedly the genuine article.

There was now no need for haste. All inducement to run to the office cabin to phone Rider had evaporated just as soon as Anne had recovered her nerve and told Bailey what Joe had said to Braidwood - that he had severed all means of communication before leaving the hut. Now the security man's thoughts could focus on the relief he felt that Anne was safe, and the problem of moving the injured scot to a place of warmth. There was nothing else to think about; the mission was over - failed. In a few days, the world would begin to suffer from the effects of Hargreaves' operation. Nothing could stop it.

As Bailey struggled along behind Anne, with Shughie draped unconscious across his shoulders he heard the murmur of an engine. At first, he believed it to be the Scammell in the distance, breasting the final rise before it descended to the metalled road beyond. A glance in that direction confirmed his suspicions for he could make out the vehicle's lights as it made very slow progress up the incline.

They were almost at the office cabin when he heard the engine noise increase, but another glance told him that the Scammell had hardly moved from where he had last seen it. In fact, he began to believe that it hadn't moved at all. It seemed to be stuck.

Perhaps the Scammell, laden with something like thirty tons of 'ballast' was too heavy for the cinder track, he reflected. Then Bailey's heart began to flutter with excitement, and he increased his pace. By the time they had arrived at the cabin he was almost running, whereupon he almost heaved Shughie through the open doorway.

He did a quick check to confirm Anne's words about the communications fit. It was as she had said, the transceiver was smashed. Around the able were a lot of boxes and clothes were draped untidily over them.

At his quizzical expression, Anne revealed that Hickson had been here. He was part of the gang, she told him, and had been moved here with his belongings to get Bailey away from the MSA.

Bailey dropped Shughie into a chair. 'Take good care of him, Anne, he's done good work for us tonight,' gasped Bailey, his breathing laboured from the exertion of carrying Shughie. 'I'm going after them.'

Anne's expression was one of amazement. 'Going after them?' she cried. 'You're mad. There are five of them and you haven't even got the means to follow them.'

'There is one chance,' he replied, the conversation not halting his preoccupation with searching the place, '*if* I can find the ignition keys.'

'What are you talking about?'

Abruptly he turned to face her. 'The Scammell is bogged down over on the materials dump. I know of one vehicle that is still in this area and which is in working order,' he explained. 'If I can find the keys I can follow them - and still get word to my boss.'

It was soon obvious that there were no keys in the cabin and, at the end of a minute, all he had discovered was, as Anne had also reported, that the telephone would never work again.

'I'll just have to hope that they're already in the ignition,' he said at last, and made for the door.

Anne looked up from tending Shughie then. 'Take care, Ian,' she implored.

Bailey looked back. 'Don't worry; I may be back earlier than you think.' Then he ran out into the night.

Chapter Fourteen

(24/25th December: 1930 - 1100)

Having suffered two false starts already, Bailey wasn't prepared to build his hopes too high on the success of a third. Nevertheless, if he failed this time it wouldn't be for lack of trying, and now - with Anne's safety assured - there was nothing to distract him from concentrating wholly on the pursuit of the Scammell.

Just how desperate he was to get after Braidwood was demonstrated by his very first action on leaving the cabin, for instead of looking for signs of the three-wheeler's presence near at hand, he plunged through the knee-high snow towards the position - somewhere in the murk - where he and Joe had found the vehicle on the day of the tour. For all he knew the vehicle could have been moved. Nevertheless, as he didn't have the time for a comprehensive search of the site, he had to pin all his hopes on the vehicle being parked where he expected it to be.

Some yards from the cabin, he halted. A quick look around told him that visibility was getting worse, even the light in the cabin doorway was just a pale glimmer. He knew that even if the three-wheeler was where he thought it was he could so easily pass by it in these conditions. This thought made him want to be getting on but he paused for a second or two to listen. At first he heard nothing unusual but then a faint sigh - different in tone to that of the wind - registered on his brain, and he knew that the Scammell was still in difficulties. He moved off again, struggling tiredly against the fettering influence of the snow beneath his feet.

When he had accompanied Joe from the cabin to the vehicle they had needed to walk no more than a few hundred yards. In the blizzard, impeded by both drifting snow and bad visibility, even one hundred yards seemed a mile. In his haste, Bailey could not hope to judge the distance he had covered at any time and soon he felt the doubts increase. Had he veered to left or right to miss the vehicle - only to be moving further out into the white wastes? He didn't know, and he couldn't see far enough to place any sort of landmark. Several times he stumbled to fall into the snow but always managed to get up instantly in response to a mental clock which was ticking away much faster than the mechanical variety, as he saw in his mind's eye the Scammell speeding away to make good its escape.

He was tiring rapidly and beginning to slow his pace when he felt, rather than saw, a high column of snow which stood directly in front of him and very close. Sluggish as his movements now were, he couldn't quite manage to avoid it altogether but brushed against it with his shoulder. Immediately the white gave way to a blackness beneath which drew his gaze like a beacon. In a split second his brain told him what it was he saw and felt with gratitude the deeply-etched tread of the giant vehicle's front wheel. Even though his relief at finding the three-wheeler was immense, he didn't stop to rest but carried on to make the climb to the cab. There would be time for rest later - *whatever happened*.

In the near total darkness, he had to rely heavily on his memory of the tour, when he had had many opportunities to study the layout and operation of the vehicle's controls. Almost blind, he found that it was a far more difficult task to find his way around the cab's console and it was only chance which allowed his hand to settle where the ignition key should be. Then he felt it. The key had been left in the ignition. Was his luck changing after all, he asked himself. Maybe, he reflected, as it was probably luck that the engine started first time.

As soon as he had found the light switches, he began to move away, operating the large windscreen wiper simultaneously. His progress was not anywhere near as rapid or smooth as that which Joe had demonstrated but even Bailey's gear-grinding efforts managed to propel the vehicle - and in roughly the right direction. To try to be accurate with the steering was difficult for the heavy contraption at the rear exaggerated every alteration of course as its weight swung the back-end further round – and in the opposite direction - than anticipated by the security man.

Without ear-defenders, the noise from the engine was terrific and he had, in any case, absolutely no chance of hearing the Scammell now. However, with the powerful lights piercing the murk ahead he could at least have the opportunity to see it in good time should he encounter it. He did not intend to allow a repetition of Braidwood's last trick.

Gradually the cumbersome vehicle ran across the Scammell's tracks - and Bailey followed them faithfully, at the same time keeping a most careful lookout for the unexpected. He didn't have to wait too long for the latter. When he arrived at the place where the other vehicle had been in difficulties he came across a number of large black gouges in the whiteness of the ground - but saw nothing of the Scammell.

Bailey's face was not invested of a happy expression as his eyes probed the darkness all around for any sign of the Scammell's presence. Such was his concentration on this task that he neglected to watch where the still moving vehicle was going and soon found it was bumping into the shallower depressions of the scarred area. Only a severe alteration of course - with its attendant whip-lash - prevented the vehicle from assuming a critical angle close to capsizing as the right-hand wheel fell much lower than the one on the left.

Bailey's trust in the three-wheeler's stability was minimal and he had erred on the side of caution in his manoeuvres in order to reduce the chance of it toppling over. With the Scammell not in the expected place, he must assume that it was already some way ahead. If he were to locate and keep it in his sights, he would have to be quick. He knew there was only one way he could do this - he must sacrifice safety for speed.

The Scammell's wheel-tracks were etched deeply into the snow, here and there marked with black to show where the tyres had churned into the cinder surface of the track. The security man noted that they moved right, which would indicate that Braidwood had decided upon a more circuitous route to take him around - rather than over - the hill. It would mean there was less likelihood of the Scammell being bogged down for a second time. But it would also give Bailey the chance - fraught with mishap as it might be - to at least make up some lost time, if not actually allow him to intercept and overtake the vehicle. However, it meant he must take the monster over the hill.

Slowly the security man brought the vehicle up the barely discernable sweep of the snow-covered track, leaving the twin tracks of the Scammell to disappear to the right. For some moments, all went well as the three-wheeler's relative lightness – and through the low ground pressure of the massive tyres - enabled it to move over the surface of the slight incline that had defeated the Scammell. However, the next two minutes saw a desperate struggle between the vehicle's purpose-built qualities of low-pressure adhesion and the slipperiness of an ever-steepening hillside. Only by continuous adjustment of the gears and acceleration did Bailey manage to avoid a permanent halt in the snow. Even so there were several close shaves when the rear wheels, each seven feet high, spun disconcertingly, the exertion and fear bringing a sweat to his skin despite the cold.

Only when the rise had begun to flatten out could he relax for a moment - but only a moment, as the descent to the metalled road still faced him. What was more, if he got down before the Scammell he would be brushed aside like a fly off a wall before the sweep of the heavier vehicle's snowplough. That was why he switched off the lights before he reached the true summit and, after continuing just beyond, stopped the vehicle and peered out into the darkness below.

At first, the task seemed beyond him. It seemed he could have little real hope of locating the Scammell's lights at that distance - a task he deemed impossible if the vehicle was already moving directly away from him and along the metalled road through the swamp. With this in mind - sharing concentration with the prospect of having to descend the steep hill - he spent the next three minutes gazing into the darkness until his eyes began to hurt.

His need to be going - to battle with his fear of driving the unstable vehicle down a steep, snowbound incline and to be physically involved in the pursuit, had him moving the three-wheeler away in quick time. But as he moved off he realised he hadn't switched on the lights which, in his alarm at the discovery, caused him to fumble the controls and stall the engine.

At that precise moment, he saw the light from the Scammell. Like the beam of a searchlight, it traversed through the darkness until it was aligned to cross the three-wheeler's path, but some distance below it. As he watched - his hands and feet operating the controls to restart the engine - he tried to calculate how long he had in order to arrive at the metalled road just *after* the Scammell.

It was a tight schedule for him to work out for, if he arrived below too soon, the inevitable would happen; too late, and he would be left too far behind to keep in touch. The difficulty therefore - heightened by the engine's apparent stubbornness to not restart - was in timing the start of his descent. It was vital, he kept reminding himself, that he should arrive on the lower track just after the Scammell had passed. That way he would be relatively safe from ramming, as the heavy vehicle wouldn't be able to turn round on the dangerous surface.

Then the engine answered his prayer and fired.

Now he must judge his timing nicely to when he must switch on the lights, as to make a descent without them would be suicidal. However, another factor hindered his timing for he could not see the road below. The Scammell seemed to be making good progress too, which was perhaps partly responsible for Bailey's subsequent misjudgement - when he switched on the lights too early.

Having committed himself by revealing his presence, Bailey began the descent immediately and the three-wheeler lumbered forward. Almost as soon as he felt the front wheel drop, he knew that something was wrong. It came as he tried to ease the wheel round to keep on the zigzag track. The weight of the rear machinery dragged the back-end round in an alarming lurch that would have toppled the three-wheeler in a very short time had Bailey not centred the wheel instantly.

By this time, the front wheel had run off the lip of the track to bump over onto the rougher ground beyond. As he didn't want to turn and invite a repetition of the real emergency he had just experienced, Bailey knew that he must control his speed·if he wasn't to arrive at the lower road ahead of the Scammell, for there was now only one way he could go - straight down.

However, that wasn't the only problem to assail his nerve-wracked body. The steepness of the incline combined - as for the ascent - with the slipperiness of surface snow to accelerate the vehicles descent even without pressure on the throttle. With the tendency for even the slightest alteration of course to precipitate a capsize, there was little he could do to slow down or run off the speed except directly downwards.

At that stage, he thought he'd lost it. It seemed impossible for him to delay the descent to arrive safely or avoid a confrontation with the Scammell: both equally prejudicial to his continued existence.

There was, however, one last hope and a very dangerous one at that. It required him to make a selection of one of the eight forward gears. The right one would slow the vehicle far more efficiently in the circumstances than use of the brakes - which would probably propitiate his downfall. Had he had the time he would have arrived at the right gear by logical elimination of the other seven. Of course, he didn't have the time for such because the vehicle was already beginning to run away out of control. He must choose and then hope he had made the right choice. It was therefore the result of the wildest of guesses that had him shove the gear-stick into a receptive slot.

The vehicle jolted as he let in the clutch, waggling the rear wheels at the same time as the engine buzzed in a higher but more uniform note. Then the massive wheels began to slow perceptibly at a rate that finally equated to a forward speed of some ten miles per hour. Below, the faster Scammell moved across the front of the three-wheeler, unable in any case to slow abruptly on the slippery surface. By the time the three-wheeler had arrived on the threshold of the lower track, the ground had levelled out to almost horizontal and the vehicle slowed almost to a halt. Slowly, carefully, Bailey swung the vehicle round to follow the Scammell, letting out his pent-up breath in a long controlled sigh.

The Scammell's speed surprised Bailey. He realised now that if was possible for Braidwood to get clear away in a very short time if he didn't keep the three-wheeler close in behind. Even then, it was quite possible that the Scammell would out-run his vehicle on the straight track.

As he thought of this, the Scammell made a gentle turn to the right, slowing by his gears only. Such was the deceleration that Bailey also had to change down in order to prevent the front wheel hitting the solidness of the Scammell's low-slung rear platform.

The turn, which Bailey followed, keeping close to the front vehicle, brought them onto the narrow metalled road that ran through the swamp. As they moved in close formation down the single-track road, the lead vehicle slowed in order to safeguard against toppling into the water.

Even though it was a metalled road, months of heavy use by construction machinery, had reduced the surface to a mass of large pot-holes. The larger excavations caused both vehicles to bounce erratically as their wheels bumped into them. Bailey knew that he could not control the vehicle for long - soon the Scammell would begin to pull away and leave him to wrestle impotently with the three-wheeler.

It was probably desperation that ignited the fuse of insanity, which ruled Bailey then. The many frustrations he had experienced in the last few days were coupled to his present one of not being physically able to stop Braidwood and his men, although he was so close. Even now, as he trailed mere feet behind the Scammell, he could only watch as it moved towards safer, faster ground. He wanted to ram the Scammell - even though his three-wheeler already lurched crazily to left and right - but knew that there was no way the overgrown beach-ball up front could hope to even dent the rear of so rugged a vehicle. To attempt another move which occurred to him - that of trying to nudge the Scammell off the narrow road - was an idea unworthy of even his unhinged mind. It seemed that there was nothing to do but sit and watch Braidwood and his gang get clean away.

Suddenly a flash came from the Scammell's cab. Then another, and he heard the slam of metal against metal as the bullets ricocheted off the three-wheeled monster. It wouldn't take many more shots to hit and shatter the windscreen, Bailey knew, and he was struck by the double-edged need to stop the firing and fight back.

But how? He had already realised that it was a matter of no-contest between the two vehicles; the Scammell could not be harmed. Then another shot came from the cab, which missed narrowly, the zing as it passed penetrating the engine noise so that he could hear it quite clearly. How to stop the man in the cab shooting at him? That was the question to which he must find an answer. Seconds passed while he tried to think of a way, seconds and a few more yards as the two vehicles moved along at ten miles per hour. Soon they would come to the end of the causeway and move onto firmer, safer ground where the Scammell could use its greater speed - possibly after it had used its snowplough to ram his vehicle. He must think of something now.

He looked at the Scammell's cab, the object of his mental labour. The cab was the answer, he thought. The cab was the only soft spot in the whole vehicle.

He must attack the cab. But how? The idea which formed in a flash was no less a result of frustration as of madness. As conviction grew in his mind as to the feasibility of the plan, he knew that the cab was now his target. It would take perfect timing and a lot of that recurring influence he seemed only now to be receiving any quantity of, *luck*. He didn't consider the danger to his own safety - there was no point - he couldn't know what would happen.

Their speed - separated by some five yards - was still around ten miles per hour - a little short of suicide on its own. For a few seconds Bailey concentrated on the bounce of the Scammell as it hit the potholes. He continued to monitor the bounces even though a bullet hit the windscreen high up in the right hand corner and starred an area around it, and even though he knew he was running out of time.

Atop the monster machine, Bailey could see the twin pencil-beams of the Scammell's lights as they pierced the darkness for some distance ahead along the metalled road. He could just discern the shape of buildings at the end now - it was time to begin.

Gently, he depressed the accelerator pedal.

At this stage, he knew he hadn't the time for a second attempt. If he mistimed the move he would lose all, for the stakes were that high: it was now win or lose, and nothing else could be considered. With that thought in mind, he brought the front wheel of the three-wheeler to hesitate for a brief second, just inches from the low rear platform of the Scammell. Then the cab of the front vehicle dipped as a wheel hit a pothole and that was the signal for Bailey to increase the revolutions of his vehicles' massive wheels until the engine was screaming.

The jolt that followed the collision all but threw him over his seat but that wasn't the most disconcerting thing which occurred at that moment. As the rear wheels of the Scammell dipped into the pothole it temporarily slowed its speed. Then, when the three-wheeler's front tyre hit the edge of the same depression, it bounced high against the tail of the front vehicle and - with Bailey increasing revolutions - caused the tyre to roll up onto the rear platform. With the pressure still on the tyre to go forward, it rolled over the lip behind the cab and dropped onto the roof.

Like a mantis atop its prey, the three-wheeler dominated the Scammel in a deadly embrace. Then, as each successive pothole jarred the vehicles, the nose of the three-wheeler dropped a little lower, the weight of that seven-foot high wheel and boom crushing the mild steel fabric of the Scammell's cab by inches each time.

Bailey was hypnotised by this to such a degree that even when the next shot was fired, splashing glass around the cab, some of which stung his face, he didn't flinch.

Then, as the Scammell hit a particularly large pothole, it shuddered and the wheel dropped sharply. Whether it would have dropped further Bailey didn't wish to discover for already the vehicle beneath his front wheel was weaving, seemingly out of control, and the security man reduced speed to slow the three-wheeler.

The result of this action was immediate. The three-wheeler slowed very quickly whilst the front vehicle carried on. As the front wheel rumbled backwards along the back of the Scammell - to fall with an alarming crash onto the compacted snow - the front vehicle ran off the road to the right, and into the water.

It was several seconds before Bailey felt that the three-wheeler was stable enough for him to divide his attention. The several large bounces of the front wheel had edged him nearer and nearer to the left-hand edge of the road, causing the security man some apprehension in the process. However, it had stopped short of the water. Now he could glance back in the direction of the Scammell.

In the darkness, it was difficult to make out shapes and, at first, he found it difficult to locate. When he did, it wasn't the truck he saw at all, only the top of the crumpled cab and a little of the superstructure immediately behind it were visible.

The rest - like nine-tenths of an iceberg - were beneath the same muddy waters that had caused Bailey such hardship on his nocturnal trip to the construction site.

He could now see what damage had been caused by the weight of the giant wheel on the cab roof. Not only had the roof given way beneath its weight, the door frames had buckled also, locking the doors in metal vices and making the window mechanisms almost useless.

He couldn't hear any screams above the noise of the three-wheeler's engine but that was just as well. What he could see - embellished perhaps in his mind's-eye - was an arm reaching with frantic movements from inside the steel tomb as it fought to release the door from the outside. But time was against them. Within seconds the Scammell had sunk down until the top of the barely open window had dipped below the rippled surface, allowing a swirling mass of water to enter the crushed metal box.

Moments later the surface of the water was calm again, with no trace of the Scammell or its occupants to be seen.

Epilogue
(27th December: 1000 - 1100)

Three days later, at a little before ten in the morning, Bailey joined four other people who had assembled in a side-ward of Peterborough General Hospital. Forming a semicircle, around the one occupied bed, were Rider, Inglefield and Anne; the girl plainly nervous by the way she hung on to Bailey and by the apprehensive look in her eyes. The last person was a doctor who was soon busy explaining his patient's condition. Throughout this, the pale-complexioned person with the grey hair looked up from the bright white sheets with eyes that though filled with pain could still acknowledge their presence with moist-eyed emotion.

As far as Rider and Bailey were concerned there was nothing in the doctor's speech that was news to either of them as both had been kept closely briefed as to any change of condition during the patient's stay in hospital. Therefore, while Anne and Inglefield listened intently to what was being said, Bailey found his mind wandering back to the night of the Scammell incident and the events that followed, events that were so closely connected with the reason for their visit today.

He had decided against attempting to reverse all the way back along the metalled road after the

Scammell had disappeared from view, for that was clearly a practice too dangerous for his shattered nerves to allow. Instead, he had coaxed the three-wheeler towards the village beyond the Plant Depot and amazed the occupant of one house when he had parked the monster somewhere in the middle of the front garden - then calmly begged the use of his telephone.

He had naturally phoned his boss first and then called in the emergency services. But that hadn't signalled the end of his work that night. There were still close to two hundred people stranded on Benwick - not to mention Anne and the injured Shughie still at the construction site - and he realised that although the ambulances might force their way through to the village, there was no way they could get through to the MSA. He must return; a not insurmountable problem at the outset as he had already made the trip once and, although he was now in hardly the best of shape, it was obvious that he was the man to ferry the frailer people to the relative safety of the village - and the waiting ambulances. He managed just the one round trip. Having stopped to pick up Anne and a now conscious but dazed Shughie, he had struggled back along the trampled snow of the eastbound carriageway towards the MSA. Dazed though he had been, Shughie would not countenance Bailey's first plan – to take them both to Grafton before returning to the MSA – and insisted on going with them.

On arrival, Bailey had wasted no time in preparing for the return trip for, although the blizzard had subsided a great deal in its ferocity, there was still snow falling, endangering a successful return with each passing minute.

With the help of Sergeant Brennan and his men, he had managed to rig a tow between the three-wheeler and two large, 7-seater people carriers - formed in a single line behind it - and each was manned by a police driver. In this way, they had been able to take off a total of fifteen people, non-staff women and children. But that still left one-hundred-and-sixty-nine men and women to face the wintry conditions until help could be got to them when daylight arrived. Sadly, Lela wasn't among either group: she was not among the fifteen crammed in the cars or those who were left to suffer the cold for she was feeling nothing now, having passed away shortly after the little boy had begun singing.

It had been a difficult journey back to the village, but as he had emulated the Scammell's route around the materials dump rather than repeat his previous climb over the hills, it wasn't anything like as dangerous the second time. The efforts of the two police drivers had undoubtedly helped him as they applied their limited control unceasingly to allow Bailey some freedom to concentrate his attention on handling the three-wheeler.

At the right-hand turn onto the causeway, he had peered into the gloom for signs of the waiting vehicles. Within seconds, he had located them as his line of sight moved to the left of the screening mass that was the Plant Depot, still some distance ahead. Like beacons, the rotating blue lights of a fleet of ambulances had guided him across the thin, slippery causeway formed by the metalled road. With him in the cab had been Anne, Shughie and Shughie's wife, Linda. Together with the others, the four had climbed into the ambulances and taken the same trip to hospital.

As his thoughts returned to the present, he reflected that Shughie and Linda had already flown to the 'States. Hasty though their flight had been, however, it was unlikely they could have beaten that of the recovered gold in reaching the same country, so swiftly had the authorities acted upon Rider's information. It was the panic, involved in getting the gold to America before the Swiss audit commenced - and the subsequent relief at the avoidance of the expected petrodollar scandal - which had helped gloss over Shughie's requirement to answer for his unlawful practices on the motorway. Any hard questions had been firmly dealt with by Rider, at Bailey's insistence.

With Hickson's death would die the dream of a Golden Highway. Rumour now appeared to suggest that it would dwindle to a dual carriageway beyond the finished section of motorway as the recession bit deeper and the extravagant, impossible claims were quietly forgotten.

The doctor was still talking when Bailey's thoughts returned to the present, but it was the change in his tone that drew the security man's attention. 'Of course, the language was quite bad at times, as our nurses will testify,' he said, the merest smile upon his lips. 'But as there were few occasions of semi-consciousness up until he regained full consciousness, the bouts were similarly none too frequent.'

'Frequent enough to tip us off as to the gang's intentions, that's all,' remonstrated Rider, reminding everyone by this reference that it had been during such a period of groggy wakefulness that the vital information had been learned, to confirm the scribbled note recovered in Simmonds' notebook. Bailey nodded in confirmation at this, knowing that but for being thrown clear in the collision, the man wouldn't have been alive to disclose the plan.

But Rider hadn't finished and he now redirected his gaze to the patient. 'That, and the quick-wittedness of a policeman who recognised something in the words you mumbled on your way to the hospital. Bad language *indeed.*'

If the patient was impressed by Rider's words, he failed to show it - unless he found them deeply disturbing, in which case his expression mirrored this reaction most faithfully. As Bailey noted this strange reaction he felt Anne's grip on his arm and, by following her glance towards the patient, knew now what everyone else had discovered whilst he had been daydreaming. The old man's eyes, almost blinded by tears, which glistened shinily, were staring still in the same direction they had looked since the visitors had first entered the room - at the girl.

Being some moments behind the rest in assessing the situation, Bailey struggled to catch up. He realised almost immediately just why the doctor's change in tone had dragged him from reverie; the man had responded quickly to his patient's show of emotion and tried to lighten the mood of the visit by his inane reference to bad language. Rider, for his part, had tried a similar ploy. No sooner had Bailey absorbed all this than he was again trailing behind the rest.

Suddenly the others seemed to be leaving. Inglefield and the doctor were already through the door before he noticed that Rider was also stepping back from the bed. 'Goodbye, Mister Simmonds,' called Rider, now moving towards the door. 'No doubt you and your daughter have a lot to talk about.'

For a few moments, silence engulfed the three people. Then, as the patient's eyes flickered questioningly in Bailey's direction, Anne broke the silence. 'It's all right, Father,' she said, emotion and uncertainty making her words falter, 'you'll be seeing a lot of Ian from now on.'

THE END

www.ingramcontent.com/pod-product-compliance
Lightning Source LLC
Chambersburg PA
CBHW070804180626
46818CB00001B/100